LATCHED

TALES OF COURAGE AND PASSION

★★★

CORONADO SERIES

★★★

BOOK ONE

LEA HART

DEDICATION
For My Daughters, My Heartbeat

ACKNOWLEDGEMENTS
I would like to thank Janell Parque
for her editorial wisdom.

CHAPTER ONE

Birdie stood in the window of her shop, arranging flowers, and heard the bells jingle on the front door. Turning, she saw her best friend, James walk in. "What a nice surprise. I wasn't expecting to see you today."

"Birdie girl, are you busy? I need cookies."

"Who's driving you to eat cookies at 10:30 in the morning?"

"The woman who's getting married this Sunday at Hotel del. I've decided that I'm going to nominate her for that show on TLC that we always laugh at."

"You mean *Bridezilla Wars*?"

"I don't think that's what it's called, but yes, that one." Slinging his hand on his hip, he narrowed his eyes. "Let me ask you this…how wrong would it be to kill her?"

"It would definitely put a damper on the wedding and *kill* your reputation. No pun intended." Snorting, she laughed loudly. "That's a good one if I do say so myself."

"Girl, when you have to tell yourself it's a good one, it rarely is."

She stuck her tongue out and then turned back to her flowers. "Whatever. Just know I'm good for bail money, should that become necessary."

"Appreciate it." He dumped his bag on a chair and then smoothed out his shirt. "I appreciate the ride or die vibe you're sending my way and won't call you from jail if there are some cute reprobates to hang out with." Walking over, he helped her step over the buckets. "Come out of there and feed me chocolate."

"Need a drink to go with it?"

"Is that even a real question?"

"No." She pressed a kiss to his cheek. "Give me five minutes." She strode back to the small kitchen, gathered supplies, and hoped the brandy she had on hand would soothe her friend's nerves. Dealing with the betrothed of San Diego wasn't easy, especially if they were plunking down a hundred thousand for a wedding.

After she set the coffee, cookies, and brandy in front of James, she took a second to study him. "Why is this one getting to you?"

"It's hard to choose just one thing." He poured a healthy dash of brandy into the coffee and then took a sip. "It could be her obsessive compulsion to disagree with every suggestion I make, or perhaps it's her whiny voice that has me about to go off the rails." He shrugged and gave her a sad smile. "It might also just be a severe case of burnout." Leaning his head on his hand, he devoured several cookies. "What's different about your face?"

She fluttered her eyelashes. "It took you long enough to notice."

"Quit being a spaz and let me see." Holding her chin, he studied her closely. "Ah, lash extensions. Good choice, they make your eyes more dramatic." He sat back and fixed his pant leg. "I'm happy to see you're finally taking my advice about vamping up your appearance. As previously discussed, the flower lady–accountant look isn't going to get you laid." Taking a cookie, he pointed it at her. "But you already knew that."

"I'm super stylish—people ask me about my clothes all the time." She dropped into a chair. "Just today I got a compliment on my shoes." Lifting her leg, she admired her new leopard kitten heels. "I have fabulous style. It's just something that doesn't attract men."

Picking up her iPad, she showed him a photo of a girl who had a half-naked selfie posted on Instagram. "If this is what I'm supposed to do, I'll need a team of professionals to achieve anything close." She studied the picture closely. "And possibly surgery." Glancing up, she frowned. "Definitely surgery."

"It's certainly a cheap, trampy look, but a *look* nonetheless." He waved his hand over the picture. "You know I'm not going to be helpful since I'm gay and don't have a clue what straight men go for." He studied Birdie over the rim of his coffee cup. "I think you're stylish. But it's women and gay men who compliment you, and that's not what you're after."

"I can't whip myself into a sex Barbie to get a date. I need to work with what I have." She let out a low groan. "Is it even possible to find someone who'd be willing to have sex with me in my current state?" She leaned back in defeat. "I don't even want a relationship. I just want to find a lover. How come it's so easy for men?" Taking her iPad back, she went through her feed and showed him an account she followed called Beard Brothers. "I want a man like this." Scrolling through the images, she pointed to one and smiled. "This right here is a man who's worth spending time with."

James grabbed it and studied it with the concentration of a Talmudic scholar. "How did I not know about this? I want one, too."

"You don't need any more men; you have plenty. I'm the one who's desperate for a date."

"I don't have any men like this," he said as he scrolled through the feed. "And, don't be greedy since there are plenty to go around." Lifting his eyes, he tilted his head. "These guys are not even your type. I bet not one of them owns a pair of loafers or a striped shirt."

"Which is the point! I'm getting a new *type,* and changing the flavor of men I go after." Snatching the iPad back, she held it against her chest. "I've decided that I want a man with muscles, tattoos, and a beard. A guy who looks like he listens to crap rock music, but has the soul of a man who loves Sinatra. My only obstacle is, they seem to go for girls who look like the half-naked selfie girl." She stared down at her cute black leggings, perfect white shirt, and pile of necklaces. "I don't inspire lust or, really, even mild interest." Sitting up straight, she squared her shoulders. "But I can learn."

James stole back the iPad, studied the bearded men, and waved his hand dismissively. "You always look lovely. But you're right; lovely isn't going to get you one of these. Once you've transformed yourself, where do you think we should look?"

Hearing the front door open, he glanced over and dropped the iPad. "Holy shit, never mind looking. One just walked through your front door. It's like we conjured him up with magic."

Birdie looked across her shop and laughed. "That's just Frisco from Team One." Tilting her head, she studied him closely. "He does fit the description, though."

"I had no idea SEALs were so good-looking. I thought it was just a myth."

Frisco stood at six-foot-two, had dark blond hair, piercing blue eyes, a lean, muscled physique, amazing tattoos, and a smile that could melt a Hershey bar. There were few women on Coronado Island that weren't willing to commit at least a dozen sins for a night of his company and bless his heart he took advantage of the bounty.

Unfortunately, she felt nothing more than familial affection for the too handsome man and didn't know why. Had there been any kind of flicker, she could've already had a little tryst and gotten herself out of a slump.

Frisco swept Birdie into his arms and rained kisses over her cheek. "Did you miss me?"

"No, and put me down since your beard is scratchy." She felt his arms loosen and slid down his long frame. "I didn't think you'd be back until next week."

"Caught all the bad guys and got sprung early." He picked up the iPad from the table. "Are you shopping for a man again, on Instagram?" Collapsing into a chair, he stretched out his long legs. "As I recall, that didn't work out the last time you tried."

Ignoring his comment, she lifted her hand. "Have you met my friend James? James, this is Lt. Frisco Jones." She watched the two shake hands and studied them closely. "Frisco, I need you to tell me honestly what you find attractive in a woman." She held up a picture of the half-naked selfie girl and then found a picture of a girl who was pretty and stylish. "Who would you choose?"

"Is this a test where I fail either way?" Crossing his arms, he frowned. "Because if it is, you can just tell me the right answer, so we can skip the part where you try and fix me?"

Birdie groaned. "Just give me an answer."

Frisco pointed to a picture. "I like the half-naked girl. I'm a man with low standards and just want fun. Let's face it, women who don't wear a lot of clothes are a hell of a lot of fun." He pointed to the girl that resembled Birdie. "This girl is someone who I'd marry. But I don't want to date her right now, because I want n.a.k.e.d. fun and that's about it."

Staring at him in reproach, she let her shoulders drop. "And, that's why I can't find a lover." She pushed her hair over her shoulder. "Men want to shtup the trashy girl and marry a girl like me. Which is why I'm never going to have sex again. Men don't look at me and think naked fun; they look at me and think responsibility." She put her head down on the table. "Let the pity party begin."

James stood and gathered his stuff. "That's my cue to leave since I have already listened to this particular diatribe one too many times." He patted Birdie's shoulder. "I'll see you tomorrow; text me when you're ready." He kissed her head, then shook Frisco's hand. "Please, help our girl because I can't take the whining for much longer." He scooted out of the way before she could pinch him and walked to the front door. "Love you."

Lifting her head, she blew him a kiss. "Love you, too. See you tomorrow."

Frisco took her hand. "Birdie, I told you that I'd sleep with you. Why don't we just do it, and then your rut will officially be over?"

"I'm not going to break my rut with you; we have no chemistry." She slipped her hand away. "I want to find someone who loses his mind for me and can't help himself." She studied his handsome face. "I wish that I was attracted to you because it would save me a lot of time and effort." She bit her lip. "I'm going to hold out for a man who sees me and thinks, 'I can't wait.' It may take a while, but I'm not settling for less."

"All right, let me know if you change your mind." He stood and stretched his back. "And I don't think it's going to take any time at all since you have a body built for sin. Unfortunately, your mind doesn't go with it. You say you don't want a boyfriend, but we both know that's not true."

"It's absolutely true. I've done the whole boyfriend thing, and I can honestly say that I'm not real interested in trying it again. Free and easy, that's me."

"Okay, you just repeat that to yourself until you believe it."

"Whatever—my birthday is coming up, and I'd like one of these men as my present."

"Your birthday isn't for another four months; you're never going to make it that long."

Snapping her fingers, Birdie smiled. "Get to it, then. You must know someone you can introduce me to."

"The guys I know aren't good enough for you."

Pointing at him, she winked. "That's exactly what I want. My ex was *good enough* for me, and he ended up cheating with his assistant. A well-educated man with a good career and excellent prospects doesn't mean a thing."

Frisco rubbed the back of his neck. "Do you want to go next door for sandwiches or do you want something else?"

"Let's go to the deli; they have chicken salad today, and it's my favorite."

"All right." He held out his hand and led her out of the shop.

"When we get back, I'll give you your financial statements for the last quarter. I've found a better investment, and you're making a little more money." She opened the door to the gourmet deli and grocery and held the door. "It's too bad my superior financial skills don't make me too sexy to resist because, if they did, I'd be fighting men off with a stick."

"I think you're sexy, Birdie." He followed her, and they walked toward the back. "Men see you and think naked fun, but when you open your mouth, they realize you're the real deal. You look like sin, but you're really a responsibility. That's confusing for a man with a reptilian brain, and they probably don't know which signal is stronger."

She thought about his statement and knew there was a lot of truth in it. "I'll work on my sin signal because that's what I'm interested in finding. S.I.N." They stood in line at the deli counter, and she wondered exactly how a sin signal worked. Nothing came immediately to mind, so she figured it was going to be like everything else in her life…a matter of research and practice.

It was time to use her brains for seduction and not numbers.

CHAPTER TWO

The following day, Birdie stood in front of the window at the Officer's Club on North Island and admired the men who were assembling the arch for her cousin's wedding. She studied the six alpha males who were swimming in testosterone and decided the one that she didn't recognize could be a candidate for her plan. Laughing quietly, she wondered what it would take to get him interested.

Giving him a slow perusal, she admired the way his T-shirt stretched across his massive chest and arms making a part of her come alive that she would've bet was dead.

The man had to be capable of heat, sin, and several things she couldn't name. "That's what I'm looking for." Perhaps Frisco knew him and could make the appropriate introductions…and if he didn't then she'd just introduce herself.

It was time for operation Naked Fun to commence.

Could she dig up the courage to convince that sexy beast of a man that what she had in mind was a good idea?

Of course, you are! Don't be a scaredy-cat. That doesn't do you any good.

This wasn't about forever; this was about right now. And that man was the one she wanted—right now. Leaning back, she noticed she'd fogged up the window, so she lifted her shirt and rubbed off the condensation. When was the last time she'd breathed that hard?

She stepped away from the window and took one last glimpse around the room, feeling satisfied with the arrangements. "This flower business may work out after all." Slipping on her headphones, she strolled outside and began checking the flowers for the cocktail hour. Andrea Bocelli's "Con te Partirò" filled her headphones and she started singing along with gusto.

Not able to resist, she glanced across the lawn and shivered when the man she was interested in looked her way. Spinning around, she fussed with an arrangement and didn't know why her fingers were shaking. Laying them flat on the table, she took a deep breath. "Not a problem. Nerves. Everybody has them." She moved the bowl of flowers around and started singing again.

This was the moment of truth. If she wanted to change her life, then she needed to be willing to do whatever was necessary. Nerves or no nerves.

Stagnation was no longer an option, and she was ready for the next step, no matter how much it terrified her.

***

As his teammates finished the arch for the ceremony, Mark heard someone singing…or a cow dying. The distinction was unclear. Glancing over at the patio, he saw a woman working on the flower arrangements with buds stuck in her ears and knew the sound was coming from her. "Who in the hell is that?" he asked no one in particular.

Frisco strolled over and slapped Mark on the shoulder. "That's Birdie. She's Josh's cousin and the resident flower lady."

"That's some kind of voice," he replied with a laugh.

Josh joined them and winced. "She's the worst singer in the family and doesn't care. I've stopped telling her how bad she is because, when I do, she just sings louder."

Blake joined the group and let out a snort. "I helped clean out her garage last month and had the pleasure of hearing her sing for two days. It felt a lot like the aversion training we had in BUD/S." Shaking his head, he shoved his hands in his pockets. "The chocolate cake she made totally made up for it, though. Hell, I'd listen to her sing all the time as long as she baked for me."

"Birdie doesn't care if people enjoy her song stylings and has told me one or a hundred times that I can put in earplugs if I don't feel like listening," Frisco added.

"What's her story?" Mark asked.

Frisco narrowed his eyes. "She's not a one-and-done girl. So forget it."

Studying his lieutenant, Mark frowned. "Maybe that's not what I'm interested in."

"Since when?"

"What the hell, man? Why do you care?"

"She's a friend of mine, and I'm looking out for her interests."

"Who says I'm not in her best interest?" Mark realized the horrible singer was the same woman that he'd been hearing so much about. Half the platoon went to her house for dinner whenever they were in town and always raved over how good her food was. They had nicknamed her "Team Mom" which made absolutely no sense since she didn't look like anyone's mom.

The woman he was looking at was curvy in all the right places with one of the finest asses he'd ever seen. Had he known that Josh's cousin was so pretty, he would've tried to wrangle an invitation a long time ago. "Introduce me, Frisco. I want to get invited to those dinners you guys always talk about."

"I'll introduce you, but just remember she's not a toy."

"Never thought she was," Mark said firmly as he crossed the lawn with Frisco bellowing her name. When she whirled around, her face lit up with a smile so freaking bright it gave the sun a run for its money.

She opened her arms to Frisco and he watched his buddy twirl her around, then kiss her cheek soundly. *Why the hell did Frisco get a kiss?*" A streak of jealousy ran down his spine, making him flinch at the unfamiliar feeling.

He'd never been envious of another man in his life and didn't know why the tiny woman was making the feeling possible.

Frisco set Birdie down and squeezed her shoulder. "The arch is finished and ready for your flowers."

"Okay, I need to get ahold of James and let him know." Birdie pulled out her phone and started texting. "He's going to bring the big ladder and help me."

Mark stood quietly and noticed she was even prettier up close. She had long chestnut hair and warm hazel eyes. When she caught his gaze, he felt as though he'd been hit in the chest.

Her luminous smile drew him in and delivered a sucker punch to his gut, the likes of which he'd never known. *Who the hell are you?* Staring at her mouth, he found himself mesmerized. Devil's candy, no way around it. Realizing that he'd said nothing, he cleared his throat. "Apologies for studying you like a science experiment." He put out his hand. "We haven't met; I'm Mark." Her hand fluttered to her chest and she swallowed. Was that a good sign or bad?

"Nice to meet you; I'm Birdie, Josh's cousin."

Lifting her hand, he held it lightly. "It's nice to meet you, too. Very nice." He took a step closer and saw the pulse in her neck flutter. *Please, let that mean she's attracted to me and not scared shitless.* He was a big man, with hard features and the last thing he wanted to do was make her uncomfortable.

Birdie smiled tentatively. "Do you work with the guys?"

"Sure do, I'm the lieutenant commander of one of the platoons from Team One." Their eyes locked and he thought the world's sound system shut down. There was absolutely no sound except their breath moving back and forth.

A large ship passed in the bay, and the sound of its horn startled him enough to speak. "I've heard a lot about you."

"All good, I hope," she said quietly.

"Absolutely, the guys think the world of you." Glancing down, he realized she was trying to get her hand back, so he reluctantly let it go.

Frisco cleared his throat, and they both turned at the same time. "So, what do you want me to take back to your car?" he asked elbowing Mark.

Smiling, Mark elbowed him back and knew they were not much better than two twelve-year-old boys. Which, surprisingly, didn't bother him as much as it should.

Birdie looked at them, and he retook her hand. "Point me in the right direction, and I'll take care of whatever you need."

"There are some boxes inside. If you could grab them, I would appreciate it."

Gently, he squeezed her hand. "Roger that."

"Thank you." Slipping her hand away, she grabbed Frisco and turned him in the opposite direction.

As they stepped away, he heard her ask Frisco if he was able to think of any candidates yet. *Candidates for what? I'm a nice guy. What about me?* Rubbing his chest, he noticed a sharp pain that reminded him of all the times he'd been shot.

Watching Birdie stride away made him realize he'd just been hit, only this time it was by a woman and not a bullet.

Ten minutes later, Mark returned to his teammates and heard Birdie laugh. The sound rippled across the lawn, brushed across his skin, and tightened his chest. Not sure if what he was experiencing was a good thing, he studied her and noticed how small she appeared surrounded by all his teammates.

Why was she the one to have such a singular effect? He'd never experienced anything like it and quietly admitted that he wanted her in the bluntest of ways. It was factual in much the same way his desire to become a SEAL had been.

Like it was part of his DNA.

Shaking his head at the wild thoughts, he joined the group and strategized his next best move.

Josh gave Birdie a big hug. "Wonderful job on the flowers. Thanks for giving us this gift. Maryann's parents appreciate it."

"Of course—I was happy to do it." Birdie hugged her cousin back and then looked around the group. "Don't forget to come by the shop this week and pick up your financial statements."

Mark turned to Ace, the newest member of his platoon. "What is she talking about?"

"Birdie's a CPA and helps out the guys by paying their bills when they're deployed. She's always done it for Josh, and as she got to know the guys, she offered to do it for them as well. She's a big-deal forensic accountant and does some work for a firm downtown."

He was surprised to hear that she was a CPA, and added smarts to the already long list of things he liked. "I thought she was just the flower lady."

"She is," Ace replied. "Her grandmother passed away about a year ago and left her a house on Coronado and a flower shop. Apparently, she needed a change because her fiancé cheated on her with his assistant."

Rubbing the back of his head, he tried to figure out what kind of idiot would cheat on her. He knew that if he had her in his life, he would be more than satisfied. Which meant he needed to devise a plan to ensure that happened.

The men from his platoon started leaving, and he decided to hang back, so he could talk to her a little more. Maybe that connection thing that had happened earlier could happen again, and he could discover what his strategy should be.

He watched Frisco kiss Birdie goodbye and then throw him a warning glance. Flipping him off, he grinned and walked toward the woman who was making his heart beat fast. It had never happened before and, the sooner he could understand what it meant, the better.

Stalking toward the row of seats that overlooked the bay, he saw her sitting with her face pointed toward the sun. As he got closer, he called out a greeting, so she wouldn't be startled, "Hi, Birdie."

When she turned slowly and smiled, he felt a hot, possessive rush splash through his body.

One look, one smile, and his goose was cooked. "What's going to happen when I kiss her?" he asked quietly as he moved closer. "She's going to fucking own me, that's what."

"Hi, Mark."

Glancing down, he fell into her smile and tried to think of something to say that wouldn't be a total pick-up line or completely idiotic.

Nothing, he had absolutely nothing.

"So, you're Frisco's commander?"

Clearing his throat, he nodded. "Yes."

"It's kind of you to come out and help the guys today."

"We always show up for each other. Doesn't matter what it is."

"It's good to have people to count on," she said as she stretched out her legs.

"Once you're in the brotherhood, you always have backup." Looking down at his boots, he tried to think of something else to say to keep the conversation going. What few social skills he possessed had fled and he didn't have one interesting thing to say. He ran his hand over his jaw and remembered you could never go wrong with compliments. "I hear you're a great cook. The guys are always talking about the dinners you make."

"Well, it's nice that they enjoy them. I always invited Josh over, and then he brought Frisco, and then they brought more friends, and so on. We've got quite a large crowd now. She tilted her head. "How come you've never joined us?"

Taking a seat next to her, he casually rested his arm on the back of her chair. "I guess they've been waiting for you to invite me, but since we never met, that probably wasn't going to happen." Looking down, he felt his gaze locked with hers. "I socialize with my team members, but I make sure to leave before they get arrested. It's in everyone's best interest if I maintain plausible deniability."

"Probably a good idea since someone has to be available to bail them out." Running her hand along her jeans, she played with a loose string. "I'll make sure to include you the next time I have a team dinner."

Seeing her mouth curve up made him think of how he'd like to taste her beautiful mouth. Dating, conversation—that's how he was going to be gain the privilege of a kiss. He couldn't just say, "Let's go to bed," and not expect to get slapped.

The woman sitting next to him wasn't like the SEAL groupies he'd found in the bars, and he knew he had to treat her right. Birdie was a woman who deserved dating and romance, and he was going to give it to her. As soon as he figured out what that exactly entailed. "Thank you; I'd love to come to dinner. I can't tell you the last time I had a home-cooked meal."

Their seats were close, so he dropped his hand near her shoulder. "I'll just hang out and wait until James comes; no need for you to be out here alone." *I want you to be under me and on top of me, and beside me,* he thought, *but not alone.*

"He should be here any minute, so you don't have to wait." She patted his leg. "It's a nice gesture, though, and very sweet."

Nobody had ever described him as sweet, and he decided it might be good if she thought he was. Looking down at his knee, he felt a jolt of electricity. "I was wondering if you're bringing a…" The sound of a horn interrupted his question, and he watched her turn around.

"That's my friend, James, and he's here to save me." Standing, she smiled. "Thanks for hanging out, Mark. I better go and get this arch finished."

He watched her walk away and muttered under his breath, "I'll save you anytime, anywhere, and any place." Groaning, he saw a guy step out of a truck and open his arms for a hug. Why in the hell did all these guys get to hug her and not him? He studied the pair and decided that shit was going to end.

He was going to be the next man she hugged.

One way or another.

"Your prince has arrived to save the day," James announced loudly.

"It's about time," Birdie trilled.

Leaning against his truck, James waved to Mark. "Hello."

"Hey," Mark called out.

Birdie slapped him on the arm and shushed him. "Don't start flirting; he plays for my team."

"Spoilsport."

Mark chuckled and hung back in case he could pick up some intel. He slid his phone out and pretended to be absorbed. Seems James wasn't any competition, and for that, he was grateful. He pretended to make a call and heard Birdie's voice carry across the distance that separated them. Biting back a smile, he listened intently.

"That's Frisco's commander," Birdie said. "Isn't he the best-looking man you've ever seen? Do you think it would be wrong to ask a lieutenant commander to sleep with me?"

"How long have you been out here? Are you experiencing sunstroke?" James asked as he put his hand on her head. "I guess you're okay." Dropping his sunglasses, he studied Mark. "He's attractive in a super alpha man way, but he's not handsome. Why can't you ask a lieutenant commander to bust your slump?" Running his hand through his hair, he smiled. "He's staring at me like he wants to kill me, so I think he's going to be real interested in your plan. Just don't break anything."

"I don't want to break anything—I just want to change my juju. The guy is built like a boxer. Look at those huge biceps." Birdie shivered. "I don't think I could break anything on him even if I tried."

Mark ended his pretend phone call and wondered what Birdie's scheme was and how quickly they could get started on it. Making his way slowly over, he decided to confirm who and what she was interested in, and then make his plan accordingly.

Walking up, he held out his hand and introduced himself with a friendly smile. "Hello, I'm Mark."

"Nice to meet you, Mark; I'm James."

"We'd better get started," Birdie said. "Lot's to do." She turned toward Mark. "It was nice to meet you and, hopefully, I'll see you at the wedding."

Leaning down, he kissed her cheek. "I will definitely be seeing you there." He nodded to James. "Nice meeting you." As he walked away, he decided her nervous dismissal was a positive sign. Silently thanking the gods for putting Birdie in his path, he knew that he was going to make the most of the blessing.

CHAPTER THREE

Birdie stood in the closet, ran her hands over her dresses, and contemplated her choices for the wedding. It was between the pale pink dress and the blue sheath. One was a little heavy because of the beading, and the other was fitted and made it hard to breathe. Unable to decide, she returned to the bathroom, took out her hot rollers, and shook her hair out. Looking in the mirror, she felt satisfied with the result and gently applied hairspray. She returned to her closet and chose the pink dress because it was flirty and fun. The beading made it appear almost to be sheer, which would be a plus, considering she was sending out the naked fun message tonight.

She slipped into it, added her gold heels, and was ready. Before she headed downstairs, she bowed her head. "Please let this night go well. If Mark turns out to be a dud or not interested, please send another candidate my way. And if you could make sure he's good in bed, that would be great. Amen." She blew a kiss to the sky and hoped her guardian angel wasn't too busy to listen to her prayers.

Walking downstairs, she called for James and saw him sitting in the kitchen, reading the paper and drinking champagne. "Well, how did I do?"

He glanced up. "Oh, Birdie, you did good. You look like a woman who's ready for the next chapter and some great sex."

"Good. I tried to vamp it up as much as I could." She twirled around. "Do I seem like I'm capable of naked fun?"

James stood and studied her closely. "Yes, the naked dress sends the right message."

"I'll have a lot of family there—it's still appropriate, right?"

"People see what they want to see. Your aunts will see a lovely pink dress, and Mark's going to see a naked dress and follow you around all night."

She lifted her glass in a toast. "Well, here's hoping because a year is too long to go without sex." She finished her glass of champagne and put it down on the counter.

"I had no idea it's been that long." James cringed and slapped his hand against his chest. "I think a couple of days is a long time. Do you need a condom?"

Birdie waved her hand in dismissal. "I'm hoping for a kiss, not a shag in the bushes. But I'll put them on my shopping list for next week because I need to be ready if Mark ends up as a candidate for my plan."

James adjusted his clothes and grabbed her hand. "He definitely wants to be your candidate, no doubt about it."

"Really? Do you think he's interested?"

"He's def interested." Wiggling his eyebrows, he nodded. "He was acting like a big old lion that was ready to pounce. It was so alpha."

"I wasn't sure." Fiddling with her purse, she smiled. "He's so handsome. His face looks hard and uncompromising, but his green eyes are so pretty with those long lashes. I like the contrast."

"Who wouldn't?" James collected his keys and phone. "Let's get you to this shindig, so you can see your prince."

"That's a perfect description of him," she said as she followed him out of her house. "Hopefully, Prince Mark will see me and know that I'm a woman who is capable of naked fun."

"Yeah, let's hope he picks up on that sin signal you've been practicing and not your usual responsible accountant one."

"Don't even suggest it's possible." Before she got in the car, she looked up and sent another prayer and hoped it worked.

They pulled up to the Officer's Club, and Birdie noticed how pretty the sky appeared. The sun was beginning to sink, and all that was left behind was a gentle glow, making everyone look a little more glamourous and attractive. A large group of people were gathered on the front lawn, waiting for the ceremony to start, and she spotted Mark standing in the center. *Have courage and believe it's possible.*

James squeezed her shoulder. "Go have fun. Dance your feet off and eat lots of cake."

She gave him a brave smile and slipped out of the car. Walking around to his side, she leaned over and gave him a big kiss. "Thank you for everything today. Couldn't have done it without you."

"Anytime." He glanced over her shoulder and laughed. "Mark is staring at your ass right now and isn't acting disinterested, so you'd better get going."

"Here we go." Standing up, she straightened her dress, fixed her shoe, and spun around with a hopeful smile on her face. She stared at Mark in his suit and felt her breath hitch. The guy was impressive in a T-shirt and shorts, but in a suit, he was devastating. His broad shoulders filled out the jacket, and she could see the fabric of his pants clinging to his massive thighs. It gave her the feeling of dynamite being wrapped in tissue paper…completely unnecessary.

"Here goes nothing," she mumbled as she started walking in his direction. God willing, she wouldn't trip and fall on her face.

***

Mark watched Birdie walk toward him, and his mouth fell open. She was in a freaking naked dress, and he was pretty sure he could see right through it. Feeling himself begin to sweat, he noticed her figure was a thousand times better than he originally guessed.

She was a hot as hell, brick house with all of her curves.

He never understood why women wanted to be skinny and were always dieting. He loved a soft woman with juicy hips to hold onto and didn't see why looking like a fourteen-year-old boy was attractive. Maybe it was just him, though since he was a big man. The last thing he wanted to worry about was breaking a woman if he kissed her too hard.

Watching Birdie move closer made desire sweep through his body, so he breathed deeply and corralled his urge to sink his hands into her hips the moment she got close. When that didn't seem to work, he prayed for mercy as the blood left his brain and his body reacted instantly.

One look was all it took.

Digging into his deep well of self-control, he willed his body to obey and was able to bring it all back down. That was until he saw her hips move in that rhythm women had. He stared intently as the beading shifted on her dress. Something was going to slip, and he wanted to be the only one who was granted a glimpse of her gorgeous body. He looked around and tried to determine if she'd caught anyone else's attention. When he didn't see anyone licking their chops, he let out a breath.

He returned his attention to Birdie and realized the dress wasn't sheer after all. Also, she didn't seem real confident in her heels since she was staring down at the ground, concentrating as she took each step. "I hope she makes it to me in one piece," he mumbled quietly.

When she looked up and smiled, she tripped and almost fell right into him. Opening his arms, he caught her around the waist and pulled her against his chest.

Gazing up, she laughed. "I almost made it. I was so close, but I saw you standing there, and I got distracted."

He felt her straighten and pull away. Tugging her back into his arms, he bent over and whispered in her ear, "You look stunning, sweetheart. Nice dress." When she moved her head, he noticed that she smelled like lilacs and summer. He had no idea where that thought came from, but he would now associate the smell of lilacs with desire.

"Thanks for the save."

Kissing her cheek, he took her hand. "Anytime." He enjoyed the feeling of her small hand in his, and knew that he was going to do whatever it took to keep it there. "Would it be okay, if I walk you to your seat?" He looked over her shoulder and frowned. "I should protect you from all of the men who are going to be staring at you in your naked dress."

Stepping away, she smoothed her hand over the beading. "This isn't a naked dress—it just looks like it. I'm not flashing anything, and it's not even short."

He shook his head. "Nope, it is a naked dress. Every man here is hoping for a shift of those beads for a little glimpse." He put his hand on the small of her back and guided her toward where the ceremony was going to take place. "I'll just stick close and make sure that you're safe."

"Who's going to keep me safe from you?" Birdie asked with a laugh.

"I'm the safest bet here because I have nothing but good intentions."

Birdie gave him a slow once over. "Do you have any bad intentions? Because I might be more interested in those."

Looking down, he let out a gust of laughter. "I have whatever you want. Good or bad."

"That's the best answer in the world." Wrapping her arm through his, she started moving toward the center aisle.

Happier than he could ever remember being, he tightened his hold. Maybe all the hard things he'd done over the years had earned him the company of this very soft and beautiful woman.

Birdie stopped and studied the arch filled with flowers. "Do you think it looks okay—even and everything?"

"Perfect." Staring down at her hair, he noticed how shiny and soft it appeared, and knew that was going to be his answer from here on out when it came to Birdie.

Absolutely fucking perfect.

They walked down the aisle, and Birdie stopped. "I see my two aunts. I'm sitting with them so I should say my goodbyes." Standing on her tiptoes, she kissed Mark's cheek. "I'll see you later."

"I'm sitting with you," he said as he put his hand on her back and started to move.

Resisting his direction, she stopped. "Save yourself. My aunts are a kick in the pants, but they have no filter." Turning, she placed her hand on his chest. "They say whatever comes to their minds, whether it is appropriate or not."

"I'm a big boy and can handle your aunts." When she turned and walked ahead of him, he admired her fine ass and wondered if she was serious about welcoming his bad intentions along with his good ones. Birdie stopped in front of two identical eighty-year-old women, and he watched her give them both big hugs and kisses and hoped he could answer the question by the end of the evening.

"Aunt Belle, Aunt Bee, this is Lt. Commander Mark Frazier." Birdie stepped away and took Aunt Bee's arm. "He was kind enough to escort me and is just leaving to find his friends." Pasting a big smile on, she waited.

He hoped she had some patience because he wasn't going anywhere. "It's great to meet you both." Sliding his arm around, Birdie's shoulders he matched her smile. "And I can't wait to get to know you both." When she dropped into a seat, satisfaction roared through his veins. Sure he was being a pushy son of bitch, but so what? Two minutes ago, she informed him that she would welcome whatever kind of intentions he might want to share and if that were true, it was up to him to cut off the competition. Full stop.

Once he was settled in his seat, he took Birdie's hand. "This is going to be fun."

Aunt Belle cleared her throat loud enough for the back row to hear. "Birdie, dear, I think Mark likes you and has some ideas about you."

"I just met him this morning. I doubt he's had enough time to come up with any."

Leaning over, he put his mouth close to her ear. "For the record, I've had plenty of time to come up with ideas—lots of them, too." He moved closer and placed his arm on her shoulder. "And the minute you're ready, I'll share every single one."

She folded her hands and looked at their thighs touching. "Why are you sitting so close?"

"I think the more important question is how could I not?" He lifted her chin gently. "We've got some powerful chemistry cooking and the sooner I can see what that means, the better chance my heart has of not stopping completely."

"Really?" she asked moving closer. "Your heart feels something?"

"Yes, ma'am. Along with several other body parts." Their mouths were inches apart, and he knew it wasn't the place for their first kiss, but damn if he didn't want to throw that rule book out. "You better quit looking at me like that."

"Like what?"

"Like you're wondering the very same things I am."

Birdie tore her eyes away, letting out a breath. "I love weddings don't you?"

"Yeah, Birdie…I do like them." A fact he wasn't aware of until this very moment. But hell, he'd go to an ice skating show if that's what she was interested in. Moving closer, he mentally put up his white flag.

"The ceremony is about to start," Birdie announced as she shifted around.

The moment her soft curves pressed against his chest, he knew he'd do anything to make her his. Turning his attention to the ceremony, he thought about the best way to make that possible.

***

Mark watched Birdie return to the reception and hoped now would be his chance. The cocktail and dinner hour hadn't allowed him to spend time with her and he hoped that he could at least grab her for a dance before the reception ended. Every time he'd moved in her direction, someone had swept her away and he was running low on patience.

Maybe after she tore up the dance floor with her cousins he'd have his opening. Walking back to the bar where the team stood together, he ordered a beer and tried to dig up some serenity. He returned his attention to the dance floor and watched Birdie's hips shake as she danced to the music. If she moved like that to music, then she was going to be incredible when and if they ever got together. A thought he didn't need to entertain while he was standing among his teammates.

Huffing out a breath, he felt Blake shove his elbow into his side. "What the hell, man?"

"What's up with you and Birdie? I noticed you've been watching her since she arrived. Every time you get within a hand's span of her, you're touching her. Are you hit?"

He thought about the question for a second and knew there was only one answer. It wasn't something he was comfortable admitting, but Blake was like a brother and had saved his life twice. "Yeah…I think that I am." He rubbed his hand over his chest. "I've been getting this weird pain, every time she smiles in my direction. I plan on asking her out on a date as soon as I can." Crossing his arms over his chest, he wondered if he remembered how. "I haven't done that since college."

Blake nodded. "Well, good luck with that. She's a good woman, and you'd be one lucky son of a bitch if she took you on. Half the team is in love with her and she's never given one guy any indication that she'd be interested. So prepare yourself, it's gonna take some work before she considers going out with you."

"Has she ever gone out with anyone from the team?"

"Not that I know of. She treats everyone like a friend and I think the guys are smart enough to know that she's not someone to fool around with."

Relief swept through his gut. "Good to hear."

"You got this brotha. Show her the best of what the Navy has to offer and don't back off until she sees how good an option you are."

"I'm the damn answer, not an option."

Blake chuckled. "I wish you both luck because I think stubborn is about to be introduced to tenacious."

"At least we'll keep each other entertained." That is if ever got a chance to speak with her again.

The night wore on and Mark wondered if the chance he wanted was ever going to happen. Birdie had been dancing with her cousins for almost two hours nonstop, and he didn't know when or if she was ever going to stop.

The band finally took a break, and he noticed she was moving toward him with another woman. "About damn time," he muttered. Just as she was about to pass him, he put out his hand to catch her. "Hey, honey."

Stopping in front of him, she smiled. "Why are you not out there dancing, Mark?"

He studied her and knew she would look the same after sex. Relaxed, happy, and flushed. *This is what I want to make her feel like when we're done.* Realizing that he hadn't answered her question, he moved closer. "I only slow dance, so save one for me." She saluted him and turned toward the bathroom.

Twenty minutes later, he noticed a guy holding Birdie tightly on the dance floor. "What the hell?" About to make a move, he felt a hand on his arm. Looking over, he saw Blake shake his head.

"Stay cool. Don't make a scene."

"I'm under control." A famous salsa song started, and he watched Birdie and the guy start to dance. "Holy shit," he muttered quietly. The team moved to his side and he didn't like the idea of all of them gawking as she moved across the dance floor.

Standing there transfixed, he heard Shane pop off. "What did you say?"

"It's like watching them have sex," he replied loudly.

He glared and then shook his head. "Shut up, man. You're talking about Birdie." He turned back to the dance floor and realized the guy was right. A fit of unexplained white anger flashed through his body despite the fact he had no right. His reptilian brain told him that no one should be doing that with her, except him.

And just because the world wasn't done with him, he noticed that her dress was almost sheer under the lights. From where he stood, she looked pretty damn naked, and he wanted to close every man's eyes in the room.

The song slowed down, and the guy dipped her and swept her slowly up the front of his body. Birdie's face was flushed, her eyes were half-closed, and he guessed that's exactly what she looked like when she peaked. Standing at his full height, he crossed his arms over his chest and bounced on the balls of his feet.

Cracking his neck, he let out a big breath when the song thankfully ended. Had she'd been out there much longer, he wasn't sure what he would've done with his new possessive feelings. He was half-off the rails, and they hadn't even kissed yet.

Birdie and the guy earned a round of applause, and they bowed and then walked off the dance floor. Not having one more ounce of good-guy left in him, he tracked her as she headed to the bar. The moment she sat, he was at her side.

Putting his hand on the back of her chair, he used the universal sign of marking territory. Fuck patience, he was done. No one else was going to get near her for the rest of the evening. "I guess you like to dance?"

"Almost as much as I like cake." Birdie looked up and put her hand on his arm. "I'm done, though, because I danced my feet off."

He motioned to the bartender. "Can we have a couple of glasses of water?" Almost instantly, two appeared before them. He lifted one and handed it to her. "Hydration. Always important."

"Thank you." Taking a big gulp of water, she leaned back. "I have to find my purse so I can call my cab."

"No," he responded loudly.

Twisting in her chair, she looked up. "Excuse you. What are you talking about?"

"I'll drive you home," he said quietly. "I don't want you to be in a cab with a stranger—it's not safe."

"Mark, I'm fine. I've done this before, and I don't want to take you away from the party." Patting his arm, she turned back to grab her glass.

"Baby, you're the party and I've been waiting all night for a chance to talk...or dance...or just sit next to you."

"Oh...really?"

"Well, yeah." He leaned away. "I thought that I'd made my interest known."

Birdie ran her hand over the water glass. "I wasn't sure since I sometimes miss the signals."

He bent down so their faces were close. The earlier arc of attraction was still there. "I'm interested. One hundred percent."

"In me?"

"No, the llama you have sitting next to you." He threw up his hand. "Are you playing me?"

She pulled him down. "Someone like you has never given someone like me a second glance. So for all I know you were just marking time until…"

"News flash; I don't waste a woman's time or my own."

Birdie looked down. "Okay."

"Okay," he repeated. "Can we grab a dance, now?"

"Mark, I'm so tired—can I take a rain check?"

"You were out there with everyone except me. One dance, and then I'll take you home."

"All right, if you insist."

"Stop, you're going to make me think you like me." Watching her smile gave him the encouragement he needed. "I think you've saved the best for last." Holding out his hand, he waited until she took his. Once she did, he pulled her in close and moved toward the dance floor.

"You may be right, Mark."

"About what?"

"Saving the best for last."

Holding her, he bent down and kissed her head as the acoustic version of "Latch" with Sam Smith singing started playing. He pressed her against his chest as they moved to the music, and the moment she melted into his body, he let out a sigh.

Finally, it began.

He wasn't sure what *it* was going to be, but he sure was happy it had finally started. Having her in his arms allowed him to relax for the first time all evening. A photographer at the other end of the dance floor took several pictures of them and he hoped that she was capturing the beginning of their love story.

The music changed, and he felt her soft curves against his hard angles and knew she was the perfect fit. *Under me, on top of me, and next to me.* Not able to resist, he took a gamble and lowered his mouth slowly toward hers. When he saw her eyes close in anticipation, he dropped his mouth, pressing his lips to hers.

Electricity ran down his spine.

Opening his mouth, he ran his tongue along the seam of her lips until she granted him entrance, allowing him his first taste. As their tongues met, a flood of want and need surged through his veins like liquid heat. *God damn,* he thought as they moved around the floor, kissing one another with abandon. This was definitely worth the wait.

Birdie let out a breathy moan of pleasure that made his skin so tight it ached. Feeling like he was being drowned in deep, dark desire, he sealed their mouths and pulled her flush against his body.

They gave and received long, feeding kisses and he knew that they had crossed the line of propriety. Gradually pulling himself together, he reluctantly released her mouth and stared down into her beautiful face. "You're a thousand times better than I imagined."

Tightening her hold, her face bloomed with color. "Thank you." Smoothing her hand over his suit jacket, she sighed. "The best for last indeed. I love kissing you."

"Ditto," he replied. Dropping his hands away from her face, he took her hand and led her away from the dance floor. A smile twisted the corner of her mouth, and he knew that their attraction was mutual. "Thanks for the dance, Birdie."

"Anytime," she said with a laugh. "You know how to dance, Mark. Don't let anyone ever tell you differently."

His mind was so blasted by lust that he was only able to let out a low growl in response. Kissing her head, he felt like he'd been hit with a Mack truck full of desire. "I'll take you home now."

"Okay," she said quietly.

After she'd collected her purse and said her goodbyes, he led her outside to his truck. Once he helped her in and made sure she was buckled up, he gave her a sweet kiss. "Time to take the queen home."

"Yes, king…take me home."

Not able to resist, he pressed their lips together and vowed he'd do whatever it took so they could kiss every day. When she pulled back and dragged in a breath, he laughed. "We'll be doing that as often as we can."

Pushing at his chest, she laughed. "You better take me home before I lose control."

"Control is overrated. But I'm a patient man, so I won't push."

Letting out a big yawn, she covered her mouth. "Sorry about that."

"Tell me where I'm going, and then you can pass out." She gave him her address as they headed out, then leaned her head against the seat and fell asleep instantly. Glancing over, he felt his whole body respond and hoped he could be patient. "Birdie girl, I'm coming after you, and I hope you're ready."

He parked in front of her house and was surprised by how beautiful it was. She lived in a two-story California Craftsman that looked like a home for a family, not a single woman. Leaning over, he brushed his mouth against her cheek and then called her name. "We're home, baby. Wake up."

Slowly, she opened her eyes. "Oh, it's you."

"Yes, it's me. Do you want me to carry you to your door?"

"No, I've got it." Sitting up, she stretched and smiled at him.

Climbing out of the truck, he walked around and opened her door. When she slipped into his arms, he leaned in. "Don't give me a naughty kiss, just a sweet one. I think that's all I can handle right now."

She obliged, leaned up, and gently pressed her lips to his. "Thank you. I had fun."

Letting her go, he watched her walk to the front door and slip inside. He stood there a moment with a shit-eating grin on his face. Best damn wedding of his life.

CHAPTER FOUR

The following afternoon, Birdie stood on the front lawn and watered her flower beds while Adele's voice filled her headphones. Arcing the water above her hydrangeas, she wondered if Mark Frazier was as phenomenal as he seemed.

It hardly seemed possible that a man like him would be interested because all she had going for her were brains, a sense of humor, and unfailing good taste in shoes. And those were not the sort of qualities a man usually found attractive.

At least not men like him.

Not that she knew what men like him went for.

Looking over at the next flower bed, she felt something tap her shoulder. Spinning around, she shrieked and soaked the man standing in front of her.

"Mark, you scared me to death."

Wiping his arms, he grinned and held out her wrap. "I was returning this—you forgot it in the truck." Slipping off his sunglasses, he started to wipe them on his shorts.

"You should've seen the look on your face when I sprayed you in the face." Lifting her hand, she covered her mouth as she tried to hold back a laugh. "Sorry about that."

"Funny, you don't appear to be sorry." Taking the hose out of her hand, he shook his head. "You seem pretty pleased with yourself."

She plastered her hand against her chest and feigned a look of innocence. "You scared me; it was completely unintentional." Grabbing for the hose, it slipped out of her hand, and she had to run and chase it as it skittered across the lawn. Once she got ahold of it, she looked down at her shirt and laughed. "Instant karma. Now we're even." She walked over, shut off the water, and tried to pull her soaked T-shirt away from her body.

"Guess we have our own personal wet T-shirt contest going," he said as he pulled his over his head.

Standing still, she froze as, inch by inch, his glorious chest and arms were revealed. "Holy mother of hotness," she said quietly.

The man displayed an impressive set of hard, cut abs and a massive, well-developed chest. *Can I run my hand up one side and down the other?* He had an intricate tribal tattoo on one of his biceps, and she wanted nothing more than to read it in braille with both her mouth and hands. "Have you ever been on a calendar?" She slapped her hand over her mouth. "Did I just say that aloud?"

"Yes, you did, and no, I've never been on a calendar. Why would I?"

She continued to stare and worried she might be drooling. "Because you're the most physically perfect man I've ever seen. I thought maybe you were in one of those 'Hot Men of the Navy' calendars." Nervously wiping the water from her arms, she fidgeted from one foot to the other. "I'm sorry. That's inappropriate. I'm objectifying you, and I know that's wrong."

Taking a step closer, he wrapped his arms around her waist. "Please feel free to objectify me anytime you want." Dropping his mouth, he gave her a searing kiss.

Her body was rocked, and she tried to make sense of the list that was forming in her head. So far, there were ten filthy things she wanted to do to him, or with him, or have him do to her.

Sexual deprivation had finally cracked her mind.

Smiling against his mouth, she wrapped her arms around him. "It feels good; you can really kiss."

"Well, that's why I do it." Kissing her again, he slipped his hands under her shirt and ran his hand over her skin. "I like your wet shirt. Can I objectify you now?"

Pulling away, she glanced down at her transparent shirt. "Well, at least I wore a pretty bra today." She grabbed his shirt and held it in front of herself as she turned toward her house. "Come on in, and I'll get you a towel."

"I have my go bag in the truck—I'm going to grab a clean shirt first, and then I'll be in."

Standing on her porch, she admired his broad back and tapered waist, whistling silently. The man was a piece of art, no way around it. Pulling her wet shirt away from her body, she called out, "I'm going to change, so make yourself comfortable, and I'll be down in a bit."

When he turned and winked, she laughed because whatever was coming next was bound to be good.

***

As Mark slipped a clean shirt over his head, he wondered if there was a "Hot Men of the Navy" calendar. Didn't seem likely, but what did he know since he'd spent most of his time OCONUS and didn't always keep up with things at home.

All that might change if he had a girlfriend, though. Yeah, he used the g-word and didn't even flinch. Twenty-four hours since he first set eyes on Birdie, and he was ready to try things he hadn't considered in years—like dating, monogamy, and shared calendars. Shaking his head as he walked up the path to the house, he wondered if he had a shot at even one of those things with Birdie.

He pushed the front door open and stepped in and felt instantly at home. The first floor was dominated by a great room, with a separate office and guest room off the kitchen. Looking around, he guessed that she'd done a lot of work. The floors looked newly refinished with a dark stain, and the walls were painted white with big photographs hung as decoration.

The kitchen was open with a large island in the middle and a farm table set against French doors that led out into the backyard. Walking over to the bookcase that took up a long wall, he studied the titles and noticed she had eclectic taste. The shelves were crammed with everything from biographies to popular fiction.

Hearing her feet on the stairs, he turned and watched her approach. His heart thumped when she threw him a smile, and he knew, one way or another, she was going to be his. As she got closer, he noticed she was biting her lip, which made him believe he wasn't the only one who wanted something to happen.

Holding out her hand, she grabbed his and led him into the kitchen. "What can I get you to drink? I have beer, wine, a full bar."

"A beer would be great," he replied as she let his hand go. "You have a great house—how long have you been here?"

"A little over a year," she replied as she walked into the kitchen. "Have a seat, and I'll get you some snacks to go with your beer while I make dinner."

"Let me take you out."

She pulled out a beer and then grabbed a jar of nuts off the counter. "Let me cook for you as a thank you for bringing me home last night." She hooked her finger over her shoulder and pointed to a row of containers on the counter. "I made my pasta sauce today because all of my tomatoes decided to ripen in the same week. I also have homemade meatballs and some rosemary rolls. You said no one ever cooks for you, so let me."

"I'm not going to argue with a home-cooked meal. Thank you." She handed him the beer, then opened the jar of nuts. "So, what made you decide on a big house?"

"My grandmother left it to me, along with the flower shop and the building that it's located in. I've decided to stay in San Diego, so I'll be finishing the renovations."

"It looks great." He sat down on a comfortable stool and watched her put dinner together. "When can I take you out this week?" When she didn't respond right away, he wondered what was making her hesitate.

Tilting her head, she studied him. "Let's just see how tonight goes, and then we can decide." She poured herself a glass of wine and then flipped on her iHome, and chose some music. "So, how long have you been in San Diego?"

"I've been here for eleven years. I grew up in San Luis Obispo, went to Cal Poly, and then came down and joined the Navy. I went through BUD/S, and have been assigned to a team here since graduating." He took a drag of his beer and then ate some nuts. "I've been on loan to the teams on the East Coast a couple of times, but it was never a permanent assignment. What about you?"

"I went to USD for my undergraduate and lived with my grandmother during college. Then I moved back to Los Angeles to get my graduate degree at UCLA. I worked for a firm up there until I moved back last year." She handed him dishes and cutlery. "Can you set the table for me?"

"Sure." He got up and set the dishes on the big farm table that looked out over her garden. Her lack of enthusiasm for setting up a date surprised him. He knew they had chemistry, so why didn't she?

Maybe it was the chemistry that was making her nervous. If he had to guess, he'd say she liked to be in control of her life and probably relationships. Especially if her ex was as much of a douche as he guessed. Whatever was burning between them wasn't going to be controlled, so it made sense that she was cautious.

He set out the dishes and congratulated himself on coming up with a nice neat explanation. The other one that was floating in his head sucked because it involved her not being interested. Which he would never accept. "So, is this what I've been missing when you have the guys over for dinner?"

"I guess, but it's no big deal. I never make anything fancy; I just make a lot of it because you SEALs eat a ton."

Laughing, he walked back to the counter. "That's true."

"The guys seem to enjoy a home-cooked meal and hanging out. Maybe it makes them feel like they have some family around."

"I've heard a lot about these dinners and think it's a big deal to the guys. I hope they tell you how much they appreciate it."

She stood with her back against the counter. "They don't say it so much as show it. It seems they've adopted me as a sister, and they're always willing to help me out. Frisco and I have become close friends, even though I always give him unsolicited advice. He's helped me out at the shop when I've had to move something around. Ace is a sweetheart and showed me how to put my garden in this year. Blake introduced me to his brother, who's my contractor, and he also helped me go through the garage. Sam and Shane built new shelves in my shop last month. The guys have helped me out a lot more than I've helped them. I just feed them and make sure their bills are paid when they're deployed."

She checked the oven and pulled the meatballs out. "Almost there." Draining the pasta, she added sauce, then tossed the salad. "I think we're ready. I hope you're hungry. Can you put the salad, bread, and cheese on the table for me?"

He took the things over and poured water into the glasses. Birdie brought a huge bowl of pasta to the table and served him a big plate and a much smaller one for herself. "This looks great."

"Anything else we need?" she asked as she studied the table.

Gazing at her, he grinned. "Perfect." He made sure she was seated and eating before he started. Taking his first bite, he couldn't believe how good it was. "You're an unbelievable cook, and I may have to marry you."

"You wouldn't be the first person to say that. Don't worry—it usually wears off."

"Yeah, I don't think that's going to happen." As he ate, he knew that whatever was happening between them wasn't going to wear off. In fact, it was probably going to get a lot worse before all was said and done.

When he took her hand and got a smile, he knew she was fatal. There was no way he was going to survive. Women like Birdie didn't come along very often, and he planned on grabbing hold and seeing what happened.

They talked during dinner, and he couldn't remember the last time he'd enjoyed a conversation more. Ends up, they had a lot to talk about despite their differences.

They both enjoyed reading biographies on historical figures as well as obscure scientific facts. He never would've guessed that he had so much in common with a woman. Maybe because he hadn't spent any significant time with one since he graduated college.

The excuse he always gave himself and the woman he met was that life on the Teams was all-consuming. Which is was. But the real reason was because he'd never found anyone he wanted to spend more than a couple of nights with.

Until Birdie.

The woman sitting across from him could likely keep him interested for a long time to come. Not only was she smart, but she was well informed…something he guessed was the result of her curiosity.

It was an entirely new experience, and he was enjoying the hell out of it. This was the first "date" that he'd been on in over eleven years, and he realized that a smart accountant with a flower shop and a horrible voice was just the thing he'd been waiting for. "I haven't had this much fun in a long time," he said as he scraped his plate clean.

"My pleasure, would you like some more?"

Glancing at his plate, he shook his head. "I'm full. Thank you for the best meal I've had in a long time."

"You're welcome." She stood and picked up some dishes. "Let me pack the leftovers for you."

He got up and helped clear the table. When they stood together in the kitchen, he turned and took her hand. "I want to take you out on a date. We could go to dinner or a movie. Maybe bowling or a sail around the bay. Anything you want. Something fun."

"I like fun," she replied, looking up.

He framed her face with his hands. "Me too." Dropping his mouth, he pressed their lips together and tasted her desire as he slicked his tongue along her lips. No way was this a one-sided thing. The moment her hand gripped his shirt, he knew for sure.

Birdie ended the kiss abruptly. "Yes, I will go out to dinner with you." She patted his chest and then took a deep breath. "I like the something you're offering."

Throwing his head back, he laughed. "You held out for a long time. What made you decide in my favor? I hope it was the kissing."

"The kissing definitely helped." Stepping back, she pressed her hand against his chest. "Really helped."

He covered her hand and leaned over so he could see her face. "When do you want to go out? Tomorrow? Tuesday?"

"Why so soon?"

"Why not soon?" He moved his arm around her waist. Is this how people dated? They waited around and played games? He didn't play games. He saw her, he wanted her, and she was going to be his.

Tapping her fingers against his chest, she fidgeted. "I'm not available Monday or Tuesday because I have plans. But I'm free on Wednesday, and would love to go out with you."

He released his hold and stood up straight with his feet set apart, and his shoulders set wide. "Birdie, who are you going out with?"

"What happened to 'Relaxed Mark' and why is 'Commander Mark' standing in my kitchen? She narrowed her eyes. "We should go on a date and see if we like one another before we start talking about who we are or are not dating."

"I'll tell you whatever you want to know. I'm asking about who you're dating because I want to know who I have to get rid of."

"Get rid of? What are you talking about?"

"I'm interested in you, and am not going to let another man interfere with that."

She threw up her hands and let out a huff. "Say that then." Twirling her hair up, she frowned. "I don't know if going out with you is such a good idea after all." She frowned. "You seem dictatorial, and I don't like that, no matter how handsome you are."

"You think I'm handsome? I'm a lot of things, but I don't think handsome is one of them."

Letting her hair fall back down against her shoulders, she laughed. "Really? That's what you got out of all of that? You didn't hear, 'I don't like bossy' and only heard the good-looking part? How's that possible?"

"I heard you. I was just focusing on the good part first." Lifting her hand, he ran his finger over her palm. "I've not had a girlfriend in a long time, so I'm a little rusty with dating etiquette. I just want to spend time together and get to know you. And get rid of any other guys who think they may have a chance."

"When you say get rid of, you mean that in a figurative sense, not a literal one—right?"

"Depends on how much of a problem they are." He shrugged his shoulders and smiled. "Truth is, no one will ever find the body."

Taking two steps back, she gave him a fake smile. "I'm deciding whether I should be worried or entertained."

"Let's go with entertained." When she took another step back, he decided that saying everything that crossed his mind wasn't a good idea. The last thing she needed to know was how far he was willing to go to get what he wanted. "So, Wednesday?"

"I guess we can go out, but I don't like bossy." She pointed her finger at his chest. "There is only room for one bossy person, and I'm it!"

He grabbed her finger, brought it to his mouth, and kissed it. "Got it, you're the boss." Entwining their hands, he stepped into her personal space. "Why do you get to be the boss and not me?" He leaned down and ran his nose along her cheek. When she shivered, he hoped like hell she was surrendering.

"I get to be the boss because I'm the girl. I'm shorter, smaller, and not as strong. If you're the boss, it would be out of balance." She put her arms out. "You're almost a foot taller than me, and probably weigh twice as much. I want to even the playing field and create a fair exchange of power." Leaning back, she shook her head. "By the way, don't use your body to get your way. I'm supposed to be able to do that."

"What if I kissed you and ran my hand up your back?" Doing exactly that, he felt her shiver. "What do you want to be bossy about anyway?"

"I'd like to be bossy about things that I think of…when I think of them."

Moving closer, she pressed her chest into his and slipped her hand underneath his shirt, and then kissed him gently. When she released his mouth, he did the only thing he could and made a last stand. "My mind is clear, Birdie, and I can be all kinds of bossy. How's yours?"

She kept her hand on his chest and ran her fingers back and forth as she let her other hand rest on the waist of his jeans with one finger inside. "Crystal clear. Are you sure you're thinking *clearly*?"

His brain went blank as all the blood traveled south. He couldn't have formed a thought if his life depended on it, so he blinked a couple of times and lied. "My mind has never felt sharper." Truth be told, she was exactly like a flashbang, wiping everything from his mind. He had years of training in recovering from them, so he used his muscle memory and tried to function. He rocked his hips into hers and watched her eyes close with desire. She didn't look like she could be the boss of anything.

Except for his heart.

She could probably be the boss of that.

Feeling her respond with more passion than he thought possible let him know he was a dead man. It was so damn good that he swore he lost a couple of brain cells.

Taking over the kiss, he slipped his hand up the back of her sweater and let his fingers play against her skin, and felt her soften. "Maybe we can take turns being bossy."

Stepping away, she covered her mouth. "You never lost concentration for a second. I have absolutely no effect on you." She shook her head. "God, that's depressing. My mind goes blank, and you don't feel a thing."

He took a step closer, and she took a step back as he tried to grab her hand.

Major tactical error. In his play for control, he made her feel like he was unaffected by her kisses. Which was the furthest thing from the truth. "My mind went blank when we kissed. I acted like a commander and not a guy who was lucky enough to kiss a woman he'd been dreaming about." He tried to take her hand again, and when she let him, he brought it up to his mouth and kissed it. "Can we try that again and I'll be a man and not a soldier?"

"Yeah, I don't think so. I'm good. I don't need a repeat." She moved around the island and put the leftovers in a bag. "Thanks for the ride home and everything. Enjoy the pasta." She walked back around and handed the bag to him.

He was being dismissed, and it was clear she wasn't going to put up with any bullshit from him. He needed a new plan fast; otherwise, she was never going to let him through the front door again. "That's it? I make one small mistake, and you're going to get rid of me? You already said you would go out with me, and you can't take it back."

Standing up straight, she slid hands to her hips and laughed. When she was done, she met his eyes without hesitation. "I can do whatever I want and have decided that I don't care to go out with you. We can be friends, and I'll include you in the team dinners. But I will not waste my time with someone with whom I have no chemistry. I've done that dance, and I'm not interested in repeating it. People show you who they are, and I've found it's a good idea to pay attention when they do. Let's just chalk this up to a one-time thing and leave it at that. No harm, no foul."

Yeah, he'd fucked up, big time. "You can't dismiss me because I said something stupid. I'm going to say a lot of dumb things, and you can't get rid of me every time I do that. We have a ton of chemistry. Didn't you feel it last night at the wedding and out on your front lawn? We have so much chemistry that we're going to explode." He opened his arms and hoped she would step into them. When she stepped further away, he cringed. "I was trying to negotiate the boss thing, and I overplayed my hand. I'm sorry that I hurt your feelings and led you to believe that I'm not affected by you."

"Listen, I have to go with my original assessment—you're attractive but overbearing and intimidating. I don't want always to fight you, and that's why I wanted to be the boss. You're certainly capable of running me over without even thinking about it, and that's what makes you a good commander. But I don't want to be commanded."

He was stricken by what she'd said. "I had no idea that's what it felt like. I'm sorry."

"You're a good man, probably the best sort of man there is. I'm sure, someday, the right woman will come along, and you'll be fine with giving it up to her." She held out her hand. "Friends?"

"No, I want to be more than friends. I think you're the right woman, and I want a do-over."

She looked around her kitchen, at the floor, at the ceiling, and finally at him. "I don't know, Mark. I think we might just be better friends." Her eyes ran over his face, and she frowned. "No matter how much I like kissing you."

A smile broke across his face, and he laughed. "I like kissing you too, so let's be friends first and see if it turns into something else. I think we could be everything and want to see if I'm right."

"I want smaller hips. We don't always get what we want."

"I do. Eventually. After a lot of work. Maybe a new bullet hole or two."

"That's not helping."

"What would?"

Birdie threw up her hands. "Fine. We can go out once more and see how it goes."

"I think it's going to go great," he replied. "Scratch that, I know it's going to be extraordinary."

She gave him a weak smile. "We'll see."

"Yes, we will." He thought about what she said earlier and knew there was one area that he wasn't going to cede control and she might as well know what she was in for. "You can be the boss of whatever you want, but I'm the boss in the bedroom."

She looked him over slowly. Tapped her fingers against her thigh. And then finally nodded. "I guess that would be okay. You have a lot more experience than I do and probably have some interesting ideas." She patted his arm. "If I don't feel like harming you after the date, then I'll probably want to see them. Or feel them. Or perhaps even hear them if you're any good at dirty talk."

He let out a big laugh and couldn't believe what came out of her mouth. She said what she thought without filtering a thing out. "God bless America. I have won the fricking lottery and you are the damn prize Birdie."

"I doubt that. But if we make it past our next date, which is doubtful, and decide to have sex, you can be the boss."

He took a step closer and took her hand. "It's not a question of *if*. It's a question of *when*." Staring at her mouth, he knew he needed one more kiss. "This isn't me trying to get my way; this is me kissing you." Gently sliding his lips over hers, he kept the pressure light as he opened his mouth and let his tongue glide over her closed lips. She wasn't opening, so he lifted his mouth and kissed the edges of her mouth.

The moment he felt her lips curve slowly upward, relief washed through him. He continued to kiss her gently and pulled her hand to his heart. "Can you feel how fast it's beating?" Moving his hips against her, he said, "Can you feel how you affect me?" He moved her hand around his back and put it under his shirt. "Baby, I'm sweating and will make sure to let you know how much you affect me from now on. Lesson learned."

She bit her lip and stepped away. "We'll see."

He watched her walk over to the counter, grab the bag of leftovers, and knew their evening together had ended. "Thank you, honey; I haven't eaten this well and enjoyed myself so much in a long time. Give me a sweet kiss, and I'll leave you be."

She handed him the bag and then kissed him gently on the cheek. "Okay." Leading him to the front door, she opened it and then leaned against it. "I'll see you later."

"I may have to see you before our date because Wednesday is too damn far away." He pulled out his phone and handed it to her. "Put your numbers in there, and I'll text you back, so you have mine."

Taking his phone, she entered her number and handed it back. "Thanks for bringing my wrap over."

Sliding his hand above her head, he leaned down and kissed her. "Good night, Birdie girl. I'll call you tomorrow."

Gently pushing him away, she laughed. "See you later." She stepped back into the house and closed the door.

"Hope you're ready because I *am* coming after you." He called out as he walked out to his truck. After he got in, he sat for a moment and thought about how he almost screwed himself out of a chance with the woman who might very well be his future.

Not a mistake he was going to make twice. From here on out, he was going to make sure he let her know how he felt; otherwise, she wasn't going to waste her time—that was clear.

CHAPTER FIVE

Birdie sat in bed, gazed out the window, and noticed the sun slanting through the trees. Running the previous evening over in her mind, she tried to determine if half of the things Mark has said were true…or even possible. She didn't have much trust in her radar since it had failed her so miserably in the past and wanted a sign from above that she wasn't about to embark on a fool's errand. Or be played.

And yes, she understood how that sentiment made no sense since all she wanted was a fling that would end the funk her love life seemed to be parked in. A little, no strings attached tryst. Something that cost her nothing emotionally but filled up her physical needs tank to the brim.

Was Mark as perfect a candidate as she initially pegged him to be?

Tired of her mental machinations, she checked the clock and realized it was time to get up. Her to-do list was long and staying in bed wasn't going to get it done.

Just as she was about to push herself away from her nest of blankets, her phone buzzed. Lifting it, she saw Mark's name. Why in the world was he calling so early? Sliding the bar, she answered it. "Good morning, Boss of the Bedroom."

"Hi, honey. I wanted to be the first voice you heard this morning. Is it too early?"

"No, I was just getting out of bed."

"Damn, that's something I'd like to see. Can you face time?"

Laughing, she shook her head. "No way. I'm not fit for public consumption in the morning, and that's nothing you need to see."

"I'm going to see it eventually. I bet you're sexy as hell with your sleep-warmed skin and tousled hair. Wish I was there."

Her heart fluttered at the flattery. "My goodness, that's some heavy-duty flirting for seven in the morning. I haven't even had coffee yet."

"Get used to it because it's going to become a regular part of your day. Now, tell me what you have going on this week."

"Well Mr. Nosy McNosy, you are a curious bear this morning."

"I'm an interested man, who wants to know when I can slide into your schedule."

"Oh well…that's…"

"The best news?"

She let out a snort. "It's news."

"I'm ready for the intel, so go ahead and give me the download."

"Alright. Monday is my day off from the shop, so I usually do my errands and chores. I'm hosting my Stitch and Bitch group tonight, so I have a lot of cooking to do. I'm making my famous chocolate cake, so I should get up and get started." Running her hand over her blanket, she wondered if he was going to end up in her bed at some point. If he kept playing his cards the way he was, it might be possible. A thing she was almost sure she wanted. "What's on your schedule?"

"We're on our down cycle and have about another month before we'll be moved up in the rotation. This week, we have new equipment to train on and a couple of night drills scheduled. Wait, what is stitch and bitch, and did you say you're making a chocolate cake?"

"I was wondering if you were going to catch that. Stitch and Bitch is my knitting group. We get together once a month to have dinner, drink wine, and knit.

"Can I come over for a piece of cake after they leave?"

"Really?"

"Yeah, really. I want to see you, so tell me what works for you."

Deciding that seeing him would give her a little more info, she nodded to the empty room. "We're usually done after nine o'clock, so you can come over after that. But you can't stay long because I have to get up early on Tuesday and go to the flower mart. I leave here at four in the morning, so I have to be in bed by ten and grab my beauty sleep." A loud shout filled her ear, and she couldn't help but laugh. "

"So, I can have a kiss and a piece of cake if I don't overstay my welcome?"

"Yes to the cake, and maybe to the kiss." A loud growl filled her ear, and she pulled the phone away from her ear. "What's up with the animal sounds?"

"Sexual frustration," he stated firmly. "I've thought of little else since we met on Saturday, and I'm half-crazy with wanting to kiss you. And you give me a maybe."

"I'm a woman; that's what I'm supposed to do. I have to figure out if I want to invest time in you before I kiss you again *or* sleep with you."

"Can't we kiss and fool around first and then figure it out?"

"Nope. If we have sex, then I could accidentally get attached to you. Even though I don't want to. Women have to fight thousands of years of evolution and ignore our brains telling us to keep every man we have sex with. I'm currently not in the keeping phase of my life, because all I want is an affair. But that's not going to stop me from doing my homework because God forbid I get stuck with someone who's a lousy match. Been there, done that, don't need to do it again."

"I'm not sure that I understand. Do you like me and want to keep me? Or do you not like me and just want to use me for my incredible skills in the sack?"

Laughing, she covered her mouth. "Let's see if I can do a better job. I've always been a relationship girl, and don't want that anymore. I want to try being a naked fun girl for a while. I'm not sure how it's going to work, so all you're going to get from me is a maybe."

"All right, Birdie Boss. I'll take your maybe and see you tonight."

Feeling relieved that she somehow muddled through the explanation, she let out a breath. "Okay, handsome. Have a brilliant day and we'll see each other later."

"Can't wait."

Sliding the phone closed, she kicked her blankets off. What she'd just told him was confusing, and that was because she was baffled herself. In her heart, she wanted a love story; in her brain, she wanted a fling. How any of it was going to play out was anyone's guess.

***

Mark walked out of his office toward his platoon and saw they were unpacking the new equipment. "How does it look?" he asked Frisco.

"This is some cool shit. If it works, then it could make a big difference for us in the field. We should have it assembled in time for the night drills."

"Good news, thanks, man." Hearing his name, he turned around and saw Blake walking in his direction. "What's up?"

"Wanted to see how it went with Birdie."

Mark studied his best friend and wondered why he cared. They'd never talked about women before and didn't understand the sudden change. "I'm seeing her tonight. She's going to let me come over for cake after her friends leave."

"I hope that you're talking about cake and not something else," Blake huffed. "She isn't a booty call girl."

Crossing his arms, he told himself not to react. "I know and can tell the difference between her and some chick I picked up in a bar. Why do you think that I'm going to mistreat her?"

"I don't; it's just that you've got no experience with women like Birdie."

He shook his head. "Why do you have such a lack of faith?"

"I just want to make sure, is all."

"For your information, I've asked her out, and she won't go until Wednesday. I don't think that I'll survive until then so I wrangled an invite for a quick visit. She's making cake for her Stitch and Bitch club, whatever that is." He unwound his arms. "I like this woman, and she's making me crazy, and if she said come over and play Monopoly, I would."

Blake started laughing. "Stitch and Bitch—I don't even want to know. You're lucky she's letting you come over because she makes an amazing chocolate cake." Rocking back on his heels, he grinned. "Can you have her wrap up a piece of that cake for me?"

Mark walked away and flipped his friend off. "I'm going to the firing range. Have Frisco call me when everything's unpacked."

Damn teammates needed to be hyping him up, not shooting him down. He was dealing with enough uncertainty and did not need any of their doubts playing in his mind. Shaking out his arms, he reminded himself that even if tonight didn't go perfectly, he could ask for a hundred more chances until he got it right.

Tenacity was his middle name and he hoped it worked as well in love as it did downrange.

***

At five-thirty, Birdie's friends started showing up for their monthly meeting. As the women came in, she got them drinks and told them to start on the antipasto platter.

Her cousin, Ana, who was in the last year of completing her doctorate, arrived and she was thrilled. They rarely had time together, so she was grateful that she could make it. Handing her a glass of wine, she smiled. "I'm so happy to see you."

"Cousin, you're glowing. Did you have your one night with 'Hot Mark' or maybe two?"

"No, not yet. I'm not sure what's going to happen with him." She fixed her cousin's ponytail. "I'm cautiously optimistic, but don't want to get ahead of myself."

"The way you two were kissing at the wedding made me think it was a sure thing."

"Who were you kissing, Birdie?" Cara asked. "Did you find a man to bust your slump?"

The group of women turned and waited. "Tell us," Cara called out.

Knowing the women wouldn't stop pestering her until she gave them something, she decided to give them a nibble. "I met Frisco's commander on Saturday at the wedding. He and I hit it off, and he may be the man to break my rut." She waved her glass around. "Rest easy ladies, I may have found the perfect man for a short, meaningless affair with."

Cara took a sip of her wine. "Why does it have to be short and meaningless?"

"I don't think the guy does relationships, and I don't want one. The thing with Justin cured me of wanting anything serious, and I'm ready to try something new. I'm just not sure Mark is the man to try it with. He's the very definition of an Alpha male and likes to be in control."

"That can be fun in the bedroom if he knows what he's doing," Cara said helpfully.

The group erupted in laughter and Birdie joined them. "True. But, I promised myself that the next time I get in a relationship it's going to be with someone who loses their mind over me. Mark isn't a man to lose anything. I doubt he'll be interested past next week. Truth be told, he was barely affected when we were kissing the other night. I was a puddle of lust, and he was cool as a cucumber. The last thing I want is to spend a lot of time with a man who can take me or leave me."

"I agree," Ana said. "If you're going to take the time, it might as well be worth it."

Birdie popped an olive into her mouth and shrugged. "He's a fling sort of guy. Which is exactly what I'm looking for. Anyway, he stopped by yesterday and ended up staying for dinner. Who knows where it will go if anywhere. He's a SEAL, so it's not like he'll be around much."

"Maybe that makes him perfect for you. A hunky man to shag every couple of months could end up being the best relationship in the world. All the fun and none of the headache," Cara replied.

The ladies all clapped and said, "Hooyah."

Laughing, she looked out at her group of friends and thought they might be right. A fling with Mark could be the answer to a lot of things.

***

Mark rolled his truck to a stop in front of Birdie's and figured he'd waited long enough. It was nine-thirty, so the party should've ended. Jumping out, he strode quickly up to the door. He knocked several times and then sucked in a breath when Birdie opened the door. God damn, she was the prettiest thing he'd ever seen. A big smile lit up her face as she gazed at him warmly, and he felt a hot, possessive rush in response. "Hi, Birdie Boss. Did you miss me?"

Stepping back, she opened the door wider. "Come on in; I'm almost done cleaning up. Are you hungry?"

"I'm hungry for some kisses and you." He stepped closer and wrapped her in his arms. Bringing her against his body, he waited to see what kind of reception he was going to get. When she let out a small breath and put her arms around him, he hugged her tighter. "Thanks for letting me come over." Tilting her head up, he lowered his head and captured her mouth. He'd been thinking about her all day, and reality far surpassed his memory of what it felt like to have her under his mouth. Before he could deepen the kiss, she pulled away.

"So, you came for cake, right?"

"I'm having my cake," he mumbled, pulling her closer. When her hand pressed against his chest, he reluctantly released his hold. "I missed you."

Pulling away from his embrace, she patted his chest. "Chocolate cake—I'll get you a piece."

Standing up straight, he discreetly adjusted himself and was relieved that he'd worn jeans. Best chastity belt in the world. He was uncomfortable, but that didn't matter because she didn't need to see how turned on he was. A few kisses and he was ready to explode.

As he followed her into the kitchen, he realized he had a ton of work to do because the tactical mistake he'd made the previous evening was still fresh in her mind. He strolled over to the fridge, studied her pictures, and noticed a list. He read it and saw that some things were checked off, others were crossed out, and a few were circled. "What's this list?"

She nudged him aside and opened the fridge, pulling the milk out. "That's my must-try list. I should take it down and redo it." She poured the milk, and Mark took the milk jug from her and put it back in.

"So, when do you want to have your first swim lesson in the ocean? We could go on Saturday."

She took the plates of cake, he grabbed the glasses of milk, and they sat down at the table. "Mark, you don't have to do that because Blake told me he'd take me out whenever I wanted to go."

"No, no way." He shook his head. "Blake doesn't need to see you in a swimsuit."

"Where's 'Relaxed Mark' gone? I like him a lot better than 'Commander Mark'." She looked over his shoulder. "Can we see if he's around?"

Staring at her, he realized he was going to have to persuade her, something he had no experience with. He told his team what to do, and they did it without question. Birdie wasn't going to follow anything he said unless she wanted to. He took her hand and pressed a kiss to her fingers. "Sorry. It's just that the idea of another man's hands on your body makes me a little nuts. Blake is one of my best friends. We were swim buddies back in BUD/S, and I trust him with my life."

Quirking her head, she studied him. "Just not with me, even though we've been friends for almost a year?"

"I know it's ridiculous." He moved closer. "Please pick me for the swim lessons because I want to be the one that helps you."

"I appreciate the offer and will keep it in mind. Let's see how our date goes on Wednesday, and then decide if we want to spend more time together."

He kept ahold of her hand. "I want to spend as much time with you as I can, so I'll plan on being available on Saturday to take you to the beach." He nodded confidently. "I'm going to get rid of that seed of doubt that I planted yesterday. I like you, and want to get to know you."

"No offense, but I've heard that before." Sliding her hand away, she frowned. "I know that I'm being a hard-ass, but I have to protect myself because I can't take another betrayal."

"I understand and am confident it's not going to be a problem. You've never met a more trustworthy and determined person than me. My word can be counted on and I want to be the one that teaches you how to swim."

"I know how to swim. I want to become more confident in the ocean because I'm going to learn to surf next spring. Living this close to the beach, it seems silly not to give it a try."

"I grew up surfing, and I'd be happy to take you out. I have a longboard at my Mom's house, so next time I'm up there, I'll bring it back." Leaning back, he laced his fingers behind his head. "I'll buy you a spring suit so you won't get cold, and that way we can keep you out long enough to get up on the board. Maybe I should get you a foam board to start—that would make it even easier. We'll start now, since we still have a couple of warm months, and by next spring, you'll be awesome."

"I guess you see this thing going well and us spending all kinds of time together…"

"I do and plan on showing you that my word is gold."

Birdie kissed his cheek. "Okay, Mark." Lifting her fork, she took a bite of cake. "So, you were a surfer? Where did laid-back 'Surfer Mark' go?"

"He went into the Navy, but I can still be laid back when I have to." Taking a bite of cake, he moaned as the delicious chocolate frosting melted in his mouth. "Damn, woman, this is the best cake I've ever had."

"Glad you like it; I'll be sure to send you home with some."

"Thanks honey." He took her free hand. "And for the record; I can't wait to get you in the water on Saturday."

"Let's get through that date on Wednesday first."

Diving back into the cake, he wondered what it was going to take to get her to fall for him. Whatever it was, he'd do it because he'd fallen already, and didn't want to be the only one with all the feelings.

CHAPTER SIX

Two days later, Mark stood in front of Birdie's door with his nerves jumping and didn't care for the unfamiliar feeling. Most of the men he worked with considered him unflappable, and if any one of them could see him now, they'd be laughing their asses off.

Knocking firmly, he waited and went over his plan for the evening. He'd decided to take her downtown for dinner and then to a club, a foolproof plan as far as he was concerned because she liked to eat and loved music.

The door opened with a whoosh and when his eyes met Birdie's, he felt a sharp pain that he was becoming familiar with. There was also an audible click, and he took it to mean that everything was falling into alignment. At least he hoped that's what was on the horizon.

Because if he didn't somehow pull a miracle out of his ass and get her to fall for him, heartbreak was going to become his best friend. "Hey honey, are you ready for the best date of your life?"

Taking his hand, she pulled him into the house. "I have to confess…I'm more than a little nervous. I changed clothes three times before you got here, and when I saw you at the door, my heart started beating fast." She looked up. "Do you think that's a good sign?"

Words failed him, so he pulled her against his body and answered with his mouth. Giving her a kiss that he hoped would communicate how far he'd fallen, he devoured her mouth. Quickly realizing where the kiss could lead, he slowed himself down.

Birdie responded by fisting her hand into his shirt and letting her tongue slide against his with abandon. The bolt of lust rocketing through him wasn't surprising, but the wave of tenderness was. Lifting his mouth, he ran his finger over her cheek. "I was a little nervous, too. Maybe the kissing helps?"

"It just makes my nerves jumble more." She let out a nervous giggle, stepped back, and smoothed out his shirt. "You're so handsome. I like your shirt and your haircut. Did you do that for our date? I had my nails done and got a little trim. I also got this dress…I think it's okay."

Looking down, he was surprised to hear her nervous chatter since she'd been nothing but confident and relaxed. "I think you're the prettiest woman I've ever seen and not because of how you look." He bent down and kissed her cheek. "But for the record, you're sexy as hell and I consider myself lucky."

"Me too," she replied quietly. "Where are we going for this super first date?"

"We're going downtown to a restaurant that Sam recommended. He told me it's where he took his wife on their first date. Apparently, she liked it because now they're married with a baby on the way. I figured that's as good of a recommendation as there is, so that's where we're starting our relationship."

"So, it's a good luck place?"

"Something like that. After we eat, I'm taking you to a club that has new bands. You seem always to have music playing, so I thought we could give it a try."

"Sounds perfect. Let me grab a jacket, and we can go."

When she returned and took his hand, he felt the click again.

They were a perfect fit, no doubt about it.

A half an hour later, Mark pulled in front of the restaurant and turned off his truck. "This is it; I hope you like it."

Birdie leaned forward and looked out the window. "Looks perfect."

Once they were inside the restaurant, Mark looked around. The place appeared like it had been around since the 1950s. The lighting was low, Frank Sinatra was playing on the sound system, and there were tables surrounded by red leather booths.

As the hostess approached, he gave her his name, and they were led toward a booth in the middle of the restaurant. Birdie slipped in first, and he slid in next to her, sitting close enough that a piece of paper couldn't slip between them.

"Are you comfortable? Would you like to move any closer?" Birdie asked sweetly.

Slipping his arm around her shoulder, he grinned. "If I thought I could get closer, believe me, I would sure try." He matched her smile. "And in case there's any confusion…I'm coming for you and have no plans of backing down."

"So, is this you stating your objective? Like, 'I'm going to storm the hill, and then I'm going to take the mountain and Birdie is coming with me?'"

"Pretty much. I want you to know what you're in for so you can prepare yourself." Running his hand up and down her arm, he dared her to argue. When she didn't pop back and put him in his place, he hoped that if she had any objections, she would share them now. Best they handle them as soon as possible because he didn't want anything standing in their way. "Nothing to say, Birdie? Anything you want to share?"

She tore her eyes away from the menu. "Since you asked, I should confess that I'm relieved by your little speech." Lifting her eyes, she gave him a sharp nod. "It gives me confirmation that you'd be down for a short meaningless affair. I think you're attractive and sexy as sin, and I'm ready to take you for a spin and see if we're sexually compatible." She patted his leg. "I gave you a speech the other day about doing homework, but I've decided to forgo it since all I want is something without complications. If you're ready for a sweaty tryst, then so am I."

She appeared to be a sane person, but what came out of her mouth disproved that. How dare she want to use him for his body. He had a damn mind and heart that was worth something too! "Just to be clear, your plan is to use me for sex and then discard me at the first opportunity?"

"Well, it sounds bad when you say it like that." She tilted her head. "Why don't we call it a mutually satisfying physical relationship that has an expiration date?"

"Hell no! You won't even commit to going to the beach on Saturday, but you want to have sex with me?" His brain was about to explode, and he had no idea how to make it stop. "I am not a toy and you can't use me and lose me."

She gave him a measured look. "I don't think that's a fair characterization of my intent. You don't even have relationships, so I'm not sure why you're snippy about my idea." She straightened her cutlery. "I thought you'd be excited by my proposal. I guess it's time to rethink everything. Which is a shame since you're the most attractive man that I've ever seen." Patting his thigh, she sighed. "I guess we'll just be friends." She pointed her finger at him. "No more kissing, though. Just friends. I'll find someone else to break me out of my rut."

Mark watched her pick up her menu and did everything he could not to shout out his frustration. "Of all the crazy-ass shit I've heard, that's the craziest. I've taken crap from my friends for the last four days. 'Don't go after Birdie. She's a relationship girl. She doesn't sleep around. Don't go after her unless you mean it." He slapped the table, letting out a groan. "And little does everyone know that you're plotting to use me for my body and then drop me." He corralled the last of his temper and let out a long breath. "So let me give you my answer. Hell no! You can't use me. If you want to have sex, then you have to stick around and see what we have. I'm not some slump-buster that you can throw away, and by the way, I don't get snippy." He moved closer and put his arm around her shoulder in possession. "We're gonna date, maybe fall in love, and have a hell of a good time while we figure out what works best. End of story."

Birdie leaned away. "I didn't think you'd be angry since men like women who don't want a relationship. Don't you guys go to that bar and pick up girls for sex?" Flattening her hands on the table, she took a breath. "I want the opportunity to use a man for sex and then move on." She flapped her hands "Why do I always have to make good choices? I've been appropriate my whole life! I'm an accountant, after all." Lowering her voice, she continued. "You know what it got me? It got me a fiancé who cheated with his assistant. What's even sadder than the betrayal is that we had boring sex. I was going to settle for boring sex for the rest of my life." She picked up her menu again. "So, excuse me if I wanted some mind-blowing sex. I'll find someone else."

"No! You have me and we're gonna burn up the sheets, the house, and anything flammable that dares to get in our way." Vowing to double down and show her that his idea was a good one, he took her hand.

She let out a long breath. "You're not going to give in are you?"

"I will give you anything you want except for a way out." He kissed her head. "I want to date and see if my instincts are telling me the truth."

"Alright…I guess that will be okay."

"Really?"

"Yes," she turned and looked up. "But please don't over promise and under deliver because if you're not a mind-blowing lover, then I may take myself out of the game." She leaned against his shoulder. "And if I eventually discover that you don't have a devoted following, I'll be disappointed because with a body like yours it should be guaranteed. All of that testosterone you have should be used for good and not evil."

He laughed so loud that several patrons turned and stared. "Birdie girl, it's never going to be dull with you, that I can see." Running his hand over her shoulder, he grinned. "And the only following I care about is you. And believe you me, I'm going to do everything I can to be *your* sex god?"

"And, I appreciate it, because if you turn out to be a dud, then I may just give up."

"Believe me, honey, I plan on rocking your world, but we're going to date and see what we have. No dropping, no using, just old-fashioned romance."

Sighing, she leaned back against the booth. "Let's just see how it goes. We may want only to do it once."

"Once is never going to be enough, hell a hundred thousand may not be either." Dropping his mouth, he devoured her and felt her surrender. It was the craziest conversation he'd ever had with a woman, and the only thing that would make it better was if they could keep kissing.

The waitress approached and said loudly, "Can I get you something to drink?"

Lifting his head, he smiled at the woman. "A martini for my girlfriend and I'll have a beer."

"I'll be right back with those."

Birdie moved away and tried to straighten her dress. "How did you know I wanted a martini?"

"I asked Frisco what you liked to drink. I did a little homework too, so I could be ready for our date." Running his thumb over his bottom lip, he shrugged. "Can't say it helped me out much, considering the bomb you just dropped. Are there any other plans that I should know about? Maybe you could tell me before we order."

"I don't think so. It was just the sex thing." Moving her silverware around, she wrinkled her nose. "I haven't had sex for a year." She looked down at her hands and kept her eyes glued to her fingers. "I'm out of practice, and if I'm honest, my ex told me I wasn't any good. This could be a total bust for you…kind of like a service project." She looked up. "I don't want to oversell myself and then have you be disappointed."

Tipping her head, he kissed her gently. "Your ex was a fucking idiot, and I'm going to thank him every day for his stupidity. We're going to be incredible together, no doubt about it. When a man tells a woman that she isn't any good, it says more about him than anything else. I plan on getting you addicted to my moves and if my name doesn't fall from your mouth like a prayer, then I'm gonna keep trying until it does. So, get ready, Birdie, because I plan on blowing your mind."

She fanned her face. "I hope you're right. But I can't have sex with you tonight because sleeping with someone on the first date would make me a tart. I'm a little desperate, but I'm not a tart."

"Understood, Birdie. Not on the first date." He gave her a solemn nod. "I knew you were a relationship girl."

"Truth is, I don't know what I am." She picked up her menu and studied it. "What are you going to have for dinner?"

"I have no idea." He looked over and laughed. "All my brain can focus on is how soon we can be together."

"Maybe this weekend." She kept her eyes glued to the menu. "We can get together if you don't have any other plans."

"All my plans involve you, and now they include *you* being naked." He let out a rough breath. "I hope that I can last until then because, right now, it doesn't feel like it."

She patted his knee. "You're a man with a lot of training and discipline, so this should be a breeze."

"You'd think so, wouldn't you?" he said quietly as the waitress delivered their drinks. Once she left, Mark lifted his glass in a toast. "Thanks, Birdie James, for choosing me."

She leaned forward and pressed a kiss to his mouth. "My pleasure, Mark Frazier."

Stepping out of the club, Mark tucked Birdie under his arm and quartered the area before they started walking toward the car. The streets were busy, and he didn't want anything unexpected to happen.

Paranoid?

Definitely.

It was his nature, and it probably was never going to change. Looking down, he saw Birdie's happy smile and knew something important was going to happen between them. "Did you have fun?" he asked as they walked toward the truck.

"It was perfect." Squeezing his waist, she leaned her head against his chest. "It may be the best date I've ever had."

He kissed the top of her head. "I love to hear that since I haven't planned one since college." When she relaxed into his hold, he pulled her a little closer.

He ran over the conversation they'd had and dinner and decided that underneath all her talk about trysts, affairs, and flings, she was a relationship girl. Not that he planned on making the point since she could believe whatever she wanted. "Do you want any dessert or coffee? We could stop in that shop over there before we go home."

"No, thank you, I'm ready to go home. I'm going to be super busy for the next two days and should get some sleep. What's on your schedule for the rest of the week?"

"We have a training op with new equipment tomorrow and won't be back until Friday night. Can I plan on taking you to go to the beach on Saturday?"

"Yes, Mark. And I'd love it if you'd teach me how to swim in the ocean."

"Good because I'm a hell of a teacher and will take you out for dinner after we're done at the beach."

"Sounds good." They walked up to the truck, and he helped her in. "Thanks for a great night. I loved the restaurant, the music, and spending time together."

"Thanks for coming out with me." He confirmed her belt was secure and then ran around and jumped in. He checked his mirrors and pulled out.

As he drove toward the freeway, he grabbed her hand and listened to her hum the song from their dance at the wedding. That's right Birdie…I will be latching on because I know what I have found.

CHAPTER SEVEN

Birdie lay in bed watching mindless TV when she heard the phone ring. Seeing Mark's name on the display made her answer it immediately. "Hey, you."

"Hi, honey. I'm at your door. Can I come in, please?"

"Sure, wait a second." Climbing out of bed, she studied her jammies and tried to decide if she had enough time to change. She didn't look great, but what could she do at ten o'clock at night?

"He'll have to take me as I am," she said to herself as she ran downstairs. Opening the front door, she studied the tired man standing on her doorstep. "Bad day at the office?" She pulled him into the house and wrapped her arms around him. "You look beat."

He encircled her in his arms and kissed her head. "If you could make this day go away for a while, I would be really grateful."

"That bad?"

"And then some," he said quietly.

"Do you want something to eat?"

"No, baby, I'm not hungry. I haven't slept in forty-eight hours and knew that if I went to my empty condo I would just add another twenty-four."

"Poor you."

"The training exercise was a goat fuck from the beginning. Everything that could go wrong did. I also got news today that a buddy of mine from a team on the East Coast has been injured, and it doesn't look good." He wrapped his arms tighter. "I just want to go to bed with you in my arms and wake up to your smiling face." Tilting her chin, he wagged his eyebrows. "We can also get started on that slump-busting thing if you want…"

"I wanted to be wearing something sexy when my rut got incinerated, do I have time to transform myself?"

"I think you're plenty sexy just the way you are."

Laughing, she led him upstairs into her room. "Clearly, you have very low standards if you think this is sexy."

They stood in the doorway, and she wondered what he thought. When she'd decorated it, she wanted to create a sanctuary and thought the king-sized bed with its white sheets and white quilt achieved it. "Let me see if I have a toothbrush for you."

Walking into the bathroom, she started searching in her cabinet. "Found one."

He followed her in and glanced around. "I like your bathroom." He tipped his head toward the shower. "Maybe we can come up with something to do on the bench tomorrow."

Ignoring the comment, she tried to act cool and pretend like shower sex was a regular occurrence. "Do you want to shower? You smell good, so you must've already changed."

"I got cleaned up at the base after we got back." He took his new toothbrush and dropped a sweet kiss on her cheek. "Thanks, baby."

She handed him the toothpaste and watched him brush his teeth. "I thought I was ready…but now that you're standing here…I'm a little nervous." Moving to his side, she rested her hand on his back. "What if I'm a big talker, and stumble when it's time to turn it into action?"

"You don't have to do a thing," he said around his toothbrush.

She watched him finish and wondered what in the world he was talking about. She always had to do something…she was a doer, not a sit arounder."

"Leave everything up to me, honey."

"That doesn't seem fair. Why should you do all the work?"

"Remember when I told you that I'm the boss in the bedroom?"

"Yes."

"I meant it." He grabbed her hip and pulled her close. "A man likes to own his woman's pleasure, and I'm hoping you'll allow me the privilege to do just that."

She trailed her fingers over his arm. "What exactly does that mean?"

"It *means* that I'm going to touch all the places that make you moan," running his finger along her arm, he smiled, "and the places that make you scream. It means that you're going to surrender your body and allow me to make you happy." He arched an eyebrow. "I hope you plan on keeping your promise and let me be the boss?"

Swallowing, she blinked several times. "Uh…I'll try."

"Can't ask for more than that."

No one had ever shown the slightest interest in owning her pleasure, so she didn't know what she was in for. Whatever it was sure sounded fantastic, though. Especially the screaming part. She'd never made more than polite noises and figured if there was a man who could make her do more, it was Mark.

Giving him a small smile, she decided he could own her pleasure, her body, and whatever else he wanted. Not that she would ever tell him that. The man was already too bossy. "Do you have pajamas?"

Laughter filled the room. "I don't wear pajamas. I sleep in my boxers if we're deployed and naked when I'm home. So tell me what you want me to wear or not and I'll oblige."

"It was a silly question. Who in their right mind squawks about illicit flings and then asks about nightwear?" She fluttered her hand toward his body. "Especially if you have someone like you offering…nakedness."

"So is that a yes to the boxers or a no?"

"It's a yes…for now."

"Perfect." He kissed her nose. "Let's get in that inviting bed of yours and get ourselves some sleep. I want to be fully rested for tomorrow."

"Okay." She gave him a faint smile. "For the record, I'm not chickening out. You're the most handsome, sexy man that I've ever met, and I want the full show. Because this could be my one-time chance and I don't want to miss the screaming and moaning."

Leaning over, he kissed her gently. "Our toothbrushes are hanging out together, so I'd say you have me for as long as you want."

Pressing her face into his chest, she kissed him. "You may not be interested in more than just the one night. No matter what our toothbrushes are doing together."

Shaking his head, he let out a growl. "That asshole did a number on you." He lifted her face and waited. "Honey, one night is never going to be enough; I can tell after just a couple of kisses. I want you with every breath in my body and don't expect that to end anytime soon." Holding out his hand, he waited.

Looking down, she realized she was at a crossroads. All her talk meant nothing if she didn't take advantage of the very thing she'd dreamed about. She laced her hand in his and tugged him into the bedroom. "I'm ready."

Sitting on the bed, she watched him take off his clothes and tried not to drool. "You're better-looking than I imagined and remind me of one of the Greek statues at the Getty.

Turning, he stood with his hands on his hips. "I've got a lot of scars and it seems that they don't bother you."

Holding out her hand, she waited until he joined her. "Forget bother, I can't wait to trace every single one of them. With my mouth."

"Damn woman, you can't be saying things like that." He lay down next to her and ran his hand over her shoulder. "You're lucky that I haven't slept in forty-eight hours because it's the only thing keeping me from laying my mad seducing skills on you."

Sliding her hand through the crisp hair on his chest, she licked her lips. "I want you fully rested, so let's go to sleep and see what kind of trouble we can find in the morning."

"I like the sound of that, but I've got to kiss you just once before we close our eyes."

"A goodnight kiss is always a good idea," she responded as he lifted her chin, then brushed his thumb over her damp lips before covering her mouth with his. She met him with a moan of acceptance as his lips moved with determination and grace that was unexpected. His tongue glided back and forth, urging her to open and let him inside. One more swipe and she parted for him. He swept in and started slowly, then grew bolder as she responded. Every lick, taste, and touch resonated inside her body and she felt more alive than she ever had.

Wrapping her arms around his shoulders, she stretched to hold him. The sheer mass of him was delicious, and when his body pressed into hers, she felt his excitement. And boy, there was a lot of *excitement* to handle. The man was enormous.

He released her mouth and let out a growl. "Baby, are we going to wait until morning when we're both awake?"

When he rocked his hips against hers, she answered by rolling hers back. "Sure, waiting is a good idea. Right?"

"Maybe we should just break you out of your rut now."

Leaning back, she slid her hand over his face. "Nope. This is a big deal, and I want you at your best."

"I'm pretty good right now." He took her hand and moved it down his stomach and over his boxers. "Ready, willing, and able."

Looking down, she saw how real his words were. He was a big man all over, and when she ran her hand up and down his length, she felt him swell even larger. Biting her lip, she felt her body clench as she thought about what he was going to feel like. "I'm going to need to be rested before I can handle this—I mean you." Reluctantly, she lifted her hand away and lay on her back. "Hit the lights and let's go to sleep."

Groaning, he rolled over and hit the switch. The room was plunged into darkness, and he lay down. "Night, Birdie."

Rolling over, she rested her head on his chest. "Night, Mark." Slowly, she felt herself relax and did a happy dance in her head. Whatever happened in the morning was not only going to break her rut, but it was also going to change her life.

CHAPTER EIGHT

Birdie woke up on a hard, warm, hairy surface—Mark's chest to be exact. Smiling to herself, she ran her hand slowly across the wall of muscle that covered his torso. "Hello," she whispered against his warm skin. "I never thought this would be my morning view."

"Morning, baby. How did you sleep?"

She didn't respond as she rolled into him and kissed him over his heart. Pulling her up, he whipped her shirt over her head. "So, it's going to be like that?" she asked breathlessly.

"Absolutely." Rolling on top, he dipped his tongue into her mouth and took possession.

As he held her tightly, she tried to decide which sensation she liked best. Their mouths mating, the feel of his calloused fingers running across her body, or the heat from his skin? Maybe all of them together.

The combination had her body humming and her heart racing. When he lifted his mouth away and grinned, happiness exploded in her brain. "This is better than anything in recent memory."

Laughter rumbled out of his chest. "Just you wait, Birdie. I'm going to own you after we're done." He dipped his head and kissed his way down the curve of her neck. "You taste good," he whispered against her skin. "I've been thinking about getting you under me since I met you, and now you're here."

Arching into his body and words, she let go of the last of her reserves. He would have no problem owning any part of her if he kept up what he was doing. "Yes," she mumbled as he dragged his fingers over her breasts. Leaning down, he kissed each one and then pulled a hard nipple into his mouth. His mouth on her skin was a revelation and a thousand times better than she imagined.

"Are you ready?" he asked a moment later.

She couldn't form words, so she grabbed his head and kissed him.

"I'll take that as a yes," he mumbled against her mouth. "God, you have the softest skin and smell fucking wonderful." He trailed his mouth down her body toward her breasts and whispered against her skin, "Soon, I'll be the person who knows you best."

His big hand slid down her thigh and slipped her underwear off, and the feel of his roughened, calloused hands did things to her skin that she'd never felt before. When his fingers traced over her birth control patch and stopped, she wondered what was wrong.

"Birdie, what's this?"

She looked over her shoulder. "My birth control patch. Which reminds me, I'd better get the box of condoms I bought the other day."

"Baby, if you're on birth control, then we don't need condoms. I can enter you bareback."

"We haven't exchanged health certificates. I can go downstairs and get mine, but where's yours?"

He got rid of his boxers. "I promise you that I'm disease-free. We get tested regularly for everything. I haven't had sex since my last deployment, and I've been tested several times since my return." He rocked his hips into her as he said it. "I've never been inside a woman without a condom, and I want to be inside you without a barrier."

"All right, but you have to show me your results later today. If you're lying, I'll kill you or have your friends do it for me." He captured her mouth again as his fingers slid between her legs. Closing her eyes at his touch, she moaned. "Oh, my." The strokes of his tongue and the strokes of his fingers set her on fire. They'd barely started, and she was close to an organsm.

"Tell me when it feels good," he whispered in her ear as he slid his finger inside. Hearing a sigh, he laughed. "No, when it feels *really* good." He curved his finger. "Here?"

She shook her head.

"Wait…here?"

When she nodded, he slipped a second finger in and moved it higher until he hit something that made her jolt.

"Found it."

Sliding down her body, he spread her with his thumbs and touched his tongue to her clit. Stars exploded. "So close," she murmured as he sucked her bud into his mouth. Rising off the bed, she tried to hold onto the white-hot pleasure racing through her body. Detonating instantly, she enjoyed the ripples of ecstasy rolling through her body.

After several minutes, she collapsed on the bed and laughed. "I didn't even know that was possible. We could stop right now, and I would be out of my rut."

Laughter erupted as he crawled his way back up her body. "Baby, we just got started. We have a lot more to do; that was the warm-up."

Lifting herself, she studied his satisfied smile. "I know you're the boss, but I want to see what I'm in for." She pushed him over and studied his massive…naked…sexy body. What had she done to deserve him? The man was breathtaking with his tan skin and thick mat of brown hair covering his chest. Her eyes moved lower, and almost popped out of her head when she saw how well-endowed he was. "I'm not sure it's going to fit." Reaching out, she ran her hand up and down his length and swore she was touching steel. His erection twitched under her fingers as she stroked him. "I guess we should give it a try and see what happens."

"Don't worry because we're going to be a perfect fit."

Rolling on top, he kissed her as his hips rocked into her heat. His tongue stroked deep into her mouth and mirrored what he would soon be doing when he entered her. She gripped his shoulders as he positioned himself at her entrance. Pushing forward slowly, he slid in and waited. "So far, so good," she mumbled as he filled her. "So very good."

"Wait till I'm buried inside you."

He drove himself in slowly and her body bowed in surrender. Making a final push, he pressed his hips and was seated completely. "More," she moaned.

"You feel like a warm glove—you're so tight."

Grinding his hips firmly, she moved in counterpoint and closed her muscles around his incredible length.

"If you keep that up, it's going to end before we even get started."

"I guess that just means that we have to do it a lot until we get it right."

"Let me show you right."

Pushing her legs wide, he pumped into her and hit the bundle of nerves that had her repeating his name. She wrapped her legs around his waist and smiled up into his eyes. "That's right." He slid out slowly and moved back in, and she threw her head back as he hit every nerve in her body again and again.

"Can you feel how hard you make me?"

He dropped his lips to her face and kissed her as he stroked her once more, making her shatter.

"Keep coming for me, Birdie." The bed bounced underneath them, the headboard rocked against the wall, and all she cared about was the orgasm ripping through her body.

It was the most intense sexual experience of her life. Was it because it had been so long or did Mark possess all the magic he promised?

Whatever it was, her body was on fire with pleasure.

"God, I love being in you," he shouted as he pumped his hips with all his strength.

Holding on as best she could, she felt his release wash through her. Once, twice, and then again. Accepting that part of him made her realize that she might not be able to let him go. The last spasm passed through his body as he sank down.

They stared into each other's eyes in silence and then blinked in mutual recognition. "You can be the boss of the bedroom whenever you want."

"I think we need to keep doing this as often as we can." Nodding his head as though he'd just given an order, he kissed her gently with an unmistakable note of possession.

"I didn't know that's what sex was supposed to be. I think that I've been doing it wrong all these years. Usually, I'm so in my head, worrying about everything. This is the first time I was completely mindless. It was like drowning in pleasure."

"We fit, Birdie. No doubt about it."

"That we do." As she closed her eyes, she realized she'd been right about Mark and he was in fact, a sex god.

***

Birdie woke up with a start and couldn't get her bearings. Lifting her head, she glanced up and saw Mark smiling. "It wasn't a dream."

"Nope. We're the real deal."

Rolling out of his embrace, she felt his hand on her arm. "What?"

"Let's stay in bed and practice some more." He pulled her back on top and kissed her slowly and deeply. He rocked his hips and slipped in with little effort. "Hi."

She stared down. "Hi. I was going to make coffee and then take a shower. I have to go to the shop this morning."

He continued to move his hips and was able to slip further in as her body welcomed him. "I like your idea, though." She kissed him as he pumped his hips. Laughing, she felt herself slide off his massive body.

Catching her, he rolled them over and pinned her with his hips. "You think that's funny? I'll show you funny." He rotated his hips, and her laugh turned into a moan. "You fit baby girl."

"I'm so close."

"Let go, Birdie." He lifted her leg over his arm and drove himself into her heat. "Now."

The command unlocked something in her brain, and she did just what he asked. She clenched him as he shouted and gave into his release. Their slick bodies moved against each other as they shattered. Fast or slow, the man knew what he was doing.

He collapsed against her, and she felt herself sink into the bed. "Mark, I can't breathe. You have to move a little."

"I think I blacked out for a second. Are you okay?"

She lay on her back and waved her hand as he rolled off. "I've lost the power of speech and may be in a sex coma. Is that possible?"

"I think it might be. You have magic super sex voodoo powers and used them on me. Don't get me wrong—I liked it. And wouldn't mind if you continued to cast your spell for a long time to come."

She sat up and searched for her robe. "I think you have the voodoo powers, not me."

He slipped out of bed, stood up, and stretched, and she couldn't help but stare. The sight of him naked took her breath away, and she sighed happily. "My goodness."

"See anything you like, Birdie?"

"I like you. When you have a masterpiece in your house, it's a good idea to look your fill, and that's exactly what I'm doing." She patted his chest as she passed. "I'm going to shower and then I'll make breakfast."

He followed her and stepped into the shower. When he turned the water on and held his arms open, she figured there was no getting rid of him. "So, we're showering together?"

"Yes, it's important to conserve water."

Stepping into his arms, she hugged him tightly. "Thanks for getting me out of my rut. I can't tell you how much I appreciate it."

"The pleasure was mine."

When he leaned down and kissed her, she knew she was in a ton of trouble. Lt. Cmdr. Mark Frazier wasn't a man to fling with; he was a man to keep. "I'm going to make you a big breakfast with pancakes and whatever else you want."

Throwing her a smile, he laughed. "Orgasms and pancakes. God damn, it's a good day."

"It certainly is," she mumbled as he held her tightly against his chest.

***

Walking down the stairs, Mark realized that he'd never been connected to a woman the way he was with Birdie. And that meant, he had to find a way to talk her into a relationship.

Was something like that even possible? He couldn't say either way since she was giving him mixed signals and delievering speeches about flings every other day.

The lyrics to their song ran through his head. "Now, I got you in my space, I won't let go of you."

That's what he wanted to do with Birdie, he just didn't know how to get her latched onto him.

As he entered the kitchen, he heard her singing along in Italian with the opera playing on her iHome. "Smells wonderful."

"Coffee is ready."

"Thanks. What can I do to help?"

She pointed to the plates and cutlery stacked on the counter. "You can set the table, please."

He followed directions and watched her mix up the batter in a bowl and knew this is what he wanted...Saturdays with Birdie.

Returning to the island, he watched her pull something out of the oven. "What did you make?"

"I made a frittata with sausage and cheese. The pancakes will be ready in a minute, is there anything else you would like?"

"Nothing. It looks perfect." He slid his arm around her shoulder and kissed her gently. "I know it's going to be delicious."

She laughed and shook her head. "You haven't even tasted it yet."

"Yes, I have, and liked it." When her face turned pink, he let out a chuckle. "Just telling it like it is."

"You can't say that in the kitchen."

"Why not?" He ran his hand over the island. "Maybe I'll put you up on this island later and show you exactly what I'm talking about." She stood with her mouth open and no sound coming out. "Did I embarrass you?"

"I've never talked about it like that before. You're a lot more comfortable discussing it than I am." She ran her hand over his. "Maybe I should be more sophisticated at twenty-eight."

Lifting her chin, he shook his head. "You don't have to be anything or do anything. Just be you. You're incredible just the way you are, and I want to make sure you know how much you affect me. I learned my lesson last week, so I'm not going to play it cool. I'm going to make sure that you know how I feel every day." Placing his hands on her waist, he pulled her close. "And for the record, I don't think anything that happens between us is embarrassing. We're adults and can choose what we do with each other and where it happens. Eventually, you'll feel safe and trust me. I know that's going to take time, but it's going to happen."

"All right, I'll think about it." She stepped around him and stirred the batter.

"No thinking necessary, just let me in, and I promise you won't regret it."

"Can you put the food on the table? These will be done in a minute."

He gave her one last kiss and followed directions. He'd said what he wanted and now had to leave her be. If he pushed, she'd likely push back, and that wasn't what he wanted.

Patience was going to become his new best friend.

***

Birdie watched Mark put the last glass in the dishwasher and walked into the laundry room. As she put the sheets in the dryer, she saw him walk in and lift a pair of her panties off the drying rack.

"I like your underwear." Twirling them on his finger, he grinned. "How many sets of sheets do you have?"

"I don't know, maybe two. Why?"

"I should buy you a couple more sets since we'll be changing them every day. Unless you want to go over to my condo and spend the night."

"That sounds like a relationship." She tilted her head. "I didn't think you had those."

"I do with you! So don't try and get rid of me. We're going to have sex twice a day, every day, for the foreseeable future."

"Was that a statement or a question?"

"That was a statement. You're always telling me what you think. Well, now I'm telling you what I want. We'll be together every day and get to know one another."

"You haven't had a date since college. Do you know what you're asking?"

"Yes, I do. My toothbrush is next to yours, and that's not something you can ignore."

"I don't understand the whole toothbrush thing, but I'll think about what you're asking." She studied him and then chuckled. "You know that if we do what you're suggesting, we may wear out body parts."

"You haven't had sex for a year, and it's been at least seven months for me, so we have a lot to make up for."

She bit back a smile. "I guess it wouldn't hurt to try."

"That's the can-do spirit I like to see in a person." He pulled her out of the laundry room. "Do you want me to drive you to the shop this morning?"

"I usually walk, but a ride would be great." She gathered her purse, and they headed out to the truck and got in. "When we get to the shop, you can park in the back next to my delivery car."

"I noticed your vintage Wagoneer last week. Was it your grandmother's?" He started the truck and pulled out.

"It was. Grams kept it in good shape, and it has low mileage. I had it checked out when I moved down, and the only thing I have to add is airbags."

"You can't drive it if it doesn't have airbags." He glanced over and frowned. "I'll have them put in for you."

She was looking out the window and waved to one of her neighbors. "I only drive it around the island. I use my other car if I have to go into town. Don't worry; I'm safe."

"I don't like it. Let me have it next week, and I'll take it in. I don't want something happening to you."

"I'm fully capable of taking care of it."

"I know, but it would make me feel better if I could do this for you. Have you found a place to have it done?"

"That's part of my problem because everyone I've called so far can't seem to figure out which ones to order and how to install them. I just have to sit down and do the research."

"I'll ask Blake or Shane. They're both gearheads, and they can probably figure it out."

"That would be great."

He leaned over and kissed her. "My pleasure. I want to do this for you, so don't drive it until we figure it out."

She gave him a side-eye. "I suppose that would be okay." Staring out the window, she wondered why he was so concerned about her safety. It was sweet as could be; she just didn't understand it. In fact, she understood very little about what was happening between them.

The only clear thing was that it was something big. Big enough to possibly crack her heart open.

Which was the last thing she was looking for. Justin's betrayal had cost her more than she'd ever admitted to herself, her friends, and her family.

Was she ready to let someone like Mark in?

Did she have a choice?

No clear answer popped into her head, and she wished that she knew what the next step should be. And there was going to be one, whether she was ready or not because Mark was moving forward and it seemed he meant to take her with him.

All her smart talk about big, muscled men meant diddly squat now that she was faced with the real deal. And, that's precisely what the man sitting across from her was. The realest deal there ever was and, if she wanted anything with him, she was going to have to unlock the very thing she thought she wouldn't.

This wasn't going to be just some roll in the hay; this was going to be something that changed her life. The sooner she understood and accepted that the better it was going to be for everyone. Because at some point, she was either going to be all in or all out. Mark wasn't the sort of man to accept anything less.

CHAPTER NINE

Later that day, Birdie locked the doors to her shop and walked next door to the gourmet grocery and deli. She waved to Tom, the owner, as she made her way back to the meat counter. Marcus, Tom's husband, came out and gave her a big smile. "What are you going to make tonight?"

"I have no idea. I'm cooking for a friend and need some new ideas. Should I make lamb?"

Marcus's eyebrows lifted. "A friend—what kind of friend?"

She leaned against the counter. "The kind that I'm cooking for."

"You cook for a lot of people. This seems different."

"Might be, can't tell yet. He's on the Teams and the most handsome man I've ever met. He's alpha and bossy, but funny and sexy too. I'm not sure what it's going to be, but I'm having fun finding out."

"I'm proud of you Birdie. You're finally getting out of your own way. Bring him in, so we can give him a once over." He folded his big arms over the case. "I think you should grill some steaks, add the twice-baked potatoes, and make a nice salad. It will please your man and give you lots of time to see if he's any good in bed."

That's exactly what she wanted to do: please Mark. He had brought her back to life, and she wanted to thank him in some way. Making dinner didn't seem like much, but she figured it was a start. "I think he's good at everything."

Marcus handed her the steaks and smiled. "Well, that's good news." He came around the counter and hugged her. "You deserve it. Enjoy."

"Thank you." She kissed his cheek and then finished her shopping. As she was checking out, Tom gave her a look. "What?"

He took her card and ran it through the machine. "Coy? Didn't think that was your style, girl."

"Apparently, I'm getting a new style," she replied with a grin.

"About time." Winking, he returned her card. "I suppose that I'll have to get all of the details from Marcus." He handed her the bag of groceries. "I hope it's the same man who brought you to work this morning."

She loaded it into her basket and nodded. "His name is Mark, and it's the same man."

"Well, don't dilly dally. Go home and take care of him."

"Yes, sir!" She blew Tom a kiss and strolled out of the store. As she walked toward her house, she thought about what her friend had said and decided that taking care of Mark might not be a bad idea. After all, he'd taken real good care of her, and she should return the favor.

Her house was about three blocks from the shop, so it didn't take long for her to arrive home. As she got close, she saw Mark's truck parked in front of her house. Opening the gate, she rolled her basket in and noticed him frowning?"

He stood and let out a frustrated breath. "Where were you? I went to the store, and it was all locked up, and then I came here, and you weren't here. I was worried." Walking down the steps, he took her in his arms and hugged her tightly. "I don't like the feeling of not knowing where you are."

She hugged him back and rubbed her hands down his back. "I couldn't have gotten far. My shop is only a couple of blocks away. I stopped at the market to get some things for dinner."

"I'm taking you out to dinner."

She slipped out of his embrace and grabbed her basket. "I suppose that would be okay, it's just that…I just thought we might be busy doing something else."

A huge smile spread across his face. "You're right; we'll probably be busy. We can order pizza, though, so you don't have to cook." He grabbed her around the waist, bent her over his arm, and kissed her dramatically. When he finally released her, he grinned. "I plan on making you so happy and satisfied that you'll hardly be able to walk much less cook." He put her on her feet and then grabbed her basket and the bags he'd left by the door.

"That's a lot of happy," she replied as she unlocked the door.

"Honey, you have no idea." He followed her in, dropped the bags on the couch, then took her basket to the kitchen and watched her unpack the food. "Are you ready for your surprise?"

"You got me a surprise?"

"I sure did, and hope you like them." He took her hand and led her over to the couch, pulled out the bags, and started opening them.

She noticed they were from the local surf shop in town and wondered what he was up to. Closing her eyes, she smiled. "I'm ready and excited." Something heavy landed on her lap, and she glanced down. Mark had bought her a wetsuit. "Oh, my God, this is so sweet; I love it." She stood and held it in front of her. "I think it's perfect."

He pulled out another one. "I got you a spring suit as well. This is probably all you'll need for the next couple of months. You can use the full one in November when it gets colder." He leaned over and took something out of his pocket and handed it to her. "I went to the base and pulled a copy of my last medical exam. Nothing needs to come between us."

She opened it and started to read. "Six-foot-three, two-hundred forty-two pounds, seventeen percent body fat." She shook her head. "That's just wrong because I have more body fat than you. Which is slightly depressing." She continued to read and noticed his resting heart rate. "Are you a cobra? Your resting heart rate is 60." Placing her hand on his chest, she felt his steady heartbeat and knew it was a reflection of his nature. Turning back to the paper, she noted he was healthy and completely disease-free. "Thank you for bringing this to me." She stood and walked toward her office. "I'll get you mine," she called over her shoulder.

"I don't need to see it, honey. I trust you."

"Found it," she called out.

"You don't have to show me this."

"I looked at yours, and think you should look at mine." He started reading her report, and she put her hand over the middle of the page. "Just skip down to the bottom. You don't need to read that part."

He moved her hand and laughed. "I weigh a hundred pounds more than you do. You're small next to me."

"I'm not small at all. You're just supersized, and don't read anymore. I don't want you to see my body fat information—not after I saw yours."

He grabbed her and pulled her onto his lap. "I think you're the perfect size. I like all your curves and soft places. In fact, you could stand to add a couple of pounds."

"I've never felt small."

He ran his mouth along her neck and slipped his hand down her jeans, and massaged her behind. "This is one of my favorite parts of you. You have a world-class ass, and I intend to enjoy it." Letting his hand linger, he smiled against her skin. "Maybe we should skip the beach, go upstairs, and continue this."

"Oh, no, you said you wanted to take me to the beach." Wiggling out of his embrace, she gave him a stern look. "No more fooling around."

Growling, he kissed her, and finally let go. "Okay, I can wait." He grabbed his bag, and they started to walk upstairs to change.

She stopped on the landing and gave him a questioning look. "Do you want to still not use condoms?"

"I thought that's why we did the whole medical info exchange. I don't want anything between us."

"But then we have to agree to be exclusive. I don't want to change your life, but I don't want to risk dying. Maybe we should just use condoms to be safe and then it won't be awkward."

"I'm only going to sleep with you and will kill any son of a bitch who gets close to you. We should be fine."

"You could've left out the last part, and I would've assumed you were normal. Now I know you have a streak of crazy." When he kept his mouth shut and pasted an innocent look on his face, she realized she'd be lucky if a streak was all he had.

He tapped her gently on the behind. "Honey, let's get a move on. We're burning daylight."

"Keep that up, and that's not the only thing that's going to burn," she mumbled, climbing the stairs.

As they changed into their swimsuits, Birdie felt Mark's eyes glued to her as she pulled on a pair of board shorts over her suit. "What?"

"Nothing."

Sliding her hands on her hips, she waited. When he dropped his hands in front of his crotch, she started to laugh. His swim trunks were tented, and there was no way of hiding it. "Did I do that?"

Stalking toward her, he lifted her and wrapped her legs around his waist. "Yes, you did. Are you happy? I'm like a freaking sixteen-year-old kid."

Wiggling her hips closer, she held his face and kissed him. "You've made me the happiest girl in the world. You're the best-looking man I've ever met and to know that I affect you in any way is mind-boggling."

"So, the way I want you isn't scaring you off?"

Throwing her head back, she let out a laugh. "Are you kidding me? I've never had a man show more than mild interest, and that includes the one I was engaged to. To have a man like you want me is a modern-day miracle."

"Do we still have to go swimming?" He tilted his mouth into a smile. "It might not be right not to pay proper respect to the miracle we've been blessed with."

Unwinding her legs, she slid down his body. "We're going, Mark. We don't have to stay out long."

Leaning over, he kissed her head. "Come on then, let's get you in the water."

Twenty minutes later, they crossed the street and stepped onto the sand, Birdie looked down the coastline and saw Hotel Del in the distance. "How much time have you spent out here since you joined the Navy?"

"I have no idea. We swim and run most days and sometimes practice Fast Ropes on the other side of the inlet. I can't even begin to calculate how much time I've spent out here in the last twelve years." He kissed the side of her head. "This is the first time I'm bringing a beautiful girl to the beach, though."

"Sweet talker." She led him to a spot near the shore and dropped their stuff. "Having a Navy SEAL help me become a better swimmer is like having an Olympic athlete teach a baby how to swim."

He stood up to his full height and snapped off a salute. "Lt. Commander Mark Frazier at your service." Grabbing her, he swung her around. "Let's go get wet."

She laughed and then wiggled out of his hold. "Let me get my rash guard on."

After she got herself together, they walked out to the water, and he went in and got wet. Standing at the surf line, she hopped around because it was cold. "Why did I suggest this?" she mumbled to herself.

"Just dive in; that's the only way to get used to it." He returned, took her hand, and pulled her along. When she moved slowly, he picked her up, walked out into the surf, and threw her in. "Boy, she can scream loud," he said as he waited for her to breach the surface.

Her head popped up, and she wiped her face, glaring in his direction. "That wasn't cool; I was working my way in. Why did you pitch me in?"

He hitched his shoulder carelessly. "It would be nightfall before you made it in, and sometimes you just need to take the plunge. We should've brought the spring suit. I thought you could handle the temperature."

"I can handle it, and am not some recruit you can throw in."

He caught up with her and pulled her against his chest. "Sorry, I was just having fun. I won't throw you in anymore and go as slow as you want."

"Thank you, now let me go. I'm going to swim out a little."

He let her go, and she turned around and started swimming for the break. The waves weren't big, so it was easy for her to manage the swells. Once she had swum a couple of laps, she turned over and floated on her back.

Mark swam next to her and moved his hand up her stomach and was about to slip his finger inside her top. Pushing his hand away, she wagged her finger back and forth. "No fooling around in the water, Commander. Safety first!" She flipped over and swam around him in circles.

He watched her circle him and laughed when she tried to stay out of his reach. "I think you're a good swimmer and may not need my help after all."

She swam closer and climbed onto his back and wrapped her legs around his waist. "Today's easy because it's so flat. I get intimidated when it's big, and don't know where the current is."

"We'll keep coming out, and I'll teach you about the current. This was a good way to start, nice and easy."

As the sun bounced off the waves, Birdie felt herself relax and decided to ask the question she couldn't get out of her mind. "Why me?"

His head swiveled around as she noticed his sharp profile. There wasn't a compromising bone in the man's body, and she couldn't understand why he was so interested. It didn't add up and, as an accountant, she needed it to before she let herself become vulnerable. The intense physical connection they had might eventually turn into an emotional one and, if that happened, she wanted to understand the risk.

He pulled her around to his front. "I guess the best answer is that something about you feels like home. My home. The place I'm supposed to be. It's never happened and, as much as I'd like to pretend that I understand why, I can't. It just is. You, Birdie James, are not a choice. All I can do is follow my instinct and hope it's leading me in the right direction."

Tightening her hold, she lay her head against his chest and closed her eyes. In the middle of the Pacific Ocean on a perfectly ordinary Saturday afternoon in the middle of September, Mark Frazier stole her heart. What that would mean eventually, she couldn't say. "Well, that's as fine an answer as any person could hope for." When he pressed his mouth against her head, she closed her eyes.

"It's the truth, Birdie. My instincts are usually right on, so I've learned to trust them over the years. As far as I can tell, they're telling me to stick as close to you as I can. So that's what I'm going to do."

His big arms tightened around her as he swam them toward the shore and she decided to go with the flow and see where they landed. As far as she could tell, it was going to be someplace extraordinary.

***

Mark held Birdie's hand as they walked back to the house and noticed that whatever he'd said when they were in the water had made her relax.

It was the truth as well as he knew it, and he saw no reason not to share it with her. As best as he could tell, the more she knew about his feelings, the better off they were. Playing it cool and trying to have the upper hand the other night had almost cost him and it wasn't a mistake he was going to make twice.

The last twenty-four hours had been fucking mindboggling, and he wanted to do everything he could to make sure they had a thousand more just like it. When they got to her house, he followed her around the side into the backyard. "What's back here?"

"Prepare to be amazed." She took him over to the side of the garage and waved her hands around. "This is my new outdoor shower. What do you think?"

"I think it's great." She'd enclosed the back side of the garage and installed a shower, toilet, and sink. "This is the best one I've ever seen."

"I know. Adam did a great job, and I think it's going to be terrific." She hung their towels on big hooks on the outside wall and went in the door and turned on the shower. "I even have hot water out here."

He closed the door and looked around. "Can't ask for more than that." When she started to peel her board shorts off, he decided there was something he could ask for…hot, banging sex against the wall. Stepping closer, he unfastened the clasp on her top and let it fall into his hands. "We can't take a shower with our suits on. We'll still be sandy." He laced his fingers into her bottoms, slid them down her body, and then threw them over his shoulder. "Better." Getting rid of his trunks in record time, he grinned. "Now, we can take a shower."

Wrapping an arm around her waist, he pulled her close and dropped his lips to hers, and lazily explored her mouth. When she pulled away and took a much-needed breath, he knew she was a force to be reckoned with.

Running his lips along her neck, he enjoyed her smooth skin under his mouth, and inhaled her scent, knowing that for the rest of his life he would associate the smell of Birdie with mind-blowing happiness. "Let me see if you're ready." He slid a hand down her body, swept his fingers along her sex, and brushed her with a rhythm that had her hips moving into his hands. "Let go and show me how good I make you feel." With her mouth against his neck, she clung to him and fell apart.

Not giving her a second to recover, he lifted her, bent his legs, and entered her in one long thrust. Pushing her back against the wall, he began kissing her with the same intensity he was driving himself into her heat. "My head is about to blow off."

When she shouted out his name several times, he figured the neighbors would have it memorized by the time they were done. She clasped him as he let himself explode. Unable to slow it down or make it gentle, he ground into her until it felt like she was inside him.

As the last of the spasms went through his body, he couldn't tell the difference between her skin and his.

They felt like one.

Dropping his head to her shoulder, he tried to take a breath as his chest heaved in and out. "I like your shower," he managed to huff out. "I hope your neighbors enjoyed hearing my name over and over."

"I guess it's one way to get introduced to the neighborhood." When she laughed against his chest, he glanced down and realized that he'd never been happier.

Unwinding her legs, she slowly slipped down his body and leaned against the wall. "I've always wanted to have sex with a man who couldn't wait to get at me. You've just fulfilled one of my biggest fantasies."

He took her hand and kissed it. "I'm happy to make every one of them come true."

"I think you're capable of doing that. But you've put me into a sex coma, so I would agree with whatever you said."

He grabbed a towel and wrapped her up and then did the same to himself. When she had herself dried off, she walked out and headed over to her barbeque.

"Don't you want to go to dinner?"

"If you don't mind, I'd like to stay home. You wiped me out, and it's going to take me a while to become fully conscious again."

"We can do whatever you want. I might've blacked out for a minute, so I'm operating in a fog of sexual satisfaction. Let me do the barbeque and help with dinner."

"Okay, that would be great." She flipped it on and then took his hand and walked up to the house. "It's going to be simple."

"Perfect," he replied as he watched her go into the kitchen and start pulling out food for dinner.

"I hope you're hungry. I bought big steaks and have twice-baked potatoes, asparagus, and salad."

"Sounds great, you're spoiling me."

She turned on the oven, put the potatoes in, and added salt and pepper to the steak. Leaning over, she kissed him. "I'm going upstairs to get dressed."

He felt the same thump in his chest as she walked away and realized it was a sign of complete happiness. Something he never experienced before. But hoped to have a hell of a lot more of when he convinced Birdie that he would be the best teammate she could ask for.

***

"Do you want a beer while you cook the steaks?" Birdie asked as she held up a bottle.

"Sure, sounds great."

She passed it over and then pulled out a bottle of wine. "What kind of music do you like?" she asked as she picked up her phone.

"I don't think it's anything you want to play for dinner. I like rock and heavy metal; choose something you like."

She looked at her phone and chose a classic rock station. "How about a compromise?"

He picked up the plate of steaks, grabbed some tongs, and kissed her head. "Perfect."

Watching him walk away, she sighed. He was perfect, and she had no idea what to do about it. She followed him out and handed him his beer, then sat down and drank her wine. "My next project is going to be adding outdoor speakers and twinkle lights. Then, when I get the pool in, I can have a big party."

"I can install the speakers, and if you tell me what twinkle lights are, I can put those in too."

"I can have Adam do it—you don't have to."

He came over and sat down. "I want to give you music and twinkle lights. Let me do this."

She kissed his arm. "Thank you." They sat together with the music floating outside from the kitchen, and she couldn't remember the last time she felt so relaxed. Hearing the timer ding, she got up to finish dinner. "Do you want to eat outside or in?"

"Whatever you want."

The weather was still lovely, so she decided to bring everything outside. She went in, checked the potatoes, put the asparagus in, and finished the salad. She gathered the plates and grabbed some candles and headed outside. While Mark was checking the steaks, she set the table and lit the candles. Once he brought the meat over, she handed him a piece of foil and went back in to get the rest. She was starved after all of the sex and swimming and was ready to eat. "Thank you for taking me to the water today. It was generous of you to get me both wetsuits."

"I had fun. The ocean is usually work for me, so it was great to be reminded that it can be relaxing."

As she watched him place food on their plates, she knew that she'd never been around a man who was so compelling. Everything about him drew her in. "What's your favorite part of your job?"

"I was drawn to becoming a SEAL because I love being in the water. Now, I enjoy strategic planning and figuring out how the team is going to accomplish the mission. Five years ago, I might've told you it was jumping out of planes." He popped a piece of steak into his mouth. "That's the best thing about my job; it's never the same, and I'm always learning something new."

She dug into her food and thought about how exciting his life must be. "How long do men usually last on the Teams?"

"Well, at my advanced age of thirty-two, I'm considered an old man. If guys last until they're thirty-six or thirty-eight, it's unusual because this is a young man's job. Our career is like a professional athlete's—we last until our body gives out."

"Except you go into the most dangerous situations in the world where people are trying to kill you. Then you pull people out and bring them home."

"Well, there's that, but we're highly trained and go in with the best people and equipment. The odds are definitely in our favor."

"That's a crazy way to calculate odds." Giving him a smile, she went back to eating and thought about the chances of him not surviving a mission. Shivering, she wiped the numbers from her mind and focused on Mark and the yummy dinner they were enjoying.

Once they were finished eating, she wrapped her sweater tighter. "Are you ready to go in? I have brownies for dessert."

"Sounds good, but I'm looking at my dessert," he said as he got up and collected the plates.

Shaking her head, she laughed. "I don't have 'dessert' in me. I went from zero to a hundred today, and am worn out." Picking up the dishes, she walked in. "I'm going to clean the kitchen and then crash." When she set everything down on the island, she took his hand. "Thank you for a great day; let me walk you to the door."

"I don't want to leave. Can't we watch a movie or something?"

"We've been together for almost twenty-four hours; don't you want to go home?"

"No."

She watched him walk over to the dishwasher and start loading dishes. "Okay, I guess." Walking out to the patio, she wondered how long he planned on staying. She collected the rest of the dishes and went back inside. "Mark…"

"I want to spend as much time with you as I can," he said before she finished. "I don't have that much time at home. I want to bond with you before I get the call for wheels up."

Seeing his open expression and sincerity, she nodded. "A movie it is."

When he threw her a grateful smile, she wondered how difficult his next deployment was going to be.

CHAPTER TEN

Mark moved his fingers over the warm woman in his arms and felt her shiver. Tugging her possessively in his arms, he licked the rim of her ear and felt her giggle. "You're awake."

"Mmhmm," she murmured. "How come I'm naked and went to bed with clothes on?"

"I didn't want you to get hot, so I took them off." His hand moved slowly toward its goal and slipped into her slick folds.

"That's considerate of you," she said as she moved against his hand.

"That's me, a man of consideration." He kissed her neck and slid his thumb over her center, making her hips surge forward. Fitting himself closely, he lifted her leg over his hip and moved the tip of his penis into her opening. Groaning against the pleasure, he asked, "You okay, baby? Are you too sore?"

Instead of responding, she reached behind and grabbed his leg. "Are you trying to torture me?"

"Maybe a little." Moving in and out slowly, he felt her muscles begin to contract and slowed his thrusts. "Not yet," he whispered, "we don't want it to end too soon. It's morning sex, so I'll try and keep it gentle and sweet."

"I feel you everywhere."

Feeling her surrender, he decided there was no sweet and gentle in him this morning. He wanted to give her everything, so he moved his finger against her center as his strokes became heavy and fast. The bed moved to the rhythm as he took her higher and higher. He bent down and lightly bit her neck as she called his name and exploded, contracting sharply around him.

Hearing his name allowed him to take his final strokes. Long moments passed as he slowly came down from the mind-bending happiness that being inside Birdie allowed him. When he was finally able to take a breath, he noticed there was silence in the room except for his heavy breathing.

When he managed finally to look over, he saw that her eyes were closed, and she had a smile on her face. "Good morning, Birdie girl. What a great way to start the day."

As she started to roll over, he felt himself slip out and noticed how wet they were. Birdie lay on her stomach with her face in the pillow, so he rolled closer and draped his leg over her. "How are you doing? Still with me?" She waved her hand, turned her head, and smiled. Rubbing her back, he gently kissed her skin. "Have I put you in a sex coma?"

She opened one eye and laughed. "Having sex with you is so intense. I feel like I float away from my body."

"Baby, I know. I'll calm down after we've been together for a couple of years, but right now I can't control my desire for you."

"Did you say a couple of years?"

When she stiffened under his touch, he wondered how vital honesty was at this point. Was she ready for his truth? Not likely, but what could he do? This was it for him. It had taken him thirty-two years to find her and a week to understand that she was the one. "Are you hungry?"

"Yes, I could eat a horse."

Pulling away, he let out a laugh. "That I can do!"

When she sat up, she looked so freaking delicious that he wanted to pull her back down and start all over. Sighing, he knew that wasn't possible and contented himself with her presence.

"I like having sex with you," she said as she trailed her hand over his chest. "I figured it was going to be amazing, but had no idea you were going to show me colors that I had no idea existed."

"Honey, we just got started." He stared into her pretty eyes and hoped he could turn what they had into something more. Something that would be impossible for her to walk away from. "Let's get up so I can feed you."

Watching her stand and slip her robe on made him wonder if they could come back after breakfast. Deciding that bringing it up was a bad idea, he followed her to the bathroom.

Stopping him at the door, she pointed across the hall. "You can use that one. I need a couple of minutes of privacy."

"I've seen every inch of you and tasted most of you. Why can't I come in?"

"I want to go potty by myself."

He still didn't understand but figured it was a girl thing. "I'll use the other bathroom and then go down and make coffee. I'm still allowed in the shower, right?"

Turning toward the bathroom, she waved her hand behind her head. "Sure, sure."

She soundly closed the door, so he walked out and went to the other bathroom. At the last minute, he closed the door and figured he was past due for a refresher course in girl rules. Apparently, he hadn't remembered the important ones because he hadn't lived with any women since he left for college at eighteen. Once he was done, he put the seat down because his mom and sisters had drilled that into him and it wasn't something you forgot no matter how long it had been.

Walking out of the bathroom, he noticed one of the rooms was furnished as a guest room, and the other two were empty. He wondered what she planned on doing with them and knew they'd be perfect for kids. Leaning against the doorway of the room that faced the garden, he thought about what kind of babies they could make together. He'd certainly be happy with a couple of each.

Laughing to himself, he realized that he was ready to start this thing for real and they'd only spent a couple of days together.

Deciding to leave his thoughts where they were, he went downstairs and made coffee. Once he had their mugs full, he hustled back upstairs because he didn't want to miss taking a shower together.

Knocking on the door, he heard her mumble something and risked stepping in. She was brushing her teeth, so he set her coffee cup down and then drank half of his cup. "I'm glad you let me back in."

"It's not like I could keep you out." Slipping her robe off, she stepped into the shower and closed the door.

Watching her, he laughed. It was damn funny that she thought a closed shower door meant he'd stay out. When she turned, he looked at her ass and felt himself harden again. He couldn't do anything about it, so he tried to think about something else; when that didn't work, he got in and decided to let the chips fall where they may.

She had her head tipped back into the water, so he gently laid his hand on her stomach and ran it up the center of her body. When she moved her head up, he cradled her face and smiled. "I like you, Birdie."

Wiping the water out of her eyes, she let her hands fall against his chest. "Turns out, I like you too."

He wrapped her up in his arms, dropped his mouth, and kissed her to her soul. At least that's what it felt like to him. What they had started wasn't about some bullshit physical attraction; it was the real thing, and if they were lucky they would recognize it in time and make sure to be as careful with it as they could.

***

Birdie stood at the counter with a frown on her face and Mark joined her, placing his hand on her shoulder. "What's up, babe?"

She kept frowning at her phone and finally glanced up. "I'm not sure. My best friend Rory said she was going to come on Monday and pulled a no-show. I didn't hear from her until Tuesday afternoon, and she gave me a weak excuse. She finally sent me an email and explained a little of what's been going on, and I'm worried. Rory's mom remarried when we were in college, and her new husband owns a dozen hotels around the world and is quite wealthy. After we graduated, Rory went to work for his corporation as an operations person and has done an incredible job. She was at some benefit a couple of months ago, and there was a photograph of her with her mom, stepdad, and his son. Unfortunately, she was falsely listed as one of his children. The next week, she started receiving notes from someone, and now it's become a regular stalking thing. The police say there's nothing they can do about it. I feel like she's out there by herself and no one's taking it seriously."

"Where does Rory live? We can introduce her to my friend, Max, who has a security firm here in San Diego as well as about five other locations. He could easily provide her with protection and put a stop to whoever is threatening her."

She looked at her phone and rested her fingers on the screen. "She lives in La Jolla but travels all the time. I'll text her and see when she's going to be back."

He grabbed his phone and texted Max to give him a heads-up. "He should get back to me in a couple of hours."

"I'm not sure if the person bothering her is interested in her money or her beauty. She's built like Sophia Loren and is drop-dead gorgeous."

Hearing his phone buzz, he checked it. "Max said to tell him where and when and he'll take care of it."

Birdie reached up and kissed him. "Thank you." She sent off a quick text and then grabbed her purse. "Let's go eat because I'm starved."

They headed out to his truck, and she was about to get in, but stopped. "What?"

"I can drive."

"Baby, let me. It's a guy thing." He could see her debating and hoped this wasn't going to be the moment she put her foot down. When she sighed and got in, he figured she was too hungry to make it a debate.

"This time, you can drive, but I want the chance sometime."

"Absolutely." He buckled her in and then kissed her. As he drove them to a restaurant on the other side of the island, he knew she was never going to give in as quickly as she just did.

The thing he admired about her was also the thing that was going to make their lives interesting. She was smart and had all kinds of opinions about how things should be done, so how they were going to manage their wants and needs was going to be interesting.

There were a few things that he didn't want to compromise on and assumed she had some as well. Looking over, he figured he'd do just about anything to make her happy, and maybe someday she would feel the same way about him.

Which might make all the compromising and negotiations they were about to get into, a lot easier.

She was a strong-minded woman, and he hoped like hell that never changed because it would mean she was his match in every way, and he wanted nothing less.

Walking into one of his favorite restaurants, they were seated quickly toward the back. The café was a regular spot for him and his buddies because it offered decent food with generous portions at great prices. Which is all a guy from the Navy ever looked for. He'd been coming since he arrived in Coronado and, as far as he was concerned, no one served a better breakfast.

When Betty approached their table, she gave him a long look and raised an eyebrow. He'd never brought a woman in the diner and knew she was taking note. "I'd like to introduce you to my girlfriend, Birdie."

The waitress, who had been serving him and his buddies for years, gave him a warm smile. "I didn't think you'd be to talk such a pretty woman into taking you on."

"Neither did I," he responded with a laugh.

Betty gave Birdie a warm smile. "What can I get you, darling?"

Birdie looked between the two of them and then shook her head. "Nice to meet you, Betty. I would like the waffles with bananas, a side of sausage, one egg over easy, and coffee, please."

"I like a woman who eats," Betty replied. "I'll give you your regular order, Mark."

After she walked away, he smiled at Birdie and noticed that she didn't return it. In fact, she was looking at him like she might like seeing some harm come to him. "Everything okay?"

"When were you going to ask me to be your girlfriend?"

Instantly, he understood his mistake and wondered how long it was going to take for him to dig himself out. Probably a lot longer than he liked based on the way she was frowning. "Well, I thought it was implied. We're only sleeping with each other, and I'll kill any guy who gets near you. I assumed that made us boyfriend and girlfriend. Do I give you my class ring to make it official?"

When she glared and remained silent, he knew whatever he'd said hadn't worked, and might've made things a bit worse. "Or…"

"Have you lost your ever-loving mind? Do you think I would become someone's girlfriend without consultation? Do you think I'm that easy?" Lifting her water glass, she shook her head and then set it back down. "We were just going to sleep together, and that was going to be it. But, no, you have your toothbrush and your plans. I knew you were bossy and a little overbearing, but I let it slide." Moving her utensils around, she sighed. "I was clearly mistaken, and you've taken my easy-going nature and run over it with a bulldozer. I do not appreciate you announcing to someone that I'm your girlfriend without asking me. I'm so upset that I am not going to be able to finish my waffles."

He got up and slid into the seat next to her. "I'm sorry. I've been coming here for eleven years, and Betty's never seen me with a woman. I thought once we agreed to be exclusive that it meant we were committed. I'd like you to be my girlfriend if you would consider it."

"I'll think about it. Right now, my blood sugar is low, and I can't make a reasonable decision. Go back to your side of the table and let me eat in peace."

He slid out of the booth and went back to his side of the table.

Betty must've heard because when she started setting down the plates, she shook her head. "You didn't ask her, did you? You just assumed." She studied Birdie. "He's a good man; he's just lousy at this. Give him a break and let's see what he's capable of."

She smiled at Betty. "I'll think about it."

"I'm going to eat because I'm not doing myself any favors by speaking."

"Probably a good idea," Birdie replied before tucking into her food.

Mark watched her eat and wondered how mad she was. It was hard to tell because she was humming as she plowed through her food. Maybe after she ate, she'd feel better.

Once her plates were clean, she leaned back. "You know, men announcing things has never sat well with me. I like to believe that I'm the captain of my ship, and your heavy-handedness is not sitting well with me."

"I know."

"It's not the idea of being your girlfriend that bothers me; it's that you didn't ask. You can't lieutenant commander yourself all over my life within the first week. The truth is, you already own my body, and I'd like to keep ahold of my mind and heart for as long as I can."

"You already own every part of me. I've barely had a thought in the last week that wasn't about you, so the idea of us not being together is inconceivable." He held up his hand. "But I understand that it's going to take you a bit longer to feel the same way. I'll back off and relax. We don't have to say what we are." Thumping his chest, he winked. "I know what we are here, and that's all that matters."

Laughing, she leaned forward and took his hand. "If this is relaxed, I'd hate to see you when you get determined about something."

He lifted their joined hands and pressed a kiss to hers. "Honey, you have no idea how focused I can become." When she shook her head, he decided not to say anything more. Best to let things be because there was no need to give her the full picture.

Plenty of time for that later.

***

They stood outside on the sidewalk, and he decided that it was time for his next move. He'd fed her and let her eat in peace, so now it was time for the next step. "Would you like to see my place? It's not far from here."

"Sure, sounds good to me."

He drove them to his condo, which was two blocks from the beach and close to the base. He'd had it for a while and hoped it was a place that she would eventually feel comfortable in. "You're the first girl who has come over."

"How come?"

"Because I've never wanted to invite anyone before you." When he saw her puzzled look, he decided to ignore it. There was little he could say to her about his past that would make her feel confident about taking him on. So he did the only thing he could and forged ahead.

As they stood in front of his condo, holding hands, he felt like he was taking a significant step into his future. Not only was he bringing a woman home, but he wanted her to stay. "Come on in, and I'll show you around."

"This is a nice place; how long have you had it?"

"I bought it about five years ago when real estate crashed." He opened the door and led her in. "It's two bedrooms and two bathrooms." Taking her hand, he led her back to his room. "Decorating isn't my thing, but it's clean." As he looked around, he wondered what she thought. He had a king-sized bed with a blue comforter and a big chest of drawers, and that was it. The other bedroom had a desk, a bunch of boxes of books, and a laptop. He tried to see it through her eyes and realized it wasn't that much different than the officer housing at the base. Glancing over, he noticed a fake smile on her face.

"It is nice and clean."

He could tell that she didn't like it. "You would never spend the night here."

"I don't hate it. Your home is nice and clean."

"You already said that." He shook his head and laced their fingers together. "I dare you to spend the night tonight!"

Letting out a snort, she let go of his hand. "You don't have to dare me, and could just invite me."

"Okay, how about on Wednesday night? I'll make you dinner, and then you can spend the night."

She put out her hand and shook his. "I'll be here!"

"Deal." He led her out of the room and walked down the hall into his office. "I'm going to get my paperwork together for you."

"What are you talking about?"

"I want to hire you to be my accountant."

"I can't be your accountant because I'm sleeping with you."

He went through his files. "I don't understand the conflict. Why can't you be my accountant?"

"Because we're involved, but not married. I can't have control over your finances because it's not considered a good business practice."

He waved his hand in dismissal. "I trust you with my health. What do I care what you do with my money?"

"No way, Mark."

He stood and handed her a bunch of files, then walked out of the room. "Yes, you will be my accountant," he called over his shoulder as he walked into the kitchen.

Returning to her, he held up a bag. "I hope everything fits in here." He shoved everything in and tried to hand it to her, but she wouldn't take it, so he tried again. "Just take a look and give me your professional opinion."

She glanced at the bag. "I'll look, and then recommend someone."

"Thanks, baby." He set the bag by the door and then led her over to the couch. "What do you want to do next?"

She put her hand on his face. "Can you take me home? I need to get started on my chores because I have to go downtown tomorrow."

"You don't want to spend the rest of the day together?"

"Don't you have things to do? This has been the longest date on record. We've been together since Friday night."

He took her hand. "I'm not done yet and want it to continue. What if I do my run and swim and then take you out to dinner? That way you have time to get stuff done and then we can have the evening together. If you still have stuff to do tonight, then I'll watch football."

"Do your dates usually last three days?"

He let out a laugh and shook his head. "No, but I don't know how much time I have before I get the call for wheels up. I need to spend whatever time I have with you, so when I'm deployed, we have a strong enough connection to withstand the separation." Taking her into his arms, he rolled her over and started kissing her face. "I want you to be mine." She started to giggle, so he continued. "Be my girlfriend, Birdie."

Pushing at his chest, she smiled. "Maybe."

Looking down into her eyes, he decided that's all she was going to give him. When she lifted her face and pressed her mouth to his, he knew the *maybe* was soon going to become a yes, though.

"You're a hard man to resist, so go get your stuff and let's go back to my house."

"Thanks, honey." After he dropped a quick kiss on her mouth, he jumped up and strode down the hall. It was a small victory, and he was going to enjoy it because there were probably going to be few and far between.

When he returned to the living room, he noticed her studying one of the folders he put in the bag and knew she couldn't resist.

"Why don't you have a mortgage on your condo?" she asked as she studied a spreadsheet.

He put his bag by the door and returned to the couch. "My dad was an engineer as well as a professor at Cal Poly. When the whole computer thing was taking off, he invented a widget. It's still used today in those monster processors that banks and the government have. My mother, two sisters, and I receive a quarterly check from all the companies that use it. I had enough cash to buy this condo without a mortgage."

Running her hand through her hair, she shook her head. "I thought you were just good-looking and sexy. Now I find out you're wonderful in bed, smart, and funny. Not to mention the whole hero thing. Holy crap, I'm swimming in the deep end, and should be in the kiddie pool."

He wasn't sure if what she said was a good thing or a bad thing. "Baby, you're all of those things and more. You're beautiful, kind, caring, smart, successful, and so sexy that I can't control myself. You probably have a lot more money than I do, so maybe it's me who's in the wrong pool. Is that why you're always trying to get rid of me?"

"I'm not always trying to get rid of you. What you are talking about?"

He was way out of his comfort zone, but maybe that's what it took to get Birdie on board with his plan. "Why don't you want to be my girlfriend?"

"Well, you didn't ask me; you announced it to Betty and assumed. I don't like being pushed into things. We've known each other for a week, and only just started dating. Why are you in such a rush? Maybe it's about conquest and has little to do with me. Maybe once you get me, you won't want to keep me."

What the hell was she talking about? Once he got her, he was never going to let her go. "Birdie, you've turned me inside out. I like spending time with you, making love, talking, and laughing. I want to do that every day, and get to know you. I want to be the person you call if you need anything. Granted, I don't have a lot of experience being a boyfriend, but I'll protect you, care for you, and do it all unconditionally." When her eyes teared up, he realized this was the moment of truth. It was either going to work or blow up in his face.

She took his hand and gave him a watery smile. "I'd be honored to be your girlfriend. Thank you for asking." She leaned over and kissed him gently

He let out a big breath. "I guess the lesson here is that I just have to ask and then it'll work out for me." He rolled her under him and kissed her with everything he had. When he felt like he had thoroughly branded her, he released her mouth. "You can also be the boss of me if you want. We'll eat what you want, go where you want to go, and do what you want to do."

She rested her hand on his face and sighed. "I just want to pick out the food and not feel like you're commanding me. After that, we can decide together."

She kissed his chest right where his heart pounded, and he quietly held her in his arms. "Whatever you want, honey." And he meant that because he just wanted her to be happy.

**

They had finished dinner and were sitting on the couch watching one of Birdie's shows. It was some sort of night-time soap drama thing, and she'd finally given up trying to explain it, which was fine by him. As long as she was curled up against him and he had his hand up her shirt, he was happy.

The show finally ended, and they made their way upstairs. When she didn't bother putting on a nightgown, he considered it an excellent development in their relationship. He would watch every single one of her shows, even *Dancing with the Stars*, if she went to bed like that every night.

She was fiddling with her clock and then glanced up at him. "I'm setting the alarm for six o'clock. Do you need it to go off earlier?"

When he saw her on her stomach with her mind-blowing ass on display, he grinned. Pulling her legs so she was closer, he started a trail of kisses up her legs. When he ran his hand over her hip and gave her a love bite, she gasped.

"My goodness, what are you up to?"

He didn't respond because his need to devour her killed his ability to speak. Gently, he pressed a kiss to her skin and knew he'd never experienced anything so perfect. The smell, the feel, and the taste of her were all he would need for the rest of his life. There was never going to be anyone who made his heart beat as wildly as Birdie.

Lifting her hips, he slipped a finger inside her folds and discovered how wet she was. Seemed he wasn't the only one who was turned on. His fingers were quickly coated with her juices as he ran his fingers around and around. When he pressed his thumb to her clit, she moaned. "I sure am enjoying my girlfriend," he said against her skin. Thrusting two fingers into her heat, he found her magic spot instantly, and she came all over his hand. "That's it, Birdie, let go."

"More," she said.

"Damn right, I'll give you more." He lifted her hips, wrapped his arm around her waist, and pushed into her halfway. Gritting his teeth, he tried to give her time to adjust. "How are you doing, baby?"

She moaned and answered by pushing against him. That's all it took for him to lose his mind and control. "God, you feel so good." Thrusting into her deeply, he felt her hips start to move. The friction built up wildly as he pistoned in and out of her wet, silky heat.

When she pulsed around him, he exploded and emptied every drop into her. Holding her tightly, he gentled his strokes and knew he was home. They collapsed together on the bed, and he heard her laugh.

"So far, you are an excellent boyfriend. I don't know what we just did, but I liked it."

"I'm about to become a better one." He rolled off the bed, went into the bathroom, and brought back a wet washcloth. He gently cleaned her up and then kissed her neck. "I'm a full-service boyfriend."

"So you are," she mumbled.

Returning to bed, he collapsed next to her and heard her sigh as she kissed him right over his heart. "Thanks for agreeing to take me on. You won't regret it." She squeezed his hand and before he knew it, she was asleep.

This was the best damn weekend of his life, and he prayed this was the first of thousands.

CHAPTER ELEVEN

The following morning, Mark walked up the stairs with the clean sheets under his arm and two cups of coffee. There was a sound he couldn't immediately identify and wondered if something was wrong with the plumbing. As he stepped into the room, he realized it was Birdie singing in her closet.

He dropped the sheets on the bed, left her cup on the table, and leaned against the door so he could enjoy the show. She was singing along with Barry White and belting out *Can't Get Enough of Your Love*. He watched her thong disappear as she pulled a skirt up over her sexy hips and was ready to take her up against the wall. When she slipped on black heels and started swinging her hips, he was at full attention.

Birdie turned around, and his mouth fell open when he saw her black lace bra lovingly holding up her beautiful breasts. She was singing at the top of her lungs, and he'd never seen anything sexier. She caught sight of him and let out a small shriek. "Keep going. I love this."

Smiling, she started dancing over to him as she sang. When she was right in front of him, she grabbed his hips, danced against him, and sang, "I can't get enough of your love, every time you're near, I scream your name, I can't get enough of your love." She started laughing and couldn't get any more lyrics out. "That concludes the morning's entertainment."

Twirling around, she grabbed a silk blouse and winked. "If you want to run now, I completely understand."

"No running. I'm holding on tight." Lifting his hand, he framed her face and kissed her firmly. "Thanks for being my girlfriend because that's the best thing I've ever seen."

"Either you have low standards or all the sex we've been having is making you think I'm better than I am." Stepping back, she began buttoning up her blouse.

As he tried to grab her, she danced out of his reach and shook her head. "One more kiss."

"No, sir, the accountant can't be wrinkled. I have to appear professional."

"So, how many men work at this firm that you're going to today?"

Lifting her eyes to his, she wrinkled her nose. "I have no idea. I usually just go in for meetings and do the bulk of the work here at my home office. I've never really noticed." She grabbed a jacket and picked up her coffee cup. "How many women do you work with?"

"You know there are not many."

She started to walk out of the room but stopped at the door. "You know, you could show up in your dress uniform dripping in medals if you wanted. Or better yet, you can come by in full combat gear. I think that would send just the right message."

He came up behind her with the dirty sheets under his arm. "Smartass. Message received."

She laughed. "I've always worked with men, and no one has ever been unprofessional. Come on, let's go get breakfast ready."

After he put the sheets in the washing machine, he returned to the kitchen and watched Birdie cook. "I want to come up with something so that if I get called for wheels up, you won't panic. I can't tell you when I get the call until we're married. And even then, I won't be able to tell you where I'm going."

He leaned against the counter and crossed his arms. "I'll call you or see you every day, and if that doesn't happen, then you can call Maryann and ask her how Josh is doing. She can't tell you anything specific, but at least you'll have something. How does that sound?"

Nodding, she remained silent. "Baby, they say it takes a strong man to be a SEAL, but it takes a stronger woman to be with him. I have a feeling that you're plenty strong."

She leaned over and kissed him. "I hope so. The idea of anything happening to you scares me to pieces."

He watched her fill their plates and decided that if she was scared, then she was starting to get attached, which was good news. Granted, he didn't want her to worry, but there wasn't much he could do.

The nature of his job meant that he put his life on the line every time he went downrange, and he knew Birdie understood that because her cousin had been on the Teams for years. "After breakfast, I'll put the sheets on the bed." It might be better to stick to mundane details than to take on the big monster that was his job.

Birdie handed the plates over. "You don't have to. I'm going to stop and get a mattress cover for the bed, and then I'll put it together when I get home."

"Why do you need a cover?"

"Because we're not using condoms and we're going to get the mattress wet. I don't know how to say this, but you have a lot in you."

Laughter spilled out of his mouth, and he found it hard to stop. "Birdie, you're so polite. Don't forget that I've been in the Navy for a long time, and there's nothing that I haven't heard or probably said."

She gave him a disapproving look. "Well, I'm not going to be crude just because you are."

He kissed her. "The good thing is that when we want to have kids, it'll work in our favor."

She kissed him back and patted his arm. "I think we should wait until the second week of dating before we plan our family." She refilled their coffee mugs and then walked over to the table. "Let's eat, so I can get to work."

The fact that she didn't lose her mind when he brought up children made him damn happy and led him to believe things were going better than expected.

Unless she was placating him or hadn't heard. As he set her plate down, he noticed she was relaxed. Which meant—what?

"So, what are you doing today?" she asked with a smile.

"Drills and PT." He wiped his mouth and lifted her hand. "I'll also add to the morning announcements and let everyone know that I have a girlfriend."

"That will liven up the morning chatter." She ran her finger over the rim of her cup. "Everyone will assume that I put a spell on you."

"No, they're going to think that I put a spell on you because nothing else would explain why you're willing to take me on."

Throwing back her head, she let out a laugh. "Doubt it. You're a catch, Mark, and I consider myself lucky."

Leaning over, he kissed her. "I think the luck is all mine."

***

Mark drove to the base and met his platoon in the hangar. The company that developed the new equipment was there, and everyone was trying to figure out what had gone wrong. As he stepped up to the group, he listened to the lead designer explain the fix they'd made. Leaning over to Frisco, he said, "I'm going to confirm this is worth another shot because I don't want to want a repeat of last week."

"Roger that," Frisco replied.

He signaled the lead engineer and walked away from the group. The first thing he needed was a solid explanation of what exactly had been done to repair the equipment because the last thing he wanted was to put his men at risk. The guy seemed confident that he'd made the fix, and offered to be available if there were any more glitches. He agreed and then made his way to his office to work on the logistics of getting the team out to the desert. Frisco and Sam followed him, and they began figuring out what they needed for the three-day op.

Blake stepped in and sat at his desk. "Let's put the two platoons together for the training op. I think it will give us a better idea if this equipment is worth anything out in the field."

"Sounds good."

"Hey, how was your weekend? Did it work out the way you wanted?"

Mark finished what he was working on, then turned around. "It was the best weekend of my life, and Birdie agreed to be my girlfriend." When his buddy appeared shocked, he wondered why. "I'm as gone as I can be, and this woman has me completely under her spell."

Blake stood and shook his hand. "Congratulations, man! How did you convince her?"

Why did everybody think he had to do so much convincing? "It's not like I had to drug her to get her to agree. Jeez, it's not that unbelievable."

"Okay," Blake replied. "But in a more real sense, it is—because you've never had a girlfriend."

"Fuck you," he huffed out. "I may not have a lot of experience, but that doesn't mean I'm not going to succeed at this. Birdie is mine, and I'm not going to fail."

Josh walked in and shook his head. "Are you serious about my cousin? A man can't even go on his honeymoon without something happening."

He got up from his chair, making it roll fast enough to hit the wall. "I'm going to say this once, and that's it. Birdie James is my girlfriend, and it wasn't easy to get her to agree. The truth is, she was planning on using me as a slump buster, and then getting rid of me. So, if you assholes want to be worried, maybe it's me you should be concerned about. This is it, and she's going to be the mother of my children, so you all can just back the fuck up. I'm going to marry this woman. Any questions?"

Frisco let out a bark of laughter. "Does she know about your plans yet?"

Shrugging, he stared at his boots. "She knows she's my girlfriend, but doesn't know about the rest. I'm going to ease her into it, and I'm sure it's all going to work out." Giving the men a confident smile, he crossed his arms. "Hell, I have my own toothbrush, and it sits right next to hers." When they gave him a look of understanding, he knew they got it. "You know, for someone so smart, she doesn't understand the significance of the whole toothbrush thing, and it kind of surprises me."

"Maybe you don't need to enlighten her," Josh said as he sat at a desk.

"Probably right," Mark responded as he rolled his chair back. He slid his keyboard closer and decided he was going to keep his long-term plans under wraps.

No need to give her any idea what their future was going to be until they were further down the road.

No need at all.

***

Birdie sat at her desk, heard the shrill noise of the phone, and almost jumped out of her chair. Looking up at the clock, she realized she'd been buried in spreadsheets for far too many hours. "Hello," she said as she started closing down folders on her computer.

"Hey, baby. I'm on my way over. Should I pick up something for dinner?"

"I had a sandwich at five, so I'm not hungry. Come on home, and I'll make you something to eat."

"Those are words that make a man happy." He let out a little growl and then laughed. "I'm going to have to make sure and thank you by setting your body on fire the moment I'm done eating."

"I had no idea that making you a sandwich would result in sexual favors; I'm going to have to remember that."

"Honey, it's not a favor. It's my damn privilege to make you as happy as I can."

Sighing, she tilted back in her chair and wondered how long he was planning on hanging around. "I'll see you in a bit, Mark."

"So, you're going to ignore what I just said?"

"No, I was waiting to see you in person so I can show how much I like it."

"Damn, Birdie."

"I'm hanging up now." As she ended the call, the sound of Mark's laughter was all she could hear. The man tilted her world in the right direction, and she hoped what they had wouldn't end anytime soon.

Getting up from her desk, she stretched, and then made her way into the kitchen. Would a sandwich be enough for him, or should she make him a quick plate of pasta? Maybe both.

She laughed as she opened the fridge and decided he would probably be happy with whatever she made and fretting like a schoolgirl was silly.

Which is how he made her feel. Giddy, excited, and utterly smitten.

Hearing the doorbell made her heart beat fast against her chest and she wondered when being around him wasn't going to set her nerves on fire. Striding to the door, she swung it open, and her tummy flipped over. Yeah, this wasn't going away anytime soon. "Hey, handsome."

Taking a step inside, he dropped his bag, and then closed the door with his boot. "Come here, and let me love on you."

She walked into his open arms and laid her head against his chest and decided there was no better place in the world. "How was your day?"

"Good." He tightened his hold and pressed a kiss to the top of her head. "I had a smile on my face most of the day because I knew I was coming home to you."

"Did the guys give you a hard time about it?"

"No. They did, however, give me a wide berth for most of the day."

"Probably afraid of catching girl cooties if they came close."

"Yeah, I'm pretty much covered in them." He leaned back and tilted her face up. "I need another dose, so they don't wear off. Would you be willing to help me out with that?"

Standing on her tiptoes, she pulled his face down. "Come here, sailor." His mouth crushed down on hers as the first tidal wave of desire moved across her body.

"Let's go upstairs, so I can show you how much I missed you today."

Stepping away, she shook her head and then smoothed down her shirt. "I'm going to feed you first so that when you do show me, you'll have the energy you need."

Slinging his arm over her shoulder, he winked. "That's a good idea because once I get my hands on you, it's going to take a good long while for me to let you go."

Fanning her face, she let out a laugh. "I better get you fed then."

She walked into the kitchen and pointed to a stool on the other side of the island. "Sit, and I'll have something ready shortly."

"Yes, ma'am."

As she assembled his sandwich, she noticed him staring. "Do I have something on my face?"

"No, I'm just admiring my pretty girlfriend."

"What did the guys say when you told them you were off the market?"

"They congratulated me and then asked what I did to get you to agree to take me on."

She passed him his plate and then grabbed a beer out of the fridge and walked over to hand it to him. "Taking you on is not that big of a deal, but holding on might be."

He held up his hands and looked between them. "Not a problem, honey. These big hands of mine are never going to let you go."

She grabbed the bag of chips and shook some onto his plate. "Sweet talker."

"I appreciate you taking care of me, Birdie." He lifted his sandwich and gave her a mile. "I usually just pick up drive-through on my way home."

Sitting down next to him, she shrugged. "Anytime."

"Did you look at my files yet?"

Sliding her glass of wine over, she took a sip. "I did." She looked over the rim of her glass and watched him eat. "I started organizing them and wondered who pays your bills when you're deployed?"

"I pay them, and they sometimes get screwed up, but I can usually fix it when I get back. Are you ready to take it on for me?"

"I've thought about it and decided that I can set up automatic bill pay and then monitor it. I do it for a lot of the guys, so talk to Frisco and see what he thinks, and then you can decide if it's something you want to do."

He finished eating and then took her hands. "I don't need to think about it. I'll give it all to you, and then I won't have to worry about it since it will be in your capable hands."

She got up and made him a plate of brownies and fruit. "I told you that I can't have access to your money because it's unethical. I'll pay your monthly bills, and perhaps give you some ideas for investments for the rest." She took a sip of wine and frowned. "Leaving all your capital in a money market isn't a good idea, and you can make some nice dividends on some low-risk investments."

Taking his sandwich plate, she then walked over to the sink and turned on the water. As she rinsed the dishes, she swore she heard him mumble something about how it wouldn't matter after they got married because she was going to be taking care of it anyway. She glanced up and saw him eating his brownies. Maybe she'd imagined it because that couldn't be right.

Once he'd inhaled his dessert, he got up and put his plate in the dishwasher. "Baby, I'm going to be gone for three or four days on a training op. I want to give you a key to the condo and a credit card in case you need anything."

"That is the sweetest, most insane thing I've ever heard." She patted his hand and then wiped off the counter.

"It's not insane. What if you need something and I'm not here?" He crossed his arms.

"I'm a big girl and can take care of myself."

"I want to take care of you, and the sooner you understand that, the better."

"If you want to take care of me, then kiss me."

Lifting her, he strode toward the stairs. "I can do better than that."

"I can't wait." Holding onto his shoulders as he mounted the stairs made her realize that she might very well be the luckiest woman in the world to have this man in her life.

Not only was he a warrior, a gentleman, and an astonishing lover, but he was also hers. Which made him precious beyond compare.

CHAPTER TWELVE

Birdie stood in the back of her shop, creating the centerpieces for one of her favorite clients, and heard the bell on the front door. "Be right there."

James called out her name, and she wondered how he'd held himself back from interrogating her earlier. He wasn't a man known for patience when it came to acquiring all the gory details of a love affair, so she assumed he must've been busy with a bride.

Seeing her friend sweep in with dramatic flair, she let out a laugh as he set his bag down with a thud. "What brings you here?"

"Ha, ha." Motioning his hands, he gave her a give-me sign. "Tell me everything that happened with Mark the Sex Machine and don't leave anything out."

She fussed with the arrangement she'd been working on and then lifted her eyes slowly. "He's better than I imagined. If you want more information, then go open a bottle of wine."

"Coming up." He squeezed her arm. "I'm so happy that he didn't turn out to be a dud."

"Me too."

"Finish up, and I'll get our grape juice." Striding into the office, he grabbed the glasses and chardonnay, then brought it back to the table. "So, was it mind-blowing because it's been so long, or is he just a talented lover?"

"He's a remarkable man who happens to be the best lover in the history of the universe."

"Slight over-exaggeration, but I'm going to let you have it since you look too damn happy for me to argue."

She waved at the bottle. "Open and serve, and I'll be back in a minute. She walked over to the cooler, put the arrangement in, and then returned to take a healthy sip of her wine. "Better."

"So…"

"I've had the most marvelous weekend of my life, and think my new boyfriend could eventually become my future husband." She heard James choke and patted his back. "I had the best sex of my life many, many times with the sexiest man on the planet. Did I mention sexy? Because that man is a god…a sex god! And, I say that with not an ounce of irony. Being with him is like driving a Ferrari."

James cleared his throat and then dabbed his neck. "You're saying he has a lot of power, but also has a smooth ride?"

"Yes! He's made of finer stuff, and I am here to tell you that I have no plans to let him go." She fanned her face. "I can't imagine going back to driving in the slow lane."

"The man must be good because you're using car analogies and that's not something I've seen you do."

Lifting her glass, she winked. "What can I say? I'm a changed woman."

"I can see that." Leaning forward, he raised an eyebrow. "Did you do anything outside the bedroom?"

"Of course!" She set her glass down. "Mark took me to the beach on Saturday afternoon and bought me two wetsuits to make sure I would have what I needed for surfing. He also introduced me as his girlfriend to someone I'd never met, and then announced it to his teammates the first chance he got."

"He sure didn't waste a moment in getting you locked down, which means he's either a psycho or crazy about you." Brushing an invisible piece of lint off his trousers, he shrugged. "Let's hope it's the latter."

She punched him in the arm. "Yeah, I'd prefer infatuated over psycho any day." Leaning back on her stool, she looked at her sandals and wondered if there was any validity to what James had said. Mark had come on strong, and she had been hoping that it was a reflection of his feelings and not his sanity. After all, they wouldn't let a crazy person command a platoon if he was nuts—would they?

No, of course not, that was ridiculous.

"Don't over-think this," James commanded. "I see those wheels spinning."

"Do you think he's crazy for wanting me the way he does?"

"Oh, Birdie, no." James wrapped his arm around her. "I think he's smart and wants to grab you before anyone else does."

Draining her glass, she shrugged. "He's excited about having a toothbrush at my house in a sort of bizarre way that I don't understand, and he wants to see me every day."

James finished his wine and poured them another glass. "And…"

"I wanted someone to break my rut with, but I think this one may be staying awhile." She looked at

James and wondered if she was a fool for being swept up in Mark's tsunami of infatuation. Was this too good to be true? Was she kidding herself?

"It couldn't happen to a better person because you deserve every happiness." He clapped his hands. "Tell me when I should start planning the wedding."

She let out a big breath. "I think the planning can wait since we're a week away from discovering all of the things that make one another crazy." She twirled her glass. "I'm falling for him, and it's scaring me to pieces. I don't even want to analyze it to death like I usually do."

"Which means you should let it happen. He's a good man, and we both know they don't come along very often."

"True." She thought about her ex and knew without a doubt that Mark was nothing like him.

James leaned back on his stool. "Perhaps you're giving him a chance because you know that he's a good man." He leaned forward. "It could be a perfectly reasonable explanation why you've decided to open your heart, or…"

"What?"

"He's put you in a sex coma, and you would agree with whatever he suggested."

She let out a loud snort. "It could be a little bit of both. I know he's a good person and he puts me in a sex coma. Either way, I like the magic the spell he's cast." Standing, she rolled her shoulders. "Let's go to my house and order Chinese and watch *Dancing with the Stars*. I forgot to call Triple-A earlier, and I need to do that so they can come and see what's wrong with the Volvo."

"Do you have a dead battery?"

"I think so; it wouldn't start this morning, and I'm assuming that's the problem."

"Well, let's get home then."

"Sounds perfect."

"Thank you, James, for being such a good friend."

He took her hand and started swinging it back and forth. "Ditto, Birdie, ditto."

***

Mark sat in the barracks with his platoon after they'd finished their debriefing and knew the training exercise had been important. They were making progress with the new equipment, and if the changes were made, it could eventually prove to be invaluable in the field.

Lifting his phone, he checked to see if Birdie had replied to the text he'd sent earlier. When he saw a blank screen, he decided not to be disappointed since he knew she had a big flower order that she was delivering tomorrow. Running his hand through his hair, he thought about reminding her to use the Volvo and not the Jeep when she delivered the flowers.

He hadn't had a chance to do anything about getting the airbags installed and hoped she remembered she wasn't supposed to use it. Leaning back, he started typing a message and then deleted it.

The last thing he wanted to do was come off as a hard ass and, if he reminded her, she would probably think he didn't trust her. Which was far from the truth. Sliding his phone into his pocket, he silently congratulated himself on his restraint.

Frisco walked over and slid his hands on his hips. "Let's head to the mess because the guys are ready to eat."

Standing, he clapped his friend on the back. "Let's hit it."

"You gonna survive the chow hall, now that you have Birdie cooking for you?"

"Not going to be easy, man. The woman is remarkable, and she's spoiled me rotten."

Frisco shook his head as they walked toward the other end of the base. "Birdie is a good woman, and I hope you appreciate how lucky you are to have her in your life."

"I know, man, and am doing everything I can to make sure she never changes her mind."

Sam and Josh joined them, and the conversation turned to the subject of the exercise they were going to do tomorrow. As Mark listened to his men, he let his mind wander to the reunion he and Birdie were going to have the following evening. Thinking of the way they connected not only physically but emotionally and intellectually made him realize he was, in fact, the luckiest son of a bitch in the world.

Once the team was settled at a table, Sam looked down at his plate and let out a sigh. "What's with you?" Mark asked.

"I wish that I was home eating my wife's cooking." He looked up and frowned. "Even if she's putting too much salt on everything."

Josh glared down at his tray. "I wish that I was still on my honeymoon with my beautiful bride. I can't remember what I ate, but it must have been good."

Mark studied his friend. "Why is Karen putting too much salt on things? Usually, she's a great cook."

Sam looked down at his tray and then at Mark. "It's the pregnancy. She's craving salt and puts it on everything, even her fruit. The doctor told her to cut back, but she's not doing it yet, so I have to monitor her without being obvious. It's a fine line since there's nothing worse than an unhappy, pregnant wife. I would rather face a nest of tangos than face my wife when she's mad. I'm not afraid to admit it, either. She scares the crap out of me."

Sam was bigger than him and a known expert on explosives. Most people thought he was a mean, scary son of a bitch. Yet he openly talked about being scared of his wife, who was five-foot-two and a kindergarten teacher. Which, in some strange way, made total sense to Mark since the last thing he wanted was to have Birdie upset with him in any way.

"I love that woman like crazy and would do anything for her, but sometimes I have to watch my step," Sam added.

"Good luck, man. I hope you both survive." Mark began eating and wondered what Birdie was going to be like when she was pregnant with their child. Probably just the same as she was now, which, as far as he was concerned, was perfect.

CHAPTER THIRTEEN

The training op had concluded, and he was looking forward to getting the team back to San Diego. Just as he was about to grab Blake for a download, he saw Ace running from the hangar toward Josh with a SAT phone in his hand. The speed at which he was moving suggested that something was about to go down since Ace was a cool operator and never ran faster than he needed to.

After he handed Josh the SAT phone, Ace motioned for him over. Jogging toward them, he lifted his hands in "a what's up" signal and noticed Ace's somber expression.

Shit.

This was going to be bad.

"What is it, Ace?"

"It's Maryann and…"

A cold chill raced over his body, and he knew instantly that something had happened to Birdie. Looking down at the ground, he willed himself to stay calm until he knew exactly what they were dealing with. Watching Josh's face, he suspected that it was going to be fucking horrible, whatever it was.

Ace gave him a sympathetic look, and he felt like howling. "What is it?"

"The helo is getting prepped to take you guys back to San Diego."

The moment the words left Ace's mouth, Josh ended the call. "Birdie was in an accident. A drunk driver ran a red light and plowed into her, and she was driving the Wagoneer."

His legs went weak, so he crouched before falling. Resting his hand on the hot concrete, he let the pain keep his panic away. Losing his shit so early in the game wasn't going to help Birdie, and he didn't plan on letting that happen.

"They had to medevac her to Scripps Mercy Hospital, and Maryann is there now. I'm her emergency contact, and they called the house, so that's why Maryann is there."

"And…" He couldn't get the whole question out because his brain closed down when he thought of the possibilities.

"They have her in a medically induced coma because she has some swelling in her brain. She's stable for now and not in any pain, according to my wife."

Standing, he let out a string of curses as he walked away. He rested his hands on his hips and looked at the sky, sending up prayers begging for God's mercy. No way could he lose Birdie.

"Bags," Frisco yelled as he ran toward them. "Helo is ready; get your ass on there." Handing Mark his bag, he then repeated the process with Josh.

"I fucking told her not to drive that car until I got airbags installed," he said to Josh as they jogged toward the helo. "Why would she do it?"

"No idea, man," Josh responded as they boarded the chopper.

The helo lifted into the sky, and Mark closed his eyes and let the images of the last week run through his mind. They had just gotten started and had so many remarkable experiences ahead of them. Bowing his head, he began repeating prayers and hoped that God was listening. He hadn't been in church since high school, but somehow the words he needed were lodged in his brain so he could let the higher power know he and Birdie needed all the help they could get.

When he felt like he'd fully expressed himself, he opened his eyes and saw Josh facing the window with his eyes closed and figured he was probably saying his own prayers. "Nothing can happen to her because I love her and she's going to be my wife." His friend nodded as the helo began its descent.

An hour later, Mark walked into the ICU waiting room with Josh and saw Maryann. The look on her face didn't make him feel very optimistic. Waiting while Maryann and Josh embraced, he felt like he was going to crawl out of his skin. "How is she?" he finally blurted out.

"Stable," Maryann replied. "I told them that you were her fiancée so you'll be able to go in. They have a family-only policy, and I figured it was the best way to circumvent the hurdle."

Mark took her hands and squeezed. "Thank you, Maryann."

"Let's go to the nurse's station and see if they'll let you two in for a visit."

"You go first," Josh said. "I'll work on getting ahold of her parents, so we can let them know what's going on."

"Thanks, man, I appreciate it." After they went through the process of getting checked in and cleared, he made his way to Birdie's room. Before he pushed the door open, he prepared himself for the worst and was glad he did because, when he walked in, he saw that she was hooked up to a ton of equipment.

Standing next to her bed, he took her hand and let his eyes roam over her body and face. The significant contusions made his legs feel weak.

None of his experiences had prepared him for seeing the love of his life injured, and he prayed this was a one-time occurrence.

The eleven years he'd spent on the battlefield in all the world's hellholes did not compare to seeing Birdie injured. He'd seen men being blown up, shot, and had brought fellow soldiers home in bags, and this was the thing that wiped him out.

Seeing the love of his life in a coma wasn't anything he was prepared for, and he collapsed into the chair next to the bed and took her hand. He pressed a kiss against her skin and lowered his head, letting go of his tears. He hadn't cried since he was a kid, but holding her small hand proved to be his undoing.

When a nurse walked in, he had no idea if a minute or an hour had passed. Wiping his face with the back of his hand, he gave her a faint smile.

"We have every reason to believe she'll recover," the nurse said as she checked Birdie's pulse. "Despite the scary-looking machines, she's doing as well as can be expected."

"Thank you, ma'am." Standing, he cleared his throat. "I'm going to grab her cousin, so he can have a chance to see her."

"All right, son, I'll be here."

Nodding, he walked out of the room and made his way to the waiting room. When he saw Josh and

Maryann holding hands, he strode toward them and crossed his arms over his chest. "Tell me the son of a bitch who ran into her is dead. Otherwise, I need you to bail me out after I kill him."

Josh snorted and pointed to a chair. "Have a seat, and I'll update you."

He did as he was told and rested his arms on his knees. "Go."

"The guy spun out after he hit Birdie and then managed to hit a light pole and died upon impact. Apparently, he's had several DUIs. The Wagoneer is totaled, and it went to the junkyard."

"That's a damn good place for it."

"No kidding," Josh replied as he stood. "I don't know why she was so sentimental about that car."

Maryann stood and took her husband's hand. "We'll go in and then head home after we're done. I'm getting in touch with the family and expect this room will be full by tomorrow morning."

"Do you want us to stay and keep watch?" Josh asked.

"No." He grabbed his bag and moved toward the door. "I'm going to grab a quick shower, and then you guys can go. I'm not leaving until I take her home."

Josh shook his hand. "Okay, go get cleaned up, and we'll meet you back in her room."

He nodded and then headed toward the nurse's station and hoped they would let him grab a shower in the doctor's locker room. Medical personnel was often ex-military, and they usually tried to help out a soldier.

The last thing he wanted was Birdie to wake up and have to plug her nose because he stank like an old goat.

What he wanted to see was a smile on her face and prayed the moment was going to happen very soon.

CHAPTER FOURTEEN

Mark woke up when he heard the nurse come in and checked his watch, noticing it was five a.m. He sat up, stretched, and then studied Birdie for a moment and saw that she looked the same. He took it as a good sign and hoped today was the day she opened her eyes.

The nurse smiled as she checked Birdie's vitals. "What do you think?"

"I like the steady beat of her heart." The woman gave him a once-over. "How are you doing, son?"

"I'll be better when my fiancée opens her eyes."

"She seems to be doing better, so she must like your company."

"Well, I hope so since we're spending the rest of our lives together."

"That certainly helps when choosing a life partner." As she took off the thermometer strip, she smiled. "No fever. We like that because the last thing we want is an infection."

"I love this woman and plan on marrying her the minute she'll let me. So we need all the good news we can get."

The nurse gave him a long, steady look. "Love is one of the most powerful medicines, so I'm sure it's going to help that she has you." She checked her tablet and then nodded. "She's scheduled for an MRI later this afternoon, so they can check the swelling in her brain. If it's gone down, they may try and bring her out today."

He lifted Birdie's hand and kissed it. "I'd sure like to see her pretty eyes, so that would be great." He understood what was ahead of them because he was a trained as a medic and had seen similar cases. "I can't bring any flowers in here, right?"

The nurse shook her head. "Not in here, son. When she gets moved to a regular room, you can bring her all the flowers you want." She finished charting Birdie's information and moved to the door. "Keep the faith, son."

Nodding, he leaned back in his chair. "Do you hear that, baby? You're doing great, so just rest. I'll be right here, so don't worry about a thing. In a couple of hours, I'll get on the phone and make sure your shop is taken care of, and your family knows what's going on. I wanted to tell you that I loved you the other day, but held back because I thought it would freak you out. I now know that was a huge mistake and, the minute you wake up, I'm going to tell you and never stop. We don't know what kind of time we have and not to say what's important is stupid. I love you and don't want you to be scared that it happened so fast. That's just the way it is. It will be the truth today, next month, and next year."

He grabbed his phone from the table and checked it. The team had blown up his phone with texts asking about Birdie, so he got himself resettled and started updating everyone. Before he knew it, an hour had passed, and the nurse came in to tell him that Birdie had family in the waiting room.

Standing, he stretched and then dropped another kiss on her cheek. "Honey, I'll be back in a bit." He gave her one last kiss and then walked out. Once he hit the waiting room, he saw Josh and Maryann. "Hi," he called out as he walked toward them.

"Figured you needed this," Josh said as he handed him a big cup of coffee.

"God bless you, man. This is perfect." Lifting the lid, he took a big slug and sat down. "Birdie is holding her own, and I'm praying that once they do the MRI later today, we're going to have some good news."

"What has the doctor said?" Maryann asked as she sat.

"I haven't seen him since yesterday afternoon. The nurses have been real encouraging, though so I'm taking it as a good sign."

Maryann patted his leg. "She's going to pull through."

"I know because nothing else will be acceptable." He drank his coffee and knew if he had to will her to a full recovery, he would. Birdie James was the love of his life, and the idea of only having her for a couple of weeks was inconceivable.

As far as he could tell, a whole lifetime wasn't going to be enough, so he was going to do whatever it took so she came back whole and happy. "Have you gotten ahold of her folks?"

Josh leaned back in his chair. "Yes, they're on a European cruise and plan on getting off at the next port, so they can fly home. They should be here by tomorrow. I let the rest of the family know, and they'll probably start showing up later today."

"Good news." Taking another gulp of coffee, he nodded. "I checked the calendar on her phone, and it doesn't look like she had any events this weekend, but we should probably go to the shop and make sure. I think she said something about her cousin, Ana, working at the shop occasionally. Maybe she can come by and help us out."

"When I spoke with her earlier, she said that she'd take care of everything. She should be here anytime," Maryann said. "I just need to get her keys to the shop."

"I have her house keys in my bag, so when we're done here, I'll grab them for you." Draining his coffee, he rolled his neck. "I'll call the guys and have them go to the shop and help Ana clean out whatever flowers they need to. I think Adam's kids help every weekend and they probably know the routine."

Josh looked at Mark. "When did she give you keys to her house?"

"She gave me a set before we left on Tuesday. I told you she's the one for me, and it's my job to take care of her."

Maryann glanced at her husband and laughed. "Josh, it was the same way with us, so don't pretend like you're shocked."

He smiled at his wife. "I guess you're right."

Looking at his teammate, he wondered why he was surprised by what was happening between him and Birdie. Best as he could recall, Josh fell all over himself when he met Maryann and made a fool of himself in the process. "You guys go in and have a visit."

Josh stood. "I never would've guessed you would fall for my cousin."

"If you would've introduced me a year ago when she came to San Diego, then I would be married by now."

Maryann laughed as she stood. "That is a whole lot of ifs, and I think everything happened when it should. If Birdie had met you a year ago, she wouldn't have been ready. So, count your lucky stars that you met when you did."

"I guess," he replied, as Josh and Maryann turned toward the door. Maybe Maryann was right, and their timing was perfect. Except if they'd been together for a year, he would've taken care of that damn Wagoneer and the accident would never have occurred. Running his hand down his face, he realized he couldn't start that sort of thinking because it became circular. Hearing his name, he looked up and saw Ana walk in. He waved and waited for her to join him. "Thanks for coming."

"I didn't get the message until after visiting hours were over last night; otherwise, I would've come yesterday."

"Josh and Maryann are in with her now, so when they come out, you can go in. She had a good night, and the nurse said her MRI is scheduled for this afternoon. They could start bringing her out of it as early as tonight."

"Thanks, Mark, I know she's going to have a full recovery because there isn't another choice." Folding her hands in her lap, she gave him a long look. "Birdie and I spoke yesterday morning, and she filled me in on how things are going with you two. I want you to know that I've not heard her this happy in a long time."

"I consider it my job to make her as happy as I can."

"Well, you can't ask for more than that, but know that I will hunt you down if you hurt her. She can't take another broken heart, so I'm hoping that what you say is what you mean."

"No hearts will be broken because I plan on marrying her." He watched Ana's eyes grow large and wasn't surprised. Claiming you were going to marry a woman that you'd known for less than a month was bound to leave people stunned.

"Does she know about this yet?"

Mark stared at his hands. "Not exactly. But when she wakes up, I'm going to make sure she knows. I may wait for the marriage part until she's fully recovered because I don't want to spook her."

"Probably a good idea," she replied with a laugh. "I have a set of keys to Birdie's house and the shop, so I'm going to get her some clothes and toiletries and bring them back. After that, I'll go to the shop and check the calendar."

"I looked at her phone and didn't see anything for this weekend. I was planning on sending the guys down to help you clean out the flowers and do whatever was needed."

"I can probably handle it if Adam's kids are available…and…"

When Ana stopped talking, Mark looked up and saw his team amble in. He noticed Blake and Ana stare at one another. Whatever was happening between the two was intense, and he wished they'd just finally go on a date and see if they had anything in common. "Thanks for coming," he called out, as he glanced over and noticed that Ana had dropped her gaze and was studying her shoes. Not one to leave things be, he motioned his friend to come over. "Hey, Blake, can you give Adam's number to Ana? She's going to go to the shop today and wondered if the kids were were available to help."

Blake moved closer. "Hi, Ana. I haven't seen you since the wedding."

"I've been busy at school," she mumbled as she studied her shoes.

Mark watched her blush and wondered if she'd ever get out of her own way. "Blake, why don't you help Ana at the shop today?"

Ana stood abruptly and shook her head. "That won't be necessary; I'll just give the kids a call and have them come by." Looking across the room, she waved to Josh and Maryann. "I better go."

Mark watched her sprint away and turned to his buddy. "What the hell was that?"

"I might've kind of sort of asked her out on a date."

"And?"

"I don't know; she never really gave me an answer either way. When I asked Birdie about it, she told me to be patient." Blake looked across the room. "The woman is a genius, and I can barely pronounce what she's getting her doctorate in, much less understand it. Maybe I should just leave it be for now."

"She was blushing and tongue-tied from the moment she spotted you. Before you got here, she was telling me she'd kill me if I hurt Birdie."

"I don't understand women."

"Don't think we're expected to," he replied as he rolled his shoulder. "Give me Adam's number, and I'll pass it on."

"Okay, I'll get the guys organized, so you can go back and see your girl."

"Thanks, man, I'm hoping we get some good news today."

"Go on; we'll take care of things."

After he shook Blake's hand, he made his way through the crowd, thanking people as he passed. He couldn't control the swelling in Birdie's brain, but he could make sure he kept her life organized while she rested. It was an insignificant thing, but it made him feel as though he was helping in some small way.

Several hours later, Mark paced outside of the room where Birdie was getting her MRI and felt like he'd been there all day when it had only been a couple of hours. Hearing the sound of doors whooshing open, he turned and saw a tech walk out with an attendant as they rolled Birdie in his direction. "How does it look? How is my fiancée?"

The tech shook his head. "You have to wait for the radiologist to read the results. He should be up in a little while."

"Can you give me a thumb's up or down?" He threw him one of his death stares to see if he could shake any information loose and noticed he didn't even blink.

"That may work on combatants, but it doesn't work on me." He stepped back into the room. Shrugging, he took Birdie's hand. "It was worth a shot."

"Always," the attendant replied as he rolled Birdie's bed toward the elevator.

While waiting for the elevator, he leaned down and kissed her. "Don't worry, baby girl. I feel like we're going to get good news. Maybe you'll be done resting soon, and they can start to bring you out tonight."

As they walked onto the elevator, he squeezed her hand. "God doesn't give you a woman like Birdie to love and then take her away. I have a lot of credit built up, and she's sticking around." Smoothing out her hair, he grinned. "You just take your time, honey."

Later that evening Birdie had been moved out of ICU into the Critical Care Unit when her MRI came back with positive results. The medical team was in the process of bringing her out of the coma by decreasing her medication slowly and were optimistic.

Mark had been holding her hand for hours and kept a running commentary going about what was going on, and knew on some level she heard him. Figuring she was a woman who liked to know what was happening, he didn't want her to wake up and be mad that she'd missed something.

The nurses finished checking her vitals, and he stretched as he looked around the flower-filled room. Ana had made a bunch of arrangements and dropped them off a couple of hours ago, and the place looked a lot like Birdie's shop and smelled terrific. If nothing else, she was going to feel at home the moment she opened her eyes. Which, God willing, would be any time now.

He picked up Birdie's phone and started going through her playlist and noticed one with his name on it. Hitting play, the room was instantly filled with the song they had their first kiss to.

Falling back into the chair, he felt an enormous smile break across his face as he took her hand. "I knew from the moment I saw you that we were going to become something. Or more accurately—I wanted us to become something."

Scratching his head, he let out a small laugh. "It had never happened before, so I figured you were the one for me. Hell, there was no figure, there is only absolfuckinglutely."

As he looked at her face, he felt some movement in his hand and looked down and then felt it again. "If you're squeezing my hand, you keep doing that. I love you and need you to come back to me. Have you had enough rest? Can you wake up? I want to see your pretty eyes looking at mine." He held his breath and focused on her face as her eyes fluttered. "That's it, baby, just keep doing that." Her eyes popped open, and she stared right at him.

Standing, he leaned over and covered her face with kisses. "I love you; I love you; I love you." He lifted his head and stared into her beautiful sable eyes and noticed she was staring at him blankly.

Like she didn't recognize him.

Fuck, he thought to himself. "Not going to panic, baby." He pressed the button for the nurses and waited. "I've been waiting for you to come back to me and I'll wait forever if that's what it takes to get your brain unscrambled." The nurse finally came in and started evaluating her condition and let him know the doctor would be in shortly.

Standing back, he didn't let his faith waver. Just a bump in a long road to recovery. Not a big deal because they would get through this.

Hearing the door open, he glanced over his shoulder and saw the doctor walk in. He bit back a remark and decided it wasn't going to help if he lost his cool. Keeping a close eye, he saw when she slipped back into unconsciousness. Not able to wait a minute longer, he asked, "What's your opinion, Doc? How is my fiancée doing?"

"It appears like she's having all the appropriate responses."

"Is she asleep or unconscious?"

"She's asleep, and we're getting normal brain activity." He pointed to one of the monitors and smiled. "In fact, she has quite a bit considering the number of drugs in her system."

"I don't think she recognized me when she woke up."

"Not unusual. We're going to give her body a chance to recover from the drugs and then take another look. Let's give her more time."

"I'll give her all the time in the world."

"She's doing better than we expected, considering the amount of trauma she suffered." He wrote his orders and then nodded. "I'll check back in the morning."

Mark returned to his seat and took her hand as the nurses finished their work. Once they'd left, he let out a sigh. "I don't blame you for going back to sleep; I sure would if I was in your position."

Leaning back in the chair, he decided to grab a quick combat nap, so he could be refreshed when Birdie was ready to wake up.

Mark had been dozing in the chair when he was awakened by his hand being squeezed. Popping up quickly, he looked over and saw Birdie's eyes open. A small smile started to form on her lips, and that's when he lost his shit. Tears streamed down his face, and he embraced her gently. "I knew you'd come back to me."

Watching her head nod slightly, he held her face gently as he pressed kisses to her cheeks. "Didn't enjoy the last twenty-fours, and I'm going to have to ask you not to do that again."

He pushed the nurses' button again and then gave her another kiss. "I knew God wouldn't take you away from me." The door swung open, and the room quickly filled.

This time, he didn't mind all the people poking at Birdie because he knew it was a sign they were moving to the other side of tragedy.

It took several hours for them to check her thoroughly and when they finished, and the room finally emptied, he took a seat. "You need anything, baby?"

"You," she whispered.

He watched her point to him and then to the bed. "Honey, I don't want to jostle you." Her brows moved together, and she pointed to the bed again. "Okay." He settled himself as gently as he could next to her and took her hand. Looking down, he saw her smile. "You can get your way without much more than pointing your finger."

Her shoulder shrugged as she gave him a satisfied smile. "I love you too; thanks for sticking around," she whispered.

Drop the mic.

His heart stopped.

"Can you repeat that?"

"I love you, Mark Frazier."

"I love you with everything I've got." Curling himself around her small body, he held her gently and thanked God for the blessing they'd been given.

Things didn't always turn out this well, and he wanted to take a moment to appreciate it. The love of his life had survived an accident, and he was going to make sure to enjoy that fact every day and let her know how he felt.

CHAPTER FIFTEEN

Mark woke up with a start and glanced down at Birdie and felt her steady breathing. His heart slowed down after the initial panic, and he kissed her gently on the top of her head. Moving slowly, he felt his hand being squeezed and his heart thumped in response. *She came back to me.*

He slipped off the bed and studied her carefully, noting that she didn't look like she was in pain. "Good morning, how are you doing?"

She lifted her hand and moved it back and forth and then motioned for him to lean down. "My throat hurts, and I don't have a voice."

He cupped her face and ran his finger back and forth across her soft cheek. "It will take time. Don't worry; you're going to be able to boss me around in no time at all." The smile she gave him in response told him that she couldn't wait. "I'm going to get the nurse, and then I'll hit the head and get cleaned up."

"Thank you," she whispered.

A tear slipped down her face, and he wiped it gently away. "You've got me, heart and soul." Leaning over, he kissed her. "I'll check and see what your parents' ETA is because they're supposed to be here sometime today." She tried to move and winced. "Let me." He helped her adjust the bed and gently lifted her, so she was sitting. "Love you, Birdie."

She pulled his hand, so his face was close to hers. "Love you more."

"I'll never get tired of hearing you say that." He squeezed her hand. "I'm going to get the nurse and then I'll be back."

She gave him a thumbs up and then motioned for him to leave.

"Yeah, I didn't think that you'd need your voice to boss me around." He blew her a kiss and then walked out to the nurses' station and let them know she was awake, and they informed him that her parents were in the waiting room.

Taking a deep breath, he walked down the corridor and prepared himself for meeting his future in-laws. Not knowing what to expect, he decided not to worry about it.

He entered the waiting room and saw a couple that had to be Birdie's parents. The woman looked like an older version of his future wife, and he immediately saw where Birdie got her big smile. Stepping over to the couple, he introduced himself. "Mr. and Mrs. James, I'm Lt. Cmdr. Mark Frazier. It's unfortunate to meet you under these circumstances, but I look forward to getting to know you both."

Before he could say more, Mrs. James enveloped him in a hug. He let out a small laugh. "Now I know where Birdie learned how to hug."

Mrs. James released her hold and patted his chest. "I've heard a lot about you over the last couple of weeks, and am so happy that you were here to keep an eye on our girl."

Mr. James stepped forward and gave Mark a hearty handshake. "Young man, we understand that you haven't left her side. Is that true?"

Standing at attention in a modified parade stance, he nodded. "Yes, sir, Josh and I grabbed a helo and came as soon as we got the news. I didn't want her driving that car until I had airbags installed, but she didn't follow directions. This was completely avoidable."

Joy took his hands. "Now, you listen to me; things like this happen, and there is no going back and second-guessing your actions. Birdie knew we were not happy about that damn car, but she was sentimental and drove it anyway. As I'm sure you already know, our girl is stubborn, and isn't easily persuaded to veer from the course she's set." Frowning, she patted his arm. "The good news is that the car has been totaled, and she's going to be fine."

He lifted his eyes and met both of their gazes. "Thank you for saying that. The nurses might be done with their morning routine, so she's probably ready to see you. I'm going to grab a shower, and then I'll get us some coffee."

"Perfect," Mrs. James responded as she gathered her things. "We'll see you in a bit." Before she walked away, she smiled. "Call me Joy."

"And call me Tom," Mr. James added. "Looks like you're going to become a permanent fixture in our daughter's life, so there's no need to stand on formality."

"Thank you." He watched them walk out of the room and let out a breath. *So far so good*, he thought as he headed for the doctor's lounge. Today was a damn good day, not only because Birdie was recovering and conscious, but it seemed that she loved him too.

Seems that old soldiers were granted a miracle now and again.

***

Just as the nurse finished checking her vitals, Birdie looked up and saw her parents walk in. Seeing her mom and dad opened the floodgates and he started crying.

Before she got herself too worked up, both her parents enveloped her in a gentle hug, and she breathed them in. Their familiar scent settled her nerves as she felt their arms wind around her.

"Well, I guess we finally got rid of that damn car," her father said firmly. "Thank God."

She and her mom started laughing, and they released their hold. Sitting back, she wiped her face. "Yes, Daddy, the car is dead, but I'm not."

"Don't say that young lady, my goodness…that is not a bit funny."

"If we can't start to make jokes, then I'm going to start crying again."

"That's fine," Joy replied. "I'll take tears over your morbid jokes any day."

"Mom, I want a shower; can you take me in? The nurse said it would be okay if I had someone help me. I need to wash my hair and brush my teeth."

"Of course, sweetie. Let's get you cleaned up; it's sure to make you feel a hundred times better." Picking up the bag off the table, she looked at her husband. "Tom, you go meet Mark in the waiting room while Birdie and I take care of things here."

He gently hugged his daughter. "Love you, Birdie. Thank God you're okay."

"Love you too, Daddy."

Her mom helped her up from the bed, and they moved slowly toward the bathroom. "Bet you thought your days of giving me baths were over."

"Oh, sweetie, a mom never thinks her job is completely done."

"I'm so happy you and Daddy are here."

"We wouldn't want to be anyplace else."

She held her mom's hand and knew deep in her heart that she was a fortunate woman, not only because she survived the accident, but because she had a lot of loving people in her life.

Together, they managed to get Birdie showered and changed into clean pajamas. Sighing with pleasure, Birdie tilted her head as her mom blow-dried her hair and brushed it out. It was blissfully relaxing, and she felt like she was a little girl again. Being fussed over and pampered by her mom went a long way toward making her feel like she was going to be okay.

When the nurse came in with a breakfast tray, she heard her stomach rumble and figured that was an excellent sign of recovery. "The fact that oatmeal sounds good must tell everyone that I'm well on the road to being one hundred percent."

"It's certainly a good sign," the attendant commented as she set down the tray.

A nurse came in and took her vitals and then gave her a nod of approval. "Looks like you're being moved down to a regular room this afternoon."

"Great news, thank you." Settling back into bed, she picked up a piece of toast and took a small bite.

Taking the napkin, Joy unfolded it and handed it to Birdie. "So, tell me about this man who's blown into your life like a gale-force wind. From your last email, I didn't get the impression it was as serious as it appears to be."

Sitting back, Birdie took a sip of tea and tried to gather her thoughts. "I somehow fell in love with him over the last two weeks." Seeing her mother's confusion, she took her hand. "But it took the accident to make me realize that my feelings are real. I remember seeing the car hurdling in my direction and knowing that I might not survive. My first thought was that I didn't tell Mark how I felt. I think that I screamed it as the car hit me, and that's the last thing I remember."

Joy put her hand on her daughter's shoulder. "Nothing like seeing death to let you know what's important."

"I can't believe that I thought we'd just have a fling and nothing more."

"So, do you think this is the man for you?"

"Maybe...possibly. Probably." She drank more of her tea and realized she made no sense. "We've only known each other a couple of weeks, so maybe it's just lust." Shrugging, she picked at the toast on her tray. "I don't even know if we would get along over a long period of time, but I guess that I want to find out. The accident has allowed me to acknowledge my feelings, and I want to see where this goes and not chicken out." She set the toast down. "I love him, and he's a good man, so I don't think it's much of a gamble on my part. As far as I can tell, he's one hundred percent in, and I want to see what that means."

Joy squeezed Birdie's hand. "Well, I think it's worth investigating. He hasn't left your side since he got the news, and he's organized everyone to take care of your life while you've been in here." Running her hand through her daughter's hair, she smoothed it out. "I think, he's all in so prepare yourself."

"The man is nothing short of a tornado, so preparation might not be possible." She shook her head. "Mark practically wrote the book on being bossy and I'm not sure how much of that is his personality and how much of it has to do with his career in the Navy. I'm not a person who wants to be bossed and told what to do, so I have to teach him to back off a little."

"Nature of the beast, dear. A person doesn't become a SEAL without having a great deal of confidence and determination. These men have to operate as if there's not a thing they can't accomplish because if they don't, it could be deadly. One of their biggest assets is their inability to give up, and that shows up in all areas of their lives. I remember talking to Sarah when Josh was going to BUD/S, and she explained what succeeding in the program takes. These men have to be exceptional before they're even considered eligible to enter the program, and then only twenty percent of them make it through. There's no way to come out of the experience not believing you're invincible. Mark, your cousin, and all the men on the Teams are the best of the best." Leaning back, she shook her head. "I don't think you could've found a more competent, confident man if you ordered him up on the Internet, so this has to be something you're willing to take on. Only you know whether he's worth the effort."

"You're right, Mom. I guess my initial assessment is that he's totally worth it."

The door opened, and Joy looked up. "Here they come."

Mark walked in with Tom following and smiled at the women. "Here's your coffee, Joy."

"Thank you."

Mark stook Birdie's hand and kissed her head. "How do you feel? The nurse said they're moving you in a little while and your last MRI is scheduled for later this afternoon."

"I have a headache, but I want to go home. Maybe they'll let me out tonight."

"Baby, I don't think that's going to happen, but maybe tomorrow they'll release you. Josh is going to bring your Volvo up for your parents to drive, and Ana's taking care of your shop, so don't worry."

"Mark, my Volvo wouldn't start the other day. Something is wrong with my battery, and that's why I took the Wagoneer. I was only going to make a delivery two miles from my store."

"The guy who hit you ran a red light and was drunk. It wasn't his first offense, and he died at the scene of the accident. Instant justice, you don't always get that."

She looked at him, horrified. "I didn't want him to die. That's not justice."

"Oh, yes, it is. You were lucky to survive that accident. You must have an angel on your side. What if the next person he hit was a van full of kids? What would you think then?"

"Let's just agree to disagree. I'm going to have to think about this some more when my head doesn't hurt."

"I'm sorry; I don't want you to be upset. But that son of a bitch almost took you away from me, and I wouldn't have survived that."

"Neither would we," Tom added.

Birdie looked at her family and knew that if the situation were reversed, neither would she. What Mark had said sounded harsh and unforgiving, but if the tables were turned, how would she feel?

Certainly not something she would answer today. She felt Mark move closer and knew that her mother had been right earlier, he was all in, and right now, that felt pretty damn wonderful.

CHAPTER SIXTEEN

Mark noticed Birdie's frightened expression and wondered if she was going to be able to get in the truck. No doubt, the memory of the accident was still fresh in her mind, and he bet this first car ride was going to be challenging. The moment her hand started trembling in his, he knew they'd be lucky to get out of the parking lot. "Let's grab a seat, no need to rush things."

"All right, I might need a second before I'm ready to go."

"Whatever you need," he said as he led her away from the curb. They sat on the bench that faced the parking lot, and he looked into the bright blue sky and tried to think of something to say that would ease her anxiety. Everything that came immediately to mind was just a platitude that wouldn't help. Maybe the best thing to do was just be patient and hope the animal comfort of his body gave her some solace. Leaning down, he whispered in her ear, "We'll take as long as you need, but we have to get you in the car today; otherwise, it will be harder tomorrow and more so the day after that."

"Mark, I realize that." She huffed out an impatient sigh. "I'm just gathering my wits, so I don't lose it when we start rolling down the highway."

"You can lose it if you want. Won't bother me a bit."

She folded her hands. "My heart tripping over itself is making it hard to move my feet."

"Let's just people watch and relax, then."

"I didn't think you were the type of man who enjoyed that sort of thing."

"There's a lot you don't know about me yet and vice versa. I'm looking forward to peeling back the layers and discovering all the interesting things about you."

"Right now, I'm going to leave my layers where they are because I don't want you to see the frightening mess that I am."

Turning, he swept a kiss across her cheek. "I'm not interested in some polished version of you."

"Well, I'm going to keep the polish on for a while, until you've fallen for me good and hard."

"I already have, Birdie. When I got the news that you were in the hospital, my world stopped. The color drained away and, I've got to tell you, I'm not interested in living without you."

"Oh, Mark, that is the loveliest thing anyone has ever said to me."

"It's true; I love you and always will."

"Love you, too." Sitting up, she straightened her shoulders and looked around. "All right, let's do this." She stood and marched over to Mark's truck and crossed her arms over her body.

"This is going to be a piece of cake." When she snorted as he helped her into the truck, he decided to keep his mouth shut. Feeding her a bunch of lines wasn't going to make the experience any better.

Once he climbed in and started the engine, he glanced over and saw her sitting stiffly as she stared straight ahead. "Ready, honey?" She nodded and closed her eyes.

As they headed toward Coronado, he glanced over several times and noticed she didn't open her eyes once. "Almost there," he said as they started to cross the bridge that would lead them to the island.

Once he parked in front of her house, she let out a big breath and opened her eyes. "You did it." Lifting her hand, he pressed a kiss to her skin. "We'll get in the car every day until you feel more confident."

"You can think whatever you want, but know that it doesn't make it true."

"I see that you're going to be a great patient."

"Whatever."

Laughing to himself, he climbed out of his truck and walked around. Sassy was back, and he took it as a good sign. She could dish whatever she wanted, and it wouldn't make a bit of difference to him. "Love the attitude."

"You said you wanted the real me." Lifting her arms, she gave him a smirk. "Be careful what you ask for."

"Bring it." He lifted their bags out of the truck and watched the love of his life swing her gorgeous ass as she walked into the house.

Did she do it to torture him or was it a promise of what he might be enjoying later on?

Shrugging, he followed her and decided it didn't much matter. It was a view he loved, and what it meant didn't matter.

Joy walked out of the kitchen, wiping her hands on a towel. "Perfect timing. Dinner is almost ready. I made your favorites to welcome you home."

Birdie gave her mom a big hug. "Thanks, Mom. You're the best."

"Mark, go put those bags away and come to the table. We're about ready to eat."

"Yes, ma'am." As he climbed the stairs, he sent up a prayer of thanks to whoever was in charge. Birdie was okay, and they were together and in love. It was a significant blessing and one he didn't want to ignore. Someone up there had given him everything he ever wanted, and he was going to do his best to make sure he earned it.

***

They sat at the big farm table and had just enjoyed Birdie's favorite dinner, which was Beef Stroganoff, green beans, Caesar salad, French bread, and angel food cake for dessert. "Mom, everything was delicious."

Joy took her daughter's hand. "So happy that you're okay."

"I second that," Tom responded as he lifted his glass in a toast. "And, we don't have to worry about that Wagoneer anymore."

"Hear, hear," Joy said as everyone clinked glasses.

"Mrs. James, thank you for the delicious meal. Now I know where Birdie learned to cook."

"Mark, my daughter is a much more accomplished cook than I am. I can do the basics well, and that's about it."

Birdie looked around the table and felt a moment of God's good grace that she was here to enjoy her family and her boyfriend. The enormity of the accident hadn't fully sunk in yet and, when it did, she hoped that she'd be able to process it. "Thanks, Mom, it was just what I needed." Feeling Mark's arm rest lightly on her shoulders, she decided that exhaustion had finally taken over. "I'm starting to get tired, and am ready to go up and take a shower in my own bathroom."

"Go on up then," Tom replied as he stood and cleared his plate. "I'm going to finish in the backyard. I just want to water the garden, and then I'll come in."

Mark began clearing the table. "I'm going to do the dishes, and then I'll be up."

Standing with her mom, she watched Mark deposit the dishes on the counter and then bend over as he loaded the dishwasher.

"I can see your attraction and understand it," Joy said quietly to her daughter.

Laughing, she kissed her mom and then headed upstairs.

Joy began putting the leftovers away and smiled. "I think my daughter is lucky to have you."

He wiped his hands. "It's me who's lucky."

"I'll do the dishes; you go on up and see if Birdie needs anything."

"Yes, ma'am."

***

Birdie was laying on the bed, flipping through channels, when Mark walked into the bedroom. "Can you help me in the shower? I can't lift my arms enough to wash my hair because my ribs still hurt."

He gave her a sly grin. "Damn, I'd love nothing better than making sure you're clean." He put his hand out and helped her out of bed. "Being here with you is not something that I'm ever going to take for granted."

Standing slowly, she took his hand. "Me either."

"As a side note, I want you to know that I'll probably be at full mast anytime I see you naked." Holding up his hands, he smiled. "But I understand that you have to heal fully before we make love, so just ignore it, and I will, too."

"Well, I hope to be fully recovered soon. Otherwise, all the hard work you did to get me out of my rut will be for nothing." Sliding her hand on her hip, she gave him an encouraging smile. "We may have to start all over again with a more intensive schedule, just to get back on track."

He slipped her bra strap off her shoulder and swept his hand over her breast. "Whatever is necessary will be done." Staring at her with admiration, he shook his head. "Maybe we should just get on that intensive schedule as a precaution."

"Might not be a bad idea." When he unhooked her bra, she felt excitement flow through her veins. What a startling contrast to the last several days. "In fact, let's just do it to be sure."

"I like the way you think."

As they walked into the bathroom, she knew that having the opportunity to face her mortality was a blessing because it made her realize what was important. The last thing she wanted to do was miss out on the chance to love Mark as deeply as she could. Playing it safe, being smart, and protecting herself didn't make any sense if it caused her to miss a minute of what they could be together. "Thank you."

As the water heated up, he gave her a questioning look. "For what?"

"For being here."

He gently embraced her. "Only place I want to be." He kissed her and then said against her mouth, "Thanks for coming back to me."

Putting her hand on his heart, she felt the steady beat. "You're a good man to come back to." She leaned against his chest and listened to the steady beat pulsing against her ear. "Your heart is your biggest muscle, and that's saying something, considering you're built like a brick wall."

He let out a laugh and held her hand as they walked into the shower. "Birdie, the only thing bigger is my stubbornness, and I promise to try and use it for good and not evil."

As he tipped her head back into the water, she sighed. "Well, we have that in common. My family considers me more obstinate than a donkey, so I guess we have that to look forward to."

"Nothing better than spirited debate." He cupped her cheek. "We can always solve our disagreements by loving on each other." He tilted his hips and winked. "Bet we can get rid of half of them in no time."

Feeling his impressive length, made a ribbon of desire unfurl. "Oh, how I wish I was ready to take advantage of you."

"Soon, Birdie." He gave her a chaste kiss and stepped back. "Let's get cleaned up, so you can rest."

"Kind of the last thing I want to do." Running her hand down his length, she bit her bottom lip.

"Soon," she said to herself as he moved his hips away.

"Soon," he repeated. "Now, behave and let me wash your hair."

"Yes, sir." She leaned her forehead into his massive chest and felt her heart fall into him completely. "Love you," she said quietly.

CHAPTER SEVENTEEN

"Morning," Mark murmured against Birdie's warm skin. "I'm going to make coffee, and then head to the base."

"I'll make it."

He dropped his lips to hers and kissed her thoroughly. "Maybe we can do more than kissing tomorrow if you feel like you're up to it. I miss making love to you."

"I was thinking the same thing. Now that I've had you, I want you—a lot."

"Shit, Birdie. You can't say something like that without warning. I'm going to be thinking about it all day now." He rocked his hips. "I always feel like I'm the one out of control, and to hear that you want me to is damn incredible."

Moving away, she sat up and smiled. "You go get ready, and I'll make you something for breakfast."

"I'd rather have you, but I guess that isn't on the menu yet." He watched her stand and pull her robe on. "What are you doing today?"

"Mom and I are going to the shop, and I'm thinking of looking for a person who can work part-time."

He stood and took her hand. "I think that's a great idea. Hey, I may have someone for you. Frisco told me the other day that his sister, Melanie, was moving down; she could be perfect for the job."

"That's a great idea. When you see Frisco today, tell him to have her call me." Moving her hair off her shoulder, she looked out the window. "I also need to shop for a new delivery car for the store, and I should take the Volvo in to make sure the battery is okay."

"Not necessary. Frisco took it to the dealership and had it checked out and then looked over it himself. The light in the back got switched on. Since you don't drive it every day, it killed the battery. I had Frisco put a new one in, just to be sure."

"Mark, you didn't have to do that. Let me pay you back for everything." She walked over to her purse and started to pull her wallet out.

He strode over and shook his head. "Birdie, don't insult me."

"I am more than capable of taking care of myself."

"So am I, so don't stage a rebellion because you're not used to someone helping you. This is how it's going to be, and you don't get to be in charge of this." He stood at his full height and crossed his arms over his chest and waited for her to come up with an argument.

"Well…"

"You can make me breakfast, and that will be thank you enough." Seeing her struggle to accept it made him realize they had a lot of work to determine what their normal was going to look like. He kept his expression blank and prayed she was going to let this one go and allow him to do what he needed to.

She pulled on his crossed arms, and he leaned down with a stern look on his face. Kissing his cheek, she whispered in his ear, "Thank you for helping and wanting to take care of me."

He wrapped her gently in his arms. "Love you, honey."

"I love you too, but don't think because I've let this go that it sets any sort of precedent."

Resting his chin on top of her head, he let out a chuckle. "All right, if you say so." He tightened his hold and decided not to say anything more. He knew that in battle, every small victory led to the next, and he'd just managed one. Keeping that fact to himself seemed to be the best course of action, so he enjoyed it silently.

"The fact that you agreed so easily makes me a little nervous, but I'm not sure what I can do about it."

"Your lack of trust is kind of unsettling."

She pulled away. "Yeah, I don't buy that statement for a minute." She crossed her arms and let her eyes drag up and down his body. "You have a plan, and I'm going to figure it out sooner than you think."

"Suspicion is not a good look."

"Get used to it because it's not going away until I have you completely figured out."

Taking her hand, he pressed a kiss to her skin. "You do whatever you feel is necessary."

She turned toward the door and called over her shoulder, "Believe me, I will."

He shook his head as he walked into the bathroom and knew he had a hell of a battle in front of him. Picking up his toothbrush, he squeezed toothpaste on it and grinned because he loved nothing better, and soon she would understand that.

***

Birdie sat at the farm table in her shop and went over her calendar and tried to come up with a schedule for a part-time person. Hearing the front door open, she looked up and saw James walk in with a big pink box from her favorite bakery. She stood and gave him a big smile. "Hello, friend."

He set the box down and then opened his arms, hugging her tightly. "I do not appreciate all of the stress you've put me through."

"Sorry about that," she mumbled against his chest. "I'll do my best to stay away from drunk drivers from here on out."

He released his hold and then sniffed. "See that you do because it scared the shit out of me." Smoothing down his shirt, he smiled. "I expect to be the maid of honor at your wedding."

She laughed and then held her middle because her ribs were still a little sore. "You have to fight Ana and Rory for the honor."

He waved his hand in dismissal. "Please, I can take those bitches with my eyes closed."

"That's what I'm afraid of." Opening the lid to the box, she swooned. "Mom, James is here. Can you make some coffee?" she called out loudly.

Her mom popped her head around the corner and smiled. "Hello, James. Lovely to see you. I'll make a fresh pot and then be right out." She blew him a kiss and went back to the little kitchen.

James pulled out her chair and waited for her to sit before he took his own. "Mark let me have a couple of minutes with you on Saturday afternoon before you went in for your MRI and, I have to say, he kept up a brave front."

"I'm sure he did."

"I had a feeling that he wasn't going to give you a choice about recovering and was ready to will you into getting better if that's what it took. Do they teach that in SEAL school?"

"It's funny that you said that because I swear I felt his focused attention." Shaking her head, she let out a laugh. "And I'm hoping it's going to turn out to be a good thing and not something that I can't handle."

Joy came out with a tray of coffee, plates, and napkins. "So happy you brought us treats, James."

"Being in a car accident sort of requires it, right?"

"Yes," she agreed as she picked her favorite.

Tom walked in with a folder of papers and printouts. "I guess that I got here just in time."

Joy got up and kissed her husband. "Go sit, and I'll get you a cup."

James shook hands with Tom. "Nice to see you again, sir. I'm sorry it has to be under these circumstances."

Tom nodded. "Well, at least our girl is okay, and we got rid of that damn car. I have several options for a new delivery van, and just need some info about how much you transport, and then we can narrow it down."

They sat around the table, looked at the printouts, and discussed the options, and when the phone rang, she got up to answer it. "Good afternoon, Island Flowers."

"Hi, honey, how are you feeling?"

"I'm feeling pretty good. We're drinking coffee and eating treats that James brought in. Dad's here, and we're looking at cars he researched. What are you doing?"

"I'm doing paperwork. Later, we have PT, time on the gun range, and then the O-Course. I'm calling to check on you and tell you I love you."

"Thank you, and I love you, too. We're going to eat around six."

"Sounds good. We need to get you in the car tonight, so let's go after dinner."

She straightened the front desk a little and remained silent. The last thing she wanted to do was get into a vehicle and had a feeling he was going to make her.

"Your silence is never a good thing."

"I should get back to work."

"Okay, we'll talk about it when I get home."

She made a non-committal response and then wiped off some dust with her finger. "Love you, see you later." She hung up the phone and stared out the windows of her shop as she thought of a strategy to avoid the inevitable.

***

After dinner, Birdie stood on the front lawn, staring at Mark in a standoff. "I told you that I'm not getting in the car."

Staring back, he was unmoved. "It will be harder if you let it go. I'm not asking you to drive. I'm suggesting a ten-minute ride, and that's it."

"No, I don't want to."

"Please, do this for me. Your parents are going home in a couple of days, and I may get called for wheels up. I want you to be able to get in the car if you need to. Don't let me be worried about you if I'm halfway across the world."

Narrowing her eyes, she slid her hand on her hip. "Jeez, lay on the guilt." She stomped to his truck and got in. "All right, ten minutes and that's it. Just know, I'm doing this for you."

He buckled her in. "Thank you." As he got in the truck, he noticed she had her eyes closed. "Maybe this time you can open your eyes for a little while."

Slowly opening them, she turned and gave him the stink eye. "How about I do what I want?"

He started the car. "Okay, sounds good to me."

"Ten minutes and no more."

Mark knew she was trying to control her fear as he saw her pulse flutter wildly in her neck. Deciding that distraction might help, he started talking. "I'm going to take you down to the beach next to the Naval Amphibious Base and show you where my career began."

"Fine."

He drove down the street and held her hand and knew he was doing the right thing. Parking the truck in the street adjacent to NAB, he looked over. "I knew you could do it."

Sitting up, she opened her eyes and looked around. "So, I did."

"Do you want to get out and take a walk on the beach? I can point out the area where we did a lot of our initial training."

"Sure, let's go."

They got out, and he took her hand as they made the short walk to the sand. "I knew that I wanted to join the military in high school. I thought about enlisting as soon as I graduated, but my mom insisted that go to college first. While I was there, I talked to the Marines, and Air Force, and once I talked to the Navy recruiter, I knew the SEAL program was for me."

"What attracted you to being in the military?"

"I wanted to serve my country." He pointed to a spot on the sand. "Let's watch the sunset." He sat down and then waited for her to join him. "I have an instinctive need to protect, and didn't know how that was going to manifest itself until I started talking to recruiters."

"What was it about being a SEAL that interested you?"

"Everything. It's like having the best, most difficult adventure of your life while protecting the country you love." He wrapped his arm around her shoulders. "I'm in a fraternity of hard men doing an impossible job. I think the most important thing that I've learned is that to survive as a small unit, you have to learn to go around big obstacles rather than through them.

"The Teams are a testosterone-filled society of tough guys and bad-asses facing impossible odds any time they're deployed. I'm telling you this because I want you to understand who I am, and why I do and say things. It's my nature to push through obstacles, and you have to let me know when I'm too much. I want you to get in a car again and be able to drive, so I'm going to encourage you as much as I can get away with."

She squeezed his hand. "Everything that I've ever attempted to accomplish has been easy. School wasn't hard and working at the firm wasn't difficult either. I've never tested myself for any reason. Which makes me the opposite of you. If I think it's going to be too hard, then I find something that I'm more likely to succeed at." She let out a sigh. "I can benefit from your influence because I'm a big wimp."

"You can't compare yourself to a crazy-ass SEAL. Most of us are certifiable. We're not normal, just the right men for the job. I think you're my perfect balance. My crazy and your sanity is going to make us unbeatable, and that's why we're going to go the distance."

"Why are you so confident? You're a man who hasn't had a relationship since college, and yet you're ready to jump into one with me."

"I know what I feel, and this is it for me. You are the love of my life. It's going to be true today, next week, next month, and at the end of our lives. I know we don't know each other well, and there are things we're going to discover that are irritating. But I know you're my woman, and the rest is just the sugar cookie."

"What is the sugar cookie?"

"When we were in BUD/S, several times a week, we would have a uniform inspection. It was thorough, and the instructors would always find something wrong. When you failed inspection, you had to run fully clothed into the surf and get wet from head to toe. Then you had to roll around until every part of your body was covered in sand. The effect was called a 'sugar cookie.' You stayed in that uniform the rest of the day—cold, wet, and sandy. The guys who couldn't accept that their effort was in vain never made it through training. The guys who understood that you were never going to have a perfect uniform did. Sometimes, no matter how well you prepare or how well you perform, you still end up as a sugar cookie. It's just the way life is sometimes. You have to get over it and move forward."

"So, what you're telling me is that no matter if we have hard times, we just keep moving forward."

"Something like that. You're not a choice for me, and we're going to face challenges, and we're always going to move forward, no matter what. I've never had an easy day in my job, and that's never going to change. I like figuring out how to make it through and don't expect simple. The last couple of weeks with you has been nothing but easy; in fact, it's like fucking Christmas every day. You are my easy and my reward for the last eleven years of hard days. I never give up, and that's why I'm so confident about us. I want my name to be the one that changes yours."

She leaned into him and sighed. "Turns out that I'm a relationship girl after all." She looked up. "I guess this has no chance of being a fling."

"It sure doesn't." He kissed her head and watched the sun dip into the ocean. They were going to be together for the rest of their lives, and nothing was going to change that.

CHAPTER EIGHTEEN

Birdie stood at the back door of her shop and watched Mark inspect her new delivery van. "It has the highest safety rating."

"It's going to be perfect for you, honey." He patted the hood. "Are you ready to go to dinner?"

"Almost, I just need to shut off the lights and lock up."

He followed her in and waited. "You should drive us over to the restaurant, and then we can come back and switch cars before we go home."

As she walked toward the front of the store, she decided that she needed to get him off track so she could delay getting into the car for a couple more days. Flicking the switch for the lights in the front, she knew exactly what would work.

Seduction.

Pure and simple.

Smoothing out her dress, she turned and walked to the back of the shop. Stopping next to her work table, she slung her hand on her hip. "You didn't give me a kiss yet."

The surprised look he gave her as he stalked in her direction made her realize she had chosen the perfect strategy. When he stood in front of her, she draped her arms over his shoulders. "Are you bored already?"

He tilted his hips forward. "Does this feel like I'm bored?"

Wiggling closer, she shook her head. "Not really."

He slid her hair over her shoulder. "I was trying to behave myself because I don't want you to think that I'm always trying to get at you."

She pulled him down and ran her mouth over to his lips. Kissing the side of his mouth, she slid her hand toward his zipper. "I appreciate your effort." Kissing him gently, she moved her hand into his pants and felt his hips move. "I love the way you smell. It's perfect."

He picked her up and put her on the work table. "If you're trying to seduce me to get out of driving, it's not going to work."

"I was just kissing my boyfriend with no ulterior motives. Can't I enjoy having a sexy man in my flower shop?" She moved her hand along his length and heard him growl. "I'm not trying to distract you."

"Really?" He leaned back and gave her an assessing gaze. "Then you won't mind if I…" sliding his hand under her dress, he moved to the edge of her panties and threw her a cocky grin, "do this?"

"Oh, well, sure, you can do that." He slipped his finger inside, and she moaned with pleasure and knew she was no longer the seducer, but the *seducee*. "If you want to."

"I'm going to slip inside you in a minute, pushing myself so deep there will be no separation between us. When we're done blowing each other's minds, we're going to get into that van, and you're going to drive us to dinner."

"Fine," she responded as his fingers drove her need higher. She had lost the battle, so it would probably be best to enjoy her defeat. Slipping her hand out of his pants, she unzipped his pants and freed him. Looking down, she saw her panties hit the floor as he moved her to the edge of the table. "At least when I drive, I'll be relaxed."

"That's right, Birdie." With one push of his hips, he slid all the way home. "Look at me."

Raising her gaze, she smiled. They were connected physically as well as emotionally, and she knew she could never let him go. She held onto his big shoulders while he pumped his hips and released her orgasm. Crying out his name, she felt his release follow her own. Dropping her head to his chest, she kissed him. "Does this mean I still have to drive the van tonight?"

"Yes, it does. But now you're relaxed, so your seduction plan worked out in the end." He slipped out of her and went over and got some paper towels and cleaned himself up. He smiled at her as put himself back together. "I knew you were up to something because you never initiate sex."

"Should I try and do that more?" she asked as she hopped off the table and searched for her panties. Going over to the sink, she took the wet towels he handed her and got herself together.

"It doesn't matter to me who gets us started, just as long as we get there. I'm the more aggressive one, so just do what feels comfortable." He kissed her cheek. "Let's eat because now I've worked up an appetite."

"I need fried chicken because there has to be a decent reward for my efforts."

"The diner has fried chicken, so you can take us there."

She grabbed the keys, turned off the lights, and they walked out. "Here goes nothing." As they stood in front of the new van, she knew it was time to face her fears. "The sex helped, but I'm still nervous."

"Nerves are okay. Not facing them, not so much."

Lifting the key fob, she unlocked the doors and climbed in. "Let's get this over with."

She watched Mark join her. "You're buying me pie to go with my dinner, right?"

"Of course."

Nodding resolutely, she put the key in the engine and then sent up a prayer. "Pie," she said to herself as she pulled out and drove down the alley.

***

They arrived at the diner thirty minutes later. The trip should've taken them fifteen minutes at the very most and Mark was grateful that she'd taken the first step. When he put his hand on her back, he noticed it was damp. "I'm proud of you, Birdie."

She made a noncommittal sound and he drew her against his side. They were shown to a table in the middle of the diner and he noticed that her brow was still puckered. "It will get easier every time you get in the car."

"I'm having fried chicken, mashed potatoes, a salad with ranch dressing, and a Diet Coke. What are you going to have?"

"Do you want to talk about it?"

"No, why would I want to relive the abject fear that rushed through my body every time we came up to an intersection? That's not polite dinner conversation, so let's choose something else to discuss."

"Baseball. We could talk about that."

"Sure, why not?"

"Do you like baseball?"

"I like the food when I go to a baseball game."

He threw his head back and let out a bark of laughter. "I love you." The waitress arrived, and he ordered, and when she left, he took her hand. "I know what you did tonight was hard."

"It was no big deal and, from now on, I'm going to try and be more like you." She squeezed his hand. "What kind of pie do they have?"

"They have whatever you want." The waitress brought their food, and they started eating. "What are we doing this weekend?"

"I'm going to the shop tomorrow for a little bit to make sure that Melanie is set up for the day." I also have Adam coming over to give me an estimate on the upstairs. What are your plans?"

"I'll do my PT in the morning while you're at the shop, and then I'll come to take you to lunch. How does that sound?"

"Perfect. I have my broker coming in after Adam. He's going to give me some ideas about what income I can generate if I make the upstairs offices or apartments."

"Should we talk about what to do with my condo? We're practically living together right now."

"I don't think we should do anything. You're going to want to escape to your place when the lust wears off and I irritate you. We're in the lover stage and can't get mad at each other because we're either eating or naked. But wait until real life happens."

"We've had real life." He moved closer. "I've experienced the fear of losing you, and I never want to feel that again." He lifted his glass and drained it. "Lover stage, life stage, whatever stage—we are together. I'm going to be deployed soon, and we're going to have to learn how to manage it."

"I'm not looking forward to your absence, but will have to learn how to live with it, since there's nothing I can do."

"I'm damn glad to hear that you don't feel like you have a choice because this is it for me. You're my person."

She wiped her hands and pulled him in. "And you're mine."

They finished dinner and, as they ordered pie, Mark saw Sam and Karen walk in and waved them over. "Hi, guys."

Birdie took Karen's hand. "How are you?"

She rubbed her tummy. "Much better, thank you. The second trimester is easier, and I have my energy back." Looking up at Sam, she gave him an affectionate smile. "I think my husband may survive after all."

Sam looked at his wife with affection. "Baby, I'm a hard-ass SEAL. I can handle my beautiful pregnant wife with no problems."

Mark laughed. "That isn't what you were saying last week. I'm glad to hear you're so confident."

Sam gave his commanding officer a dirty look. "Thanks for sharing. I'll be sure to return the favor when Birdie is pregnant."

Karen started laughing. "I was driving him nuts, and made hell week look like a picnic." She leaned over and whispered to Birdie, "I can't keep my hands off him because of these crazy hormones." She took Sam's hand. "Apparently, you get double the hormones with twins."

Sam chuckled. "I'm enjoying the hell out of this pregnancy thing and look forward to meeting our children."

"Good answer, Sam! Karen, do you know what you're having yet? I'm working on the blankets, and can make them gender-neutral if you want."

Sam took his wife's hand. "We are having one of each."

Mark stood, shook his CPO's hand, and then gently hugged Karen. "Congratulations. That's fantastic."

Birdie got up and hugged them both as well. "I'm so happy. I better start knitting faster."

"Since I'm eating for three, we'd better get started. See you guys soon." Karen waved as Sam saluted, and they went to their table.

"Do twins run in your family?"

The waitress brought their pie, and she lifted her fork and shook her head. "No twins on my side. Why are you asking me?"

"Just wondering. I guess we'll just have them one at a time." He started eating his pie and noticed her unhappy expression. "What did I say?"

"There is no *we*. I will be the one carrying the child. All you have to do is have sex. Jeez!" she took a big bite of pie and then pointed her fork at Mark. "Your job will be to make sure that I'm as happy as can be while I grow a child in my body. I hate when men say 'we are having a baby.' You are not the one gaining weight and having your organs pushed around while a bowling ball sits on your bladder." She returned to her pie and mumbled to herself. "You get to have an orgasm and send your seed, and that's it. What is this *we*?"

He smiled and knew she not only loved him but eventually would give him some babies. "Thanks for clearing that up." He kissed her head. "I will cater to your every whim and worship you after you deliver our child. I got it. No problem."

She smiled approvingly. "You can say *we* after the baby arrives because we'll both be responsible for the child."

"Well, I'm glad *we* have that all worked out. Let's go home and practice."

"Alright, we might as well."

Keeping any further comments to himself, he knew that she had become precious to his soul. And he was never going to let her go.

CHAPTER NINETEEN

Mark tightened his hold as Birdie lay across his body. "I like when you come at me." Moving his fingers back and forth over her soft skin, he wondered how long they could stay in bed. "When I met you, I knew that mouth of yours was going to be dangerous, and I was right. Devil's candy, no doubt about it."

"I had to go with the element of surprise since you always push me off when I've tried before. I had to catch you sleeping, so I could have my way with you."

"Baby, you can have your way with me whenever you want because your mouth on any one of my body parts is a blessed event. Happy anniversary to me."

She rested her head against his heart. "It's hard to believe that it's been three weeks."

"It's been the best three weeks of my life, that's for damn sure."

"I was wondering if I was becoming," she leaned up and whispered in his ear, "sex-crazed."

"God, I hope so, because if I drive you half as crazy as you make me, then there is some justice in the world."

"Are you mocking me?"

"No, I just don't want to be the only one out of control."

"Yeah, no need to worry about that because the more I have you, the more I want you."

Smoothing his hand over her hair, he felt a wide smile split his face. "It's just how it's going to be with us, and we should enjoy it. We can't take it for granted, though, because there are going to be plenty of times when we can't act on it." Lifting her face, he took a moment to make sure she was paying attention. "I want you to turn to me every day in some way, and I don't mean with just your body. The habit I want to create with you is connection. I'd like to be the one you rely on…the one that you count on. I'll do the same with you because when you stop turning toward the person you love, then that becomes a habit. And that's the last thing I want since I'm going to ask you to marry me pretty soon." When she didn't look surprised, he wondered if she'd heard him.

"I kind of guessed that's what you had in mind."

"That's it? No objections?"

"Nope." She leaned over and kissed him. "Do you want pancakes or waffles for breakfast?"

Stunned.

Where in the hell had the easy agreement come from?

Deciding he didn't need to know, he pressed their mouths together and said against her lips, "Whatever you want. Take your shower, and I'll change the bed."

"Yes, sir."

"I like when you obey orders." Hearing her laugh, he studied her retreating figure and knew he should be satisfied with clearing the first hurdle.

There were a hundred more before she became his wife, but at least they'd started.

SATURDAY AFTERNOON

Mark arrived at the shop around one o'clock and waved to Melanie as he walked in. "Is she in the back?"

"Yes, she's in the office with her broker, and said to send you back when you got here."

"Thanks." When he entered the back of the shop, he saw Birdie sitting at her desk, studying a spreadsheet, as a man leaned over and pointed to something. "He'd better not be looking down her shirt," he mumbled to himself. "Otherwise, he'll be in deep shit."

Birdie glanced up, pushed back from her desk, and threw him a smile. "Hi, babe. Come in and meet Clay. He was just giving me some info on comps in the area for similar buildings."

Putting his arm around her, he threw the man a hard stare. If that didn't send the message that she was his and he'd protect her in any way necessary, then he didn't know what would.

"Clay, I'd like you to meet my boyfriend, Lt. Commander Mark Frazier."

Clasping the guy's hand, he shook it firmly and continued to stare.

"Nice to meet you, sir. Birdie's told me a lot about you."

"Clay is the husband of Veronica, who's in my knitting club, she owns that cute kitchen shop in that little shopping center with that statue in the middle."

Feeling his muscles relax, he squeezed Birdie tighter. "Nice to meet you, Clay."

"I've spent way too much money in her shop and always tell myself that I'm just going to stop in for a visit, but I've never managed to walk away without buying something."

Clay laughed. "When my wife graduated from culinary school, I thought she was going to spend all of our money on kitchen supplies. At least with the shop and catering business, we've got a way to support her habit." Stacking the papers, he slid them into a folder. "Take your time with the information and let me know if you have any questions. The nail shop is up for lease renewal, so I'll get in touch with you next week and let you know where we're at."

"Sounds good, let me walk you out, so I can give you some flowers to take home to Veronica."

Clay turned to Mark. "Nice meeting you, and thank you for your many years of service to our country."

Mark nodded. "Take care." He watched Birdie walk into the shop and pull out a premade bouquet and wondered when the hell he was going to calm down. Seeing her motion to him, he headed in her direction and hoped like hell it happened soon because if it didn't then he was going to insult half the men on the island.

"Come on, grumpy pants, let's get something to eat."

"I'm not grumpy."

"Sure." Birdie turned to Melanie. "Do you need anything before I go to lunch?"

"No, I can handle it. I'll make a couple more bouquets for the grocery store since they only have two left."

"Sounds good. Don't forget there are drinks in the fridge in my office and cookies are in that blue container."

"Thanks, Birdie."

Snapping her fingers, she headed to the back. "Almost forgot my purse."

Following hot on her heels, he cornered her in the doorway and put his arms around her shoulders. "Give me a kiss."

"You need a little loving, Mark?"

"I need to know you're mine and no other man is going to catch your eye."

Raising on tiptoes, she pulled him down. "You are all that I can see, feel, and hear, and I can't imagine that ever changing."

Kissing her times, he felt himself settle. "Thanks, honey."

Pushing him away, she grabbed her purse. "Let's go because I need a cheeseburger and fries. Loving you takes a lot of energy, and I need to refuel."

"I know that's not a compliment, but I'm going to leave it alone for the sake of peace."

"Choosing your battles is never a bad idea."

Laughing, he took her hand and led her out of the shop. "I know that better than most. They waved to Melanie as they headed to the door, and he wondered why she put up with his possessiveness. He was off the charts crazy about her and knew he had to get it under control. "Hey, honey, why did you introduce me with my full rank? You've never done that before."

"I thought it showed respect and allowed Clay to acknowledge all that you've done for our country." Looking up, she frowned. "Was it okay?"

"It's fine; it just surprised me is all since I wasn't sure how you felt."

"I think people would like to acknowledge what you've done, and if I introduce you that way, then it allows them to show their appreciation."

"Speaking of serving my country, we're almost done with our stand-down phase, and I'm about to go downrange. I want to make sure everything is taken care of at home, so when I'm out on the other side of the world, I won't worry about you."

"You don't have to worry about me. Just tell me what you need me to do for you while you're gone."

"Let's figure it out over the weekend, and then we can go to the bank on Monday."

"Why do we have to go to the bank? I can schedule your bills to be paid monthly and then confirm it's been done. There's no need to make a trip to the bank."

"I'm not talking about my bills being paid; I want you to have access to my accounts in case you need anything."

"Mark, you know that I'm financially secure, right? I've taken care of myself for many, many years, and if we're ever together on a permanent, legal basis, then we can discuss it. But right now, I don't want access to anything."

Stopping abruptly in the middle of the sidewalk, he turned. "What are you talking about, 'if'? There's no if. There's only when."

She pulled his hand. "Let's go eat, and we'll talk about it at home tonight, not on the street."

Not budging, he shook his head. "Did you mean what you said this morning about understanding my intentions, or were you placating me?"

"I'm not discussing this on the street, so you can either take me to lunch or go home." Yanking her hand away, she looked from side to side. "What's your decision?"

Realizing he was about to lose his shit, he took a deep breath. "Sorry about that." Holding out his hand, he let out a breath when she took it. "I'll take you to lunch and behave."

"Thank you."

Knowing what he had to do, he started formulating a plan of action, and once he had the first five steps organized in his mind, he relaxed. The next step was executing, which thankfully wouldn't be a problem.

***

Mark sat in his favorite sports bar, waiting for Sam to show. Scanning the different screens, he saw that baseball, football, and hockey were available, and knew none of the games would keep his attention.

When Sam strolled in, he let out a breath of relief and signaled to the bartender that he needed two beers. "Thanks, for coming by. I know you want to spend time with your wife, so I'll be quick."

"I'm good, no worries. She's at a water aerobics class and stays in as long as she can because it's the only time she feels weightless. What do you need advice on?"

"I'm going to ask Birdie to marry me before we go down range and I need to buy her a ring, and wondered where you bought Karen's." Leaning back, he waited while the waitress deposited their drinks.

"Are you serious, man? It's only been a couple of weeks. Don't you want to wait and see if you make it out of the happy sex phase?"

"I don't plan on ever leaving that phase with Birdie, and I'm sure she's the one. How long did it take you with your wife?"

"You have a point because I knew within the first month she was going to be my wife." Holding up his hands, he shook his head. "But it took me a year to talk her into it, and then we didn't get married until a year after that. She wanted to wait because I was only her second boyfriend. She's younger than Birdie and didn't want to rush anything. It just about killed me, and honestly, I never felt comfortable until she said the I do's at the wedding. In our line of work, we deal with uncertainty every day, and I never sweat it because I know we'll find a way to accomplish the goal. Karen, on the other hand, had me sweating until the last minute and gave me a run for my money. It was all worth it, though, because look at us now...we have twins on the way and I'm married to the best girl in the world."

"If Birdie makes me wait two years, I'll go nuts. I just want to lock her down."

Snorting, Sam slapped the table. "Don't use *lock her down* when you ask her. Just a suggestion. He dug his phone out. "Let me give you the name of my cousin who's a jeweler. He helped me pick the right ring, and I trust him." Clicking, he sent the info to Mark. "Good luck with the ring and the proposal. Have you thought about how you are going to do it yet? That stuff is important, and she'll want a good story to tell everyone."

"I have an idea, and have a few details to work out, but I think it's a winner. Thanks for the advice and info." They finished their beers and watched the game, while Mark plotted and planned his next moves.

Nobody was better at executing a plan, and he knew Birdie would soon agree.

CHAPTER TWENTY

Leaning forward, Birdie took one last look in the mirror and considered herself date ready. Mark had texted her earlier, telling her to dress up and be ready by six, and she was following orders. Good things usually resulted from his directives, and she didn't expect this to be any different.

She heard the doorbell and wondered why he hadn't used his key. Strolling downstairs, she opened the door.

Lord have mercy, the man stood in the doorway in his dress whites.

Her heart stuttered.

Her body heated up.

And she couldn't believe the most handsome man in the world was her boyfriend. Everything about him was perfect. His hat sat low on his face, and he had several rows of medals covering his chest.

Polished and flawless.

He held a beautiful bouquet. "Hi, sweetheart, ready for our date?"

Taking in all six-foot-three of his glory, she felt emotion clog her throat. Seeing him like this allowed her to note once again who she was involved with. Not only was he the best boyfriend in the world, but he was a real-life hero. She moved aside and put her hand on her heart. "I didn't know I was going out with the Lt. Cmdr. tonight; I thought I was going out with that naughty man I've become so fond of."

"One and the same, honey." Taking off his hat as he entered, he handed her the flowers and then leaned down to kiss her cheek. "You're the prettiest woman I've ever seen."

"I'm not as pretty as you." Taking his hand, she led him into the kitchen. "What's the occasion for your dress whites and medals?"

"We're having a special date."

She watched him walk over to the fridge and pull out a bottle of champagne that he must've put in earlier. When he held it up, she saw that it was Veuve Clicquot Rose, her favorite. "Are you going to drink pink champagne?"

"Ana told me it was your favorite, so, yes." He pulled out glasses, poured the champagne, and then gave her one. "To the best month of my life and the woman who gave it to me."

They clinked glasses and kissed, then she took a sip and tried to figure out what he had planned. "Can you give me a hint?"

"Wait and see."

"Where are we going?"

"Follow me." He took her hand and led her outside.

Seeing the patio transformed into a romantic setting, she wondered how and when he'd managed to install speakers and twinkle lights. "You made magic, Mark." Twirling around, she took it all in as laughter spilled from her mouth.

Happiness, pure and simple. He'd given her that from the moment they met, and she finally accepted that he was, in fact, as good as he seemed. Pulling him down, she kissed him slowly and felt his hand graze her cheek.

Sweet and heat all in one kiss.

Mark Frazier cracked her heart open, and she knew there would never be another. Even if they didn't work out, he was always going to own her heart.

Forever.

"I want to make magic for you every day," he said against her lips.

"You already have."

Pulling away, he gave her a satisfied grin. "Let's sit and enjoy our champagne."

Following orders once again, she sat down and watched him pick up a remote and heard music fill the patio. "And a soundtrack to go with all the magic."

"Your cousin helped me with the playlist, and I hope you like it."

"Perfect, just like you." Sitting back, she felt his big hand drape over her shoulder and felt a wave of peace that she never thought was possible. It was as though everything in her world clicked into place and the man sitting next to her had made it possible. Seeing the last of the sun disappear over the fence, she sighed and knew all she had to do was love him as has hard as she could for as long as possible.

"How did you do all of this? We've been together since Friday, and you must've had some magic fairies working for you?"

"A man never gives away his secrets. I'm an excellent planner, and able to execute any objective."

Not satisfied with the answer, she tried to figure out how he'd accomplished everything. "Is this why you wanted to go to Balboa Park yesterday?"

"Magic is best enjoyed and not explained." The side gate opened and he stood. "Dinner is served."

She watched the owner of her favorite Italian restaurant, Vigilucci's, walk in with two boxes filled with food.

Mark spoke with him quietly and then shook his hand. "What the heck?"

Mario blew her a kiss and waved. "Buena fortuna, bella."

"Grazi," she called out.

Standing, she moved to the table and watched Mark start to unpack the boxes. "What can I do to help?"

"Sit and enjoy. I'm serving you tonight, so relax." He pulled out the plates that were filled with salad and then the ones with their main course as well as the cutlery rolled in napkins. "Let's eat."

"Thank you for this wonderful surprise."

"Sweetheart, this is just the beginning."

"Should I be nervous?" Seeing his smug expression, let her know that a romantic dinner was just the beginning. Was she ready for whatever he had planned?

"Nothing to worry about, it's all good."

He dug into his food, and she did the same. It would probably be a good idea to have as much fuel as possible for whatever was next. "So…"

"I've always been a man who knew what he desired. In high school, I knew that I wanted to serve my country and join a Special Forces team, and I made that happen. When I want something, I don't equivocate once I've made my decision. When you're on the Teams, you do the impossible every day, and that becomes your normal, and a challenge is just something to get through. I'll never give up on something once I've decided it's mine."

Listening carefully, she knew he was telling her something important; she just didn't know what it was leading to. "I have no doubt…"

He stood abruptly and came around the table, taking her hand. "I love you, Birdie James, and you're the one for me."

"And you're the one…" she watched him get down on one knee, "what are you doing?"

"I will love you for the rest of my life and promise to protect you, take care of you, and listen. Will you do me the honor of becoming my wife?" He pulled a box out of his pocket and opened it.

Covering her mouth in disbelief, she gasped and couldn't catch her breath. Staring at his beautiful face with love shining in his eyes, she felt a tear slip down her face.

"What do you say, honey?"

"What?"

"Will you marry me?"

Nodding, she felt her heart skip a beat.

"Are you saying yes?"

She kept nodding as tears fell down her face.

"Baby, you're going to marry me, right?"

"Yes, I will marry you, Mark Frazier."

He took the ring out of the box and slipped it on her finger and stood, picking her up in his arms. "Damn, you made me sweat."

Laughing and crying at the same time, she held him tightly. "I love you, and would be honored to spend my life with you."

"Can't ask for more than that," he said before crushing their mouths together.

Feeling dizzy with excitement and love, she kissed him back with everything she had. When he released her mouth, she dragged in a deep breath and held up her hand. "I'm engaged to the love of my life."

Letting her slide down his body, he held her hand. "You sure the hell are."

Gazing at the ring for the first time, she admired the solitaire in a classic setting. "This ring is beautiful."

"Thank you for making me the happiest man in the world. I will never disappoint you. I love you with everything that I am." He let out a big breath. "I was nervous, and that was harder than I expected." Kissing her, he let out a whoop. "But you said yes!"

"This is some kind of date."

"Just the beginning, we've got a million more ahead of us." He gathered her into his arms and hugged her tightly.

Pulling away, she grabbed a napkin to wipe her face. "I'm a mess, and don't want to get anything on your uniform."

"Maybe it's time to get out of it and consummate this engagement."

"That, sir, is a fine idea." Looking up into his happy face, she laughed. "I can't believe you asked me to marry you. Are you sure?"

"Baby, I've never been more certain of anything in my life. You are the one for me, and I'm the one for you. The rest is just details."

"I love you, and am looking forward to whatever adventures come our way." When she kissed him, it felt different…as though it was the beginning of everything. "Let's go inside and get you out of that uniform. I think we have some celebrating to do."

He picked her up. "I like the way you think, and believe it's about time to start making some babies."

"Let's just start with the marriage first and then worry about the babies later."

"Sure, honey, whatever you want."

As he took her upstairs, she knew he was just going along to get along, and how much of a challenge that was going to be—had yet to be revealed.

CHAPTER TWENTY-ONE

Waking up curled around his fiancée gave Mark a bone-deep satisfaction that was unparalleled. A calm had settled into his gut, and he wondered how soon he could get her down the aisle.

Would it be possible to do it before he went out on another deployment cycle or was that too ambitious to consider? Wrapping his arms tighter, he lifted his head and looked over her shoulder. "Morning Mrs. Frazier."

"Not a Mrs. yet, just a fiancée."

"You could be a wife by the weekend."

"I could also be an exotic dancer, both possible, but highly unlikely."

Rolling over her, he caged her in. "How long are you going to make me wait?"

"We've known one another for a month, so I think a nice long engagement is appropriate."

"We've got no use for appropriate. We love each other and are going to be together for the rest of our lives, and we should get started on our happy ever after as soon as possible."

Moving her hand down his chest, she smiled. "Okay, I have an idea on how we can do that."

When her hand moved to his hardened shaft, he shook his head. "You're trying to distract me with sex."

"Any objections?"

Pushing her legs apart with his knees, he shook his head. "None that I can think of." He shifted his hips and felt her legs fall open. "One happy ever after, coming right up." Sliding in with one push, he groaned. "Twice a day, every day for the rest of our lives."

Laughter filled the air as he pulled out and slid back in; once he was buried as deep as she'd take him, she moaned. He kept up a slow, leisurely pace as he spoke into her ear, "Do you want me to move a little faster?" Not waiting for a response, he pushed his hips deeper. "Fast or slow, baby?" Pulling out, he watched her eyes pop open. "Fast or slow, it's your choice."

"If you want me to marry you then you better show me how you plan on making me a satisfied woman."

"Oh, you'll be more than satisfied." Slipping back in, he set a rhythm that he knew worked, and was rewarded with his name on her lips and her body exploding around him. Allowing himself to finally let go, he emptied himself into the woman who made him the happiest man in the world.

After he managed to draw in a full breath, he rolled off and took her hand. Glancing over, he saw that she had fallen back to sleep. He ran his hand up and down her back and started making plans for their incredible future together.

***

Mark held Birdie's hand as they sat on the patio of the Hotel del Coronado, drinking champagne. "Where are we going to get married?"

"I haven't even thought about that yet."

"We could have it here or over at the officer's club like your cousin."

"Lots of time to think about it." She smiled. "Thank you for last night. It was perfect, and I can't wait to tell everyone how romantic my bad-ass SEAL fiancé is."

"Did I give you a good engagement story? Sam told me it was important, so I hope to God I gave you a decent one."

"It couldn't have been more perfect."

"Good, I had fun planning, and think there may be more romantic nights in me."

"I feel like the luckiest woman in the world, and I love you."

"Thanks for agreeing to marry me, and I promise to work hard on being a good husband."

She squeezed his hand and nodded. "I have to figure out how to become a Navy wife. Is there a handbook or something?"

"I'm sure there is, and think the first chapter is about how you're supposed to let your husband get at you as much as he can when he's home."

"That's funny because I seem to know that already. Maybe I don't need the book after all and have great instincts."

"You do have great instincts, but to be sure, we should go home and practice."

"They worked fine this morning, so you better let me eat."

Their breakfast was delivered, and he handed her a fork. "Eat up because you're going to need your energy."

Laughing, she took it and dug in. "Your eyes have gotten darker, so I know it's going to be a wild ride."

"You have no idea."

They finished their meal and headed out of the restaurant toward the boardwalk. "So, when does your platoon get moved up on the rotation?"

"It looks like it's going to be in the next two weeks. Can we go have a quickie wedding in Vegas? Then we can plan something bigger in a couple of months."

"Are you nuts?"

"No, we love each other, and you said yes, so what difference would it make if we get married sooner rather than later? Are you going to change your mind if you discover something you don't like about me?"

"No, I'm not going to change my mind. I only get one wedding, and I'd like to enjoy it. I hate Vegas anyway."

"We could go to the courthouse then, and you can plan a big event for a couple of months from now."

"Why are you in such a rush?"

"I love you and don't want to wait. I'm going downrange in a couple of weeks, and want to know that you're taken care of, so I can concentrate on my job."

"I'm capable of taking care of myself, so you don't need to worry. I'm going to keep myself plenty busy while you're gone."

Smirking, he raised an eyebrow. "And what are you going to be so busy with?"

"I'm going to start the renovations for the space above my shop and then have the garage redone. I also have the shop, and I've been offered several accounting projects. Add to that packing my condo in Los Angeles and moving my furniture. I'm a busy woman...places to go, people to see."

"The Navy will not contact you unless we're married, so if something happens to me, you'll have to hear it from my mom."

"I'm not going to be rushed, Mark and nothing is going to happen to you." She patted his arm. "Let's talk about living arrangements. I hope you feel comfortable moving into my house because I want to stay there."

"Baby, I don't care where we live as long as it's together. Let's sell my condo, and then you can use the money on your house."

"I don't think we should do that. It would be better to rent it out because of the tax advantages."

"Do you want to get a prenuptial agreement? You have a lot of assets to protect, and I don't want you to think that I'm marrying you for your money."

"I thought you were marrying me because of the mind-boggling sex." Letting out a loud laugh, she poked him in the side. "No, I don't want a prenup because once I marry you, I'm not letting go. Do you want one? You have plenty of money."

"No, I'm going to give you complete control of the finances and just need to be able to buy a new truck every five years. Leave me enough money for that, and I'm good."

"I think you're going to want to have a say in things and don't want you to get mad if I make a decision that you don't agree with."

"You told me you wanted to be the boss, so be the boss of the money."

"I don't remember asking to be the boss of the money."

"You made a big deal about being the boss, so don't think you can shirk your power so easily. You asked for it, and now you have it, so don't complain."

"That sounds bossy."

"I find it interesting that you only seem to care about picking the food. When am I going to see Birdie Boss?"

"I'm plenty bossy; just you wait and see."

"Bring it, lady, because I'm ready." Leaning down, he whispered, "I love you, and want to make it official."

"I love you too, but don't try and run me down the aisle."

He sighed and started walking. "Think about sooner rather than later, please."

"I will, but I'd like to have a wedding that I am excited about since this is the only one we get."

Arriving at the house, they walked through the gate. "I guess it's time to go to the shop."

"I'm going to check in at the base. What time are you going to be done today?"

"I only need a couple of hours, so I can be back home by five. What would you like for dinner?"

"Whatever you want is fine with me. I've eaten the worst food over the past eleven years with few exceptions." Looking up at the house, he ran his hand over his face. "I can't believe I'm marrying the prettiest woman in the world who is smart, sexy, and a great cook." Kissing her hand, he winked. "Do you like your ring? We can exchange it if you want something else."

"I love it. I may want to have it sized down a little, though."

"Let's go this week and have it done; then we can pick out our wedding bands. I bought them from Sam's cousin, who's a jeweler, and he had a big selection."

"Can you wear a wedding band when you're deployed?"

"Of course. Once it's on my hand, it's never coming off."

Pressing her head into his chest, she sighed. "We're starting our lives together. It's unbelievable."

"I knew when I saw you that something was going to happen and I was right."

Pulling her head back, she looked up. "What's it like always to be right?"

"Don't know because it's all I've ever been."

Hitting his chest, she snorted. "Sure."

"Birdie."

Turning, she waved to her mail person. "Good afternoon."

He waved and held up a big envelope. "I'm not going to put this in your box because I don't want to bend it."

She walked to the gate, and Mark followed her.

"Thanks." She took her stack of mail and motioned for him to come closer. "Gus, I want you to meet my fiancé, Lt. Commander Mark Frazier. He's moving in, and his mail will be coming here now."

"Congratulations, Birdie, I'm so happy for you. Sir, a pleasure to meet you, and thank you for your service."

"Nice to meet you, Gus. Thank you."

"I'd better get on with it." He waved, then turned back to the street.

She handed Mark the stack of letters and opened the big envelope. "This is from the photographer from Josh and Maryann's wedding." She pulled out a stack of pictures and gasped. "They're from the wedding."

Looking over her shoulder, he studied the images. The photographer had sent the pictures of them during their first dance and had captured their first moments together. The attraction simmering between them was visible in every photo, and there was no mistaking that they were falling for one another. "These are incredible."

"We have a picture of our first kiss. Who gets that?"

Leaning closer, he noticed the heat pouring off them. "That was the moment our love story began." It was hard to believe someone had caught the moment that he fell for the woman who was going to become his wife. "I want a copy of these to put in my bag, and the kiss picture for my helmet."

"I guess we found the photographer for the wedding." She lifted her shirt and wiped the tears from her face.

"Baby, if you ever get nervous about how quickly we became engaged, just look at these pictures because they will remind you that there was never going to be a choice for us."

"I think you're right. I'm going to call Sandy and thank her, then order a bunch of copies. Do you mind if I order engagement announcements from her?"

"Can we just order wedding invitations?"

"No." She took her stack of mail and turned toward the house. "I know you can be patient and it would be great if I could see a bit of it."

"I'll take you upstairs and show you instead."

They walked up the steps and went in. "Welcome home. I hope we have many happy years in this house."

He took the photos out of her hands, set them on the table, and put the other mail on top of it; sweeping her into his arms, he carried her upstairs. "Let's get working on that happy."

"I love you, Mark."

"Thank God," he replied as he held her close.

CHAPTER TWENTY-TWO

Birdie stood in the kitchen, drinking her coffee, and making a list for the team party on Sunday. She decided to order a jumpy jump for the kids and thought about hiring Melanie to help out with the smaller children. Looking up, she saw Mark come down the stairs and felt her tummy flip over in happiness.

Now that they were engaged and he had most of his clothes here, he seemed more relaxed. In fact, he was the very picture of a happy and contented man.

Which he should be, considering he'd gotten everything he wanted in a month. How her fling had turned into a boyfriend and now her fiancé, she wasn't sure, but she decided not to question her good fortune. He was, after all, everything she ever dreamed of and more.

He kissed her, and then refilled his coffee cup. Lifting the foil on the plate that she'd left for him, he grinned. "What did you make? It smells great."

"I made you a veggie omelet, and those are banana nut muffins. Eat your fruit this time because you forgot yesterday."

"Yes, dear." He grabbed a chair. "You're acting like a wife already, so why don't we run down to the courthouse and make it official? Then you can really boss me around."

"I don't think so, and by the way—where is that romantic man who proposed to me?" Smoothing down her top, she looked out the window. "I'm not running anywhere because I plan on floating down the aisle in bridal perfection. That's something that can't be rushed." She grabbed her list and sat next to him while he ate. "Can you give me Max's number? I got a text from Rory, and she's ready to do something about the notes that she's been receiving. I want to make sure she follows through, so I was thinking of taking her to his office."

"I'll write it down for you or give you his card if I can find it. Is Rory coming on Sunday?"

He smiled as he ate his fruit, and when he was done, he held up his empty bowl, so she could see he'd finished it. She nodded in approval and kissed him. "Good job."

"I've invited Max to the party, so maybe they can meet and set something up for next week."

She got up, refilled her coffee cup, and poured a glass of juice for him. "I invited her, and I think she's planning on coming." She held up her hand and flashed him her ring. "It fits perfectly now."

He took her hand. "I thought about getting you a bigger ring, but your hands are too small for anything larger." Turning her hand left and right, he shrugged. "I guess it's big enough so that no one can mistake that you're taken." He kissed her hand. "All it needs is the wedding band we picked out yesterday."

"We've only been engaged for three days, and I've chosen a photographer, a caterer, and a location. I've moved at lightning speed, so be happy."

He finished his muffin, drank his juice, and got up to put his dishes in the dishwasher. Leaning against the counter, he studied her. "You're incredible, and I'm lucky you agreed to marry me."

"You got that right, mister, and don't you forget it."

"Love you, Birdie."

"Love you, Mark."

"What's on the schedule today?"

"I'm going into the shop, and then I'm coming back here to meet Adam and Bernie. We're going to start on the office renovation and finish the closet upstairs. Is there anything else you want me to include for the office?"

"No, I think we got everything. Please use the checks that I left you to pay for the rest of the renovations. I went to the bank yesterday and added you to all of the accounts. All you have to do is go down there, sign, and give them your Social Security number."

"I think we should wait until we get married."

"You can think whatever you want, but it's already done. So go down there and sign your name. I'm not going to compromise on this."

She stood and crossed her arms. "Let's go into the office because I want to show you something."

He took her hand, and they went into the office. She sat at her desk, and he grabbed a chair while she opened one of her cabinet drawers and pulled out a bunch of files. "I want you to understand how much money I have because you seemed to be worried about me." She opened the first folder. "This is the value of the building and the income that I generate from the tenants in the building. The final number is the reserve I keep for any repairs that the building needs." She opened another folder and pointed to the figure at the bottom of the spreadsheet. "This is the income from my flower shop." She opened one more folder. "This is my income from the company that I work with downtown. I also have the money from the sale of my condo, and have a fairly healthy savings account." She pulled out a final folder and pointed to the bottom of the page. "This is my current net worth."

He read the figure at the bottom of the page and sat back, crossing his arms. "I still want to pay for the renovations. You know what I have in the bank, and I can easily afford it. I want to take of you and our family. I will be the one paying for this house—for our house. Six million dollars or not."

She closed the folders. "I'm sure we can work something out."

"We *can* work something out by using the checks I left you."

She knew that he was going to dig in, so she gave him a faint smile and decided to proceed with her initial plan. And deal with the consequences when they came knocking.

Mark shook his head. "I can see you cooking something up and hope that you'll consider honoring my request."

She flapped her hands. "Jeeze, why did you have to pull that card?"

He kissed her head. "I'm going down to the base for a couple of hours, and then will bring the last of my clothes over."

"Okay."

"Let's go to the fish place for dinner, and then come home to work on those children we are going to have."

"We're still in practice mode because I want to have plenty of time to enjoy being married to my handsome husband for a while. Which reminds me, how do I plan a honeymoon when you are on active deployment?"

"We have to wait until we're done and on the down cycle again. Sorry, we're going to have to wait."

"That's fine because you're worth waiting for."

CHAPTER TWENTY-THREE

Birdie and Mark stood in the kitchen eating the bagels as they watched the guys put up the jumpy jump and the rock wall toward the back of the yard. "Baby, you sure went all out for this party. Are you sure we need all of this?"

She finished her bagel and wiped her mouth. "Do you remember when you said that I could be the boss? Well, I'm the boss of the parties."

He studied her as he finished his coffee. "So, let me get this straight. You are the boss of the food, money, and parties."

"Yes, I think that about covers it, for now." Putting up her finger, she waved it back and forth. "I'll probably want to add to the list later on."

"I'm sure you will." He kissed her and then took her hand. "Come on, boss, and show me where you want the tables and chairs set up in the backyard."

"As I recall, you enjoyed being bossy this morning in the bedroom, so I think our balance of power is working out just fine."

"No complaints here, and just know I plan on showing more bossiness before everyone shows up this afternoon, so be ready." She erupted in laughter, and he realized the sound still made his chest feel tight. Like happiness was trying to bust out of him and didn't know how. It had been true from the moment he first heard it, and he imagined it would have the same effect at the end of their lives.

All he had to do was keep giving her reasons to laugh.

SUNDAY AFTERNOON

Their house was filled with two SEAL platoons and Birdie's friends because the team dinner had turned into an engagement party. Moving around the party, Birdie made sure everyone had what they needed, and Mark was doing the same.

Looking around with satisfaction, she knew the life ahead was going to be rich and full, not only because of the man she was marrying but because of all the people in their lives.

She saw her best friend, Rory, arrive and let out a little scream. "I'm so glad that you were able to make it." Studying her, she noticed she looked stressed but as beautiful as ever. "Come in and let's get you a drink. I am so happy to see you."

"I'm sorry that I've been incommunicado for the last couple of weeks. I was hoping that if I traveled enough, I could shake this, but unfortunately, I'm still receiving the creepy notes."

"Max is going to be here today, so once you two talk, I'm sure he'll have a solution."

Waving her hand, she smiled. "Who cares about me? Let's talk about you." Lifting Birdie's chin, she nodded. "You are in love, and it has to be the real deal because you never looked this way with Justin." She took a step back and held her at arm's length. "I can feel the happiness rolling off you." Looking around, she asked, "Where is the man who's responsible for this?" Pulling up Birdie's hand, she whistled. "He picked out the perfect ring; that's a good sign."

"Let me get you a glass of wine, and then we can hunt up Mark."

As they walked into the backyard, she spotted Mark talking to some of the guys. "He's over there, so let me introduce you, and we can find out if Max is here yet."

They made their way through the crowd and joined the group. "Hi, guys, I want to introduce Rory. We've been best friends since grade school, and she's the keeper of all of my secrets. Fortunately, we have a mutual no-destruction policy, so nothing gets out."

Mark took Rory's hand. "I'm happy to meet you. I've heard a lot about you, and look forward to getting to know you."

"Good to meet you, Mark."

Leaning over, he looked at Birdie and asked, "Is she always this serious?"

"When she's meeting the man I'm going to marry, then, yes. Absolutely."

The serious expression on Rory's face gave way to a spectacular smile. "Come here and give me a hug because I have a feeling we're going to become good friends."

Hugging her, he looked over her shoulder and winked. "I got the best friend's approval."

"You sure did, honey."

He stepped away and took Birdie's hand. "Let me introduce you to the guys."

"Please do," Rory replied with a laugh. "If I knew that there were so many good-looking sailors in the world, I would've come down to Coronado a lot sooner."

Mark let out a booming laugh. "Despite what she just said, I want everyone to behave. Starting at my left, we've got Travis, Blake, Frisco, and Ace."

"Nice to meet you," they all murmured together.

Rory studied the group and laughed. "Darn, I think I just inherited a big brother, and I hope he doesn't kill all of my fun." Leaning forward, she put up her hand conspiratorially and stage-whispered, "We'll be sure not to tell him when we start the strip poker game later." She looked at all the guys. "Right?" The men stood silently, and Rory laughed. "Gotcha!"

Birdie took her arm. "Quit torturing these men because now all they're going to be thinking of is you with your clothes coming off." She shook her head as she pulled Rory away.

Waving over her shoulder, Rory blew a kiss to the group. "Spoilsport," she said as they walked toward the table with drinks.

Birdie ignored the comment and led them toward the table that was overloaded with food. "Let's grab a plate and catch up."

"Sounds lovely," James commented as he joined them.

Once they had plates full of food the group found a table underneath the big tree.

James carefully placed his napkin on his lap and then looked at Birdie. "I knew the love train was coming at you, but I didn't think it was going to crash into you."

"How could she resist such a handsome man?" Rory asked.

James hitched his shoulder. "Fair point." He covered Birdie's hand. "I was there when she met Mark, and she was a smitten kitten from the start, and planned to use him as a slump buster."

Rory almost choked. "Are you serious? You were going for a fling?"

"Yes. I was going to use him for his body, and one month later, I'm engaged to be married. It just goes to show, that you never know what's going to happen." She smiled at her friends. "Now, I get to enjoy his body for the rest of my life."

Rory hugged her close. "I'm happy for you and can't believe the love of your life has so many good-looking friends. Lifting her glass of wine, she nodded. "This is going to work out for me as well." Leaning back, she pointed to Mark and his group. "Travis is good-looking, and I may have to go over there and chat him up after we eat."

James's head popped up as he whistled. "Look, Birdie, there's a man who looks like he's from that Instagram account you're obsessed with."

Turning, she looked at the big man and didn't recognize him. He appeared to be a couple of years older than Mark and had the same presence. "He must be from the Teams."

"Yeah, he's got that SEAL vibe," James said as he drained his drink. "Big, capable, confident, and sexy."

She studied the man and noticed he was as tall as Mark and built like a bear. He had broad shoulders, and his chest stretched his polo shirt. "Maybe that's Max."

Rory glanced over her shoulder. "If that's Max, then having a stalker may work out after all."

Birdie laughed and looked at her friend. Maybe a SEAL is just what she needed. No man had ever managed to stand up to Rory, so perhaps a man from the Navy was just the right answer.

***

Mark caught up with his friends and saw Max walk in; waving him over, he embraced him in a bro hug. "Thanks for coming."

"Wouldn't miss it," Max responded. "Had to meet the woman who was willing to take you on." He looked around and then back at Mark. "Where is she?"

Mark clapped him on the shoulder. "Right over there. Birdie is the beauty in the red dress."

Max lifted his chin in the direction of the table. "Who is the woman who looks like an Italian movie star sitting with her?"

"That's Rory; she's the one who's been receiving those letters, and Birdie wants her to talk to you."

Max narrowed his eyes and drank his beer. "She's a stunner, so she's probably a pain in the ass. Not that it matters one way or another because we'll take care of the stalker problem right away."

"I'll introduce you two after they're done eating," he said as he shoved his elbow into his friend's side. "That's my woman's best friend, so I want you to treat her right."

"Man, that's all we do at SAI. Nothing to worry about."

He noticed Ana had joined Birdie and her group of friends and looked across at Blake. "Are you going to ask her out again?"

"No, she won't look me in the eye and walks away from me as soon as she can. As far as I can tell, that's not a sign a woman is interested."

"She's just really shy."

"Maybe, but I don't have the time or energy to try and get her interested."

"Fair enough." Seeing Birdie and her friends move in their direction, he decided not to say more. Birdie and Ana's heads were together, and he wondered what was going on. "What are you two whispering about?"

Birdie took his hand. "I have great news! Ana has finished the last of her lab work, and she's about to finish her doctorate." She pulled her cousin in. "We can soon address her as Dr. Ana James."

Ana looked down and moved her foot back and forth. "It's not that big of a deal."

"It sure as hell is, Ana," Blake said firmly. "That's a remarkable accomplishment."

"Thank you; I'm happy to be finished. This has been a long road."

Travis draped his arm over Ana's shoulder. "What are you getting your doctorate in?"

Glancing at him, she gave him a small smile. "Neuropsychology." Looking down again, she took a sip of her wine.

"Congratulations, that's awesome. What kind of lab do you want to work in after you're done?"

"I'm not sure. Once my paper is published and I apply for grants, I'll see where the best opportunity is. Thank you, by the way."

Travis glanced at Blake. "Isn't that great, Blake?"

Lifting his beer in salute, he nodded. "Absolutely."

"We have a doctor in the family," Mark said as he wrapped his arm around Birdie and pulled her in. "Should we make our announcement?"

"Mark, everyone already knows." She shook her head. "I didn't realize that men in the Navy were bigger gossips than high school girls."

"We like to call it exchanging intel, not gossip."

"Is that like when you give a stink eye and call it evaluating your opponent?"

"Something like that. In more important news, I thought you would like to meet Max; he's the one who is going to help Rory out."

Max lifted his hand and waved. "Nice to meet you, Birdie. Didn't think there was a woman out there to take this beast on, and I'm happy to know you."

"Likewise." Turning to Ana and Rory, she smiled. "My best friend and cousin."

"Nice to meet you, Max," Ana called out.

Rory moved toward Max and held out her hand. "I'm happy to meet you and look forward to coming into your office and discussing my current situation. I've foolishly ignored it, hoping it would go away, but it's gotten worse, so I hope you can help me."

Max stared at Rory and swallowed loudly. "Please, come by first thing in the morning so we can evaluate everything and put together a plan." He handed her his card, and she leaned forward and embraced him.

"Sorry, I'm a hugger." She let him go and then patted his chest. "I hope I didn't make you uncomfortable; it's just that I'm so relieved that you're willing to help me."

"Absolutely. I'm glad my group is going to be able to solve this for you." Stepping back, he crossed his arms and frowned.

Mark watched the exchange and realized Max had come across a force greater than him. How that was going to turn out was going to be interesting to see. "Let's go grab some dessert," Mark said loudly to the group.

The sun was setting, and he was ready for the party to be over so he could take his fiancée upstairs. He knew he didn't have much time left at home and wanted whatever he had left to be spent with Birdie.

Not that he didn't love his friends, he just loved her a whole lot more.

As they walked back into the house, he stopped her near the stairs. "Thank you for putting this shindig on. It means a lot to the guys that we can get together and relax before we go downrange." He kissed her and held tightly to her ass. "But, I'm ready for them to leave, so we can go practice our happy."

"You've had plenty of happy today, and we're not kicking out our guests so you can get at me."

"Are you sure about that?"

"They are welcome to stay as long as they want."

They walked inside, and he mumbled, "No, they are not."

As they walked into the kitchen, Mark noticed the only people left at the party were his platoon, Blake, Max, and the wives. "Does anyone want coffee?" he called out.

Several hands went up, and he moved over to the coffee maker and felt Birdie hip check him. "What, honey?"

"I'll make the coffee, and you make sure everyone gets some dessert."

"Roger that." He moved over to the island and passed out plates. "Come and get it."

Karen stood and walked over to Birdie. "Let me help you make it."

Sam watched his wife. "Remember, no coffee. You already had your cup this morning."

She turned to her husband and stuck out her tongue. "Spoilsport, I can at least smell it."

Birdie hugged Karen. "Let me make you a cup of tea instead."

Karen squeezed Birdie back and threw her husband a dirty look. "Thank you. I think you are my new favorite person."

Mark looked at Sam and shook his head. "Coffee Nazi, you may have just killed your chances tonight."

Sam shrugged his enormous shoulders. "I have to make sure she's following the doctor's recommendations. She has two babies growing in there, so this is considered a high-risk pregnancy." He smiled at Mark. "I have a secret weapon with my wife anyway, so I'm not all that worried. When I rub her feet, she's pretty much putty in my hands."

Karen looked at her husband. "I heard that Sam, and it's not true."

"Damn," Sam replied as he crossed his arms.

Mark sat in the living room with all his men and studied each one. "You guys know we're going to be wheels up within the next week, and I want to make sure everyone has their lives squared away. If you need anything, let me or Frisco know. We want everyone to be focused when we're out there." The guys nodded and started talking about what was coming up for them in the next several months.

He noticed that Max was ready to head out, so he stopped him. "I didn't get a chance to ask you to put a security system in the house and upgrade the locks. Do whatever you think is necessary. I want Birdie to be secure when I am deployed."

"I'll have Derick come out this week and take care of it. Do you remember him? He was on my squad and retired about six months before me. He was shot up pretty bad on our last mission, and they were never able to clear him for duty."

"I remember him—crazy smart with computers and his specialty was breach."

"That's the guy. He's one of my partners, along with Frank. I'm hoping when you retire that you'll come and join us."

He took his friend's hand and shook it. "Let's hope I have a couple more years before I come knocking on your door."

"I'll call you in the morning and let you know when Derick can start on the system. He'll probably come over tomorrow for an eval and then put a plan together. Let Birdie know what's going on, so we don't surprise her."

"Copy that. Good luck with Rory; I hope you can get to the bottom of it quickly because I know Birdie's worried and thinks she isn't taking it seriously enough."

"We will, one way or another, it will be taken care of."

"Appreciate it."

"Stay safe, and I'll talk to you when you get back."

"Roger that." He watched Max walk out to his car and felt confident that he'd not only secure the house but take care of whatever was threatening Rory.

Returning to the kitchen, he saw Frisco with his arm on his fiancée. He used his commander's voice and said loudly, "Lieutenant, get your hands off my woman."

Birdie laughed as she watched Frisco throw Mark a dirty look. "Leave my friend alone."

"Yeah," Frisco replied loudly. "I was friends with her first, so don't try and break us up."

"It doesn't matter who was first, and all that matters is who she's in love with and going to marry."

"Whatever, man." Frisco kissed Birdie, took his pie, and went around the island to sit down.

"Just ignore him, Frisco, because I'm going to."

Frisco ate his pie and smiled at Mark. "Sounds like a plan."

Standing next to Birdie, Mark put his arm around her. "Do I get my dessert now?"

She handed him a plate. "This may be all the *dessert* you get tonight."

"I'll take whatever you're willing to give me." Looking at the people gathered, he knew what he and Birdie had was a once-in-a-lifetime thing and wanted to take a second to appreciate it.

After all, not too many people were as lucky as them.

Having a chance to spend the rest of your life with your soulmate was no small thing.

That he knew for sure.

CHAPTER TWENTY-FIVE

Birdie heard Mark's phone ring at five a.m. and knew the team was being called for wheels up. Opening one eye, she watched him reach over and grab it. Taking a moment to breathe him in, she buried her face in his arm and waited.

"Baby, my platoon is wheels up."

Her eyes opened instantly, and she nodded. "Let me make coffee, while you get ready." Getting up quickly, she put her robe on, kissed his arm, and made her way downstairs. Heart pounding madly against her ribs, she felt her hands shake and knew she couldn't let him see.

He needed to focus on his job and not worry about her, so she breathed deeply and got herself together. Placing a muffin and a banana in a bag, she waited for the coffee to finish. Hearing him come down the stairs, she drank in the sight of him and made a mental picture to hold in her heart. She poured his coffee into a travel cup and handed him the breakfast bag. "Please, eat the banana, not just the muffin." Taking his hand, she walked him to the door.

He stopped her, dropped his bag, and set his breakfast on the table. Engulfing her in his arms, he snugged her close. "Love you, Birdie."

She squeezed him and then stepped back. "Love you more. Be safe and come home to me." Pasting a smile on her face, she picked up his bag and handed it to him. "Don't be late because the world needs saving."

He took his bag, his coffee, and his breakfast. "See you soon. Love you." They kissed hard at the door. Then he walked down the steps and got into his truck. She waited at the gate and waved as she blew kisses.

Walking back into the house, she closed the door and went back upstairs. She flipped the blankets over, crawled back into bed, pulled the covers over her head, and fell apart, crying like she never had.

One breakdown was all she was going to allow herself; after that, she was going to get on with the business of life and make Mark proud. She needed to be brave while he was deployed because it's what he deserved.

He was doing the impossible, and the least she could do was hold it together.

One way or another.

Birdie walked up to her shop and saw Melanie sitting outside. "Good morning."

"Morning."

As she opened the door, she looked over and gave her a small smile. "If you need anything while your brother is deployed, please let me know."

"Thanks, Birdie. I appreciate it."

Nodding, she walked through the shop and took comfort in the fact that everything was set up for the week. As long as she kept herself busy, then she would manage Mark's absence without losing her mind.

At least that was the plan.

Walking into her office, she turned on the computer and, while it warmed up, she pulled out the photo of her and Mark and put it on her desk. She took a moment to look at it and sent up a little prayer asking to keep him safe. He was doing the impossible in facing the world's evil, and she wanted him not only to survive the battle but not be marked by it irrevocably.

Which, of course, was impossible.

No one came back from the battlefield without scars, and all she wanted was for him to return with nothing they couldn't recover from.

Looking at her phone, she decided to call Rory and check-in. She hadn't heard from her since the party, so she assumed that Max was taking care of things, but would like to hear the particulars. When there was no answer, she left a message and hoped she heard back quickly.

The second call she made was to her mom, and when she didn't get her either, she left a message inviting her for the weekend.

Where was everyone when she needed to talk?

Deciding there was no one else she wanted to speak with, she pulled up the latest project from the accounting firm and decided to dive in. Nothing comforted her like spreadsheets and, right now, she needed it more than ever.

The beautiful rows of numbers filled her screen, and she felt calm knowing that there was only one answer to a formula. Something that had always comforted her was especially true today because having Mark out chasing the world's horrors was the least comfortable thing in the world. Which made her realize she needed him in ways she hadn't begun to understand.

Considering they'd barely had a month together, she wondered what she was in store for twenty years down the road.

***

Mark sat inside the C-17 and looked around, realizing it resembled a flying moving van and flophouse. Boxes of ammo, piles of communication gear, weapons, and some good size shipping containers filled the space.

Everything they could need for the next ninety days in an unpredictable war zone was packed inside the giant transport plane. Seats and tiny windows lined the sidewalls, and some of the guys had strung up hammocks between the shipping containers or laid out bedrolls on the floor.

Looking at his tablet, he reviewed the snatch and grab they were going to take on once they landed. It certainly wasn't going to be the most difficult one they'd ever had, but it wasn't without risk.

Which honestly is why he'd chosen the Teams. He loved the adrenaline rush of being out in the field and meeting the expectations of the mission. He was like a lot of warriors before him and had a desire deep in his heart for battle, to fight for what was right, and live his life on the edge of adventure.

Now, he had a whole new adventure in front of him as he began to build a life with Birdie. Sliding his phone out of his pocket, he looked at his screen saver and couldn't believe the beautiful woman kissing him in the picture was going to be his wife.

How in the hell he managed to talk a woman like her into pledging her life to him was something he would never understand.

Putting his phone back in his pocket, he cleared his throat and looked at his tablet. Now was not the time to think about Birdie or any of the overwhelming, incredible emotions she evoked in him. Now was the time to focus on the mission and taking care of business.

He'd never had to split his focus before, and it seemed he was about to learn how because nothing less would be acceptable. He had the lives of the men he commanded in his hands, and they were about to enter the deadly business of a snatch and grab, so he needed to pack all those thoughts of Birdie and his life at home away and get his head in the game.

"Hey, man."

Looking up, he saw Frisco slide into the seat next to him. "Ready to rock and roll, brother?"

"Always."

"A little fun in a South American jungle is just what we've been missing."

"Haven't been on this side of the world in a couple of years," Mark responded as he opened a file. "We've got an HVT that's been grabbed by a drug lord, and she's got intel that the CIA doesn't want anyone to get their hands on."

"If all we've got to worry about is some fucking drug runners, then this is the easiest thing we've done in a year."

"Yeah, spending quality time with the Taliban, al-Qaeda, and all the other wannabe terrorists littering the sandbox puts things in perspective."

"Talk about a new perspective…can't believe you took the plunge with Birdie."

"Told you I wasn't playing."

"Either you've got some kind of crazy faith in your instincts, or you're insane as shit."

"She's one of your close friends, so you know that I'm the luckiest son of a bitch in the world."

"Yeah, she's a good one, that's for damn sure. But marriage?" He scraped his hand over his face and shuddered. "Can't imagine ever wanting it."

"Either did I until I met Birdie." Leaning back, he studied his close friend. "It's going to happen for you someday, and I'll enjoy telling you I told you so when it does."

"Hope you're patient because that shit is not happening for a very long time."

Looking at the body of the aircraft, he smiled. "Yeah, I used to think the same thing."

Sitting forward, Frisco cracked his back. "I'm ready to be out there getting some."

"Yeah, me too. I always feel peaceful when we're downrange because the sounds and smells feel so familiar. Give me the acrid scent of the gunpowder and the random boom of mortar fire, and I feel right at home."

"I like how it focuses my mind and the little complexities of life melt away. Yesterday, I was sitting in the burger joint thinking about nonsense, and today everything is stripped down, simple, and clear. I feel like I've been handed a free ticket to the best wild adventure in the world where I get to roam armed to the teeth through some of the most dangerous, exotic places on earth."

"Doesn't get much better than that. Damn lucky to be a part of this, and I never want to take it for granted because every mission holds the possibility of being the last one."

"Not this time, brother. This one is going to be easy."

"Yeah, here's to hoping." Leaning his head against the side of the plane, he closed his eyes and thought about what they were about to take on and knew they could more than handle it.

Another easy day in paradise.

CHAPTER TWENTY-SIX

Twenty-four hours later, Mark crouched on the swampy bank that faced the compound with his platoon. Hearing the anguished cries of the CIA agent, he knew they didn't have the luxury of waiting for the SWCC operators to be in position. "Whiplash, confirm your location."

"Blackbird, we're twenty mics out with Raven in flight pushing to your location."

"Roger that." Mark looked at Frisco and nodded. "Take it out."

"We're running thin; do you want to join us?"

"No, I've got SVT coming in on step, Raven on my pause, and I need to be on overwatch, so you guys don't get your six covered in lead."

"Roger that."

"Catch you on the other side." He nodded to Frisco, Caid, Ace, and Sam as they moved toward the river. Watching them slip in silently, he nodded to Travis, and they moved west a half-click and got into position. Pulling his receiver out of his kit, he took control of the drone and began confirming the location of the guards at the compound. Speaking quietly into his mic, he said, "Whiplash, assault forces moving to target early, requesting immediate fire support."

"Copy that, Blackbird, pushing to your location at fifteen mics."

"In position. Target acquired," Travis reported.

Lifting his nocs, Mark confirmed Sam was in position. Once he saw his hands raise out of the water, ready to catch the first guard, he nodded to Travis. Five seconds later, Travis took the man out and Sam caught him before hitting the water.

"Frisco, are you set?"

"Affirmative."

"Hold, Frisco, we've got a guard at one o'clock facing the tower." Travis took him out next. "Done. Clear to door."

Watching the men approach the gate, Mark took a moment to scan the surrounding area. Once they were inside the compound, he had them up on his screen. "Two squirters coming out the back door."

Caid's body cam feed came up on the corner of the screen, and he confirmed that they'd been taken care of. "Clear."

"Any additional traffic reported?" Travis asked quietly as he moved his gun through the quadrants of the compound.

"TOC informed me we had an increase in known QRF's eight clicks from the secondary location ten minutes ago. So we're going to have a full party by the time we exfil. The package we're extracting is not only worth a lot of ransom money but a ton of political capital."

"Not to mention the intel on the phone."

"Yeah, just another day at the office, grabbing important shit and saving people. Ain't no thing," Mark replied as he kept his eyes trained on the body cam feeds of his men. They had moved on target and were clearing rooms.

Gunfire erupted in the building, and Mark watched carefully. So far, so good…they hadn't met with anyone that wasn't taken out immediately. Ace and Caid quickly relieved the guards of their weapons and their lives as he heard the clatter of guns fall from their lifeless fingers as the men slumped onto the floor.

"Sitrep?" he barked into his mic.

"Target is secure; standby for confirmation."

"I've got the cell," Caid reported.

"Target confirmed," Frisco said clearly.

"Roger that." Looking into his screen, he let out a curse. "Frisco, you've got two aggressor vehicles approaching from the North about one mic out. Take the truck at the west door and meet us at extract."

"Copy," Frisco replied.

Travis packed up quickly and then stood point. "Ready to move out."

Mark nodded and quickly packed up his gear, slung his M4 over his shoulder, and then stood. "Whiplash, we have enemy QRF approaching from the North."

"Copy that."

"Frisco, you need to start your exfil NOW! We'll meet you at secondary extract." Mark nodded to Travis, and they began running along the bank. Low-hanging branches scraped against their backs as they moved across the muddy ground. Hearing the team take off from the compound in his mic, he knew the exfil was going to shit.

"We're in contact on the rear and taking rounds," Ace reported.

"Copy that," he said into his mic as he motioned to Travis to move up the bank.

"We've got a truck a thousand yards out," Caid barked.

"Got them," he replied as he watched Travis pull out a rocket. Taking his sniper rifle out of his hand, he watched him lift his M4 and load the small rocket onto his gun.

"Rocket out," he stated as Frisco and the team roared past.

They hit the target and then ran along the road. "Meet you at the rally point," Mark said as they cut across a field.

Caid slowed down enough for Mark and Travis to jump in. Pounding on the side of the truck, he yelled, "We're in."

Hitting the accelerator, the truck moved down the road. Frisco pounded him on the back. "What's the status of the boats?"

"Lost Whiplash on the run." Two additional trucks filled with QRF were coming in hot on their six. Lifting his M4, he and Travis began laying down fire. They took out the driver of the first truck almost immediately and then had another two moving toward them rapidly. "Whiplash, the secondary extract is burnt; moving to tertiary extract. I have eight packs. One pack with a gunshot wound. This will be a hot extract."

"Copy that, one mic out to your location."

They had another two trucks filled with QRF coming at them, so he knew they were getting wet. "Splash it," he ordered. They were taking on heavy fire, and he felt the familiar graze of a bullet across his shoulder. Ignoring it, he continued to engage the men who thought they could get a piece of him or his team.

Caid drove the truck down the bank of the river into the water as the SWCC boats came around the bend of the river. They laid down suppressive fire, which allowed Mark and the men to crawl out of the truck. Ace took the package and swam for the boats, and the rest pulled up their guns, ready to take out whoever got close.

Seeing a Tango on the bank of the river with a handheld rocket launcher, he lifted his gun and was about to release a bullet when the world around him exploded.

"Too close," he said as he flew into the air along with Travis.

"Fuckers!" Frisco shouted as he went over the side of the boat and swam toward Mark.

Caid followed and went after Travis. "He's hit."

"Mark too," Frisco shouted as he pulled Mark toward the boat.

Caid shoved Travis in the boat and then Frisco did the same with Mark. Once they were clear, the boat moved off target, and the second boat laid down suppressive fire.

Cutting through the water, Frisco looked at Mark and Travis and let out a stream of curses. Ace began working on Travis, and Caid moved over to evaluate Mark's injuries.

Mark's eyes opened for a moment, and Frisco stared at them. "Listen, you son of a bitch; you'd better hold on because I don't want to explain to Birdie how I let something happen to you. She'll never let me hear the end of it." Mark squeezed his hand and then closed his eyes again. "Shit."

"We secured the package, and these two stubborn assholes are not done yet, so we've got nothing to worry about," Caid said as he opened his bag and began pulling out supplies. "Not today, man, not fucking today."

CHAPTER TWENTY-SEVEN

Birdie stood in the middle of the bridal salon in downtown San Diego with her mother and future mother-in-law. She'd spoken to the owner earlier in the week, and she had assured her that several dresses would be perfect.

They were getting along famously, and she was thankful that Mark's mom was friendly and open. Opening the door to the dressing room, she saw there were five dresses for her to try on, and she was excited. Not only because trying on beautiful gowns was fun, but more importantly, because it was what she was going to wear while she promised her heart and life to Mark.

Closing the door, she sat down and took a moment to let her racing heart slow down. It had been tripping over itself occasionally since yesterday, and she didn't know if it was anxiety or merely missing Mark. Her stomach had been upset, and a feeling of dread kept pushing its way to the surface.

Not wanting to think of it as a bad omen, she had been fighting all the negative feelings since she woke up yesterday, and figured it was something she had to get used to when Mark was deployed.

She slipped off her sandals and then looked at herself in the mirror. "Be strong," she instructed herself. "This is the first of many deployments, and you will not lose it."

"Are you ready for me?" Barbara, the owner, called out.

Nodding to her reflection, she pasted on a smile. "Absolutely."

Barbara opened the door and nodded to the dresses. "I know you like Elie Saab, so I pulled two. Let's start with those."

"Okay." Seeing the one that Barbara held up, she was struck by the feeling that she'd just found the dress she was going to marry Mark in. Her breath caught and the buzzy feeling she got when she spied the perfect pair of shoes ran over her body.

"Let's start with that one."

"Perfect," Barbara replied.

She walked into the reception area, and her mother covered her mouth and gasped. "What do you think?"

Carol stared at her with tears in her eyes. "That is perfect, Birdie."

Joy stood and walked over to her daughter, taking her hand. "Well, this will do nicely."

"You sure, Mom?"

"Completely." She wiped her face. "I've thought about what I might feel when this day arrived, and I can honestly say it's far more overwhelming than I ever would've guessed."

Carol stood and joined them. "I wasn't sure if I would ever see this day because my son gave me no indication that he was interested in finding someone to spend his life with." Taking Birdie's hand, she pressed a kiss to it. "Clearly, he was just waiting to meet you, because you're perfect for him."

"Thank you, Carol. I can't tell you what that means to me."

Barbara approached with a tray full of champagne. "Are we ready to celebrate?"

Birdie grabbed a glass and lifted it. "Yes, we are. I'm going to become Mrs. Frazier in this dress." She waited for everyone to lift their glass and then said, "To the best man in the world, may God keep him safe." They clinked glasses and knew that all that mattered was Mark's safe return. He was her heart now, and there would be no life without him.

Once she had changed back into her clothes, she returned to the reception area and saw her mom sitting with the assistant. Birdie walked over and heard her mom say she was going to pay for the dress. "No way, Mom. I'm not going to let you do that."

Joy turned and leveled her daughter with one of the looks she reserved for the courtroom. "Birdie James, you are my only child, and your father and I will be paying for this wedding. You behave and use the good manners I taught you."

"Thanks, Mom, but I think the dress is really expensive."

"Well, it's a good thing that I have only have one wedding to worry about." She stood and kissed her daughter. "I love you, and am happy that you've found such a fine man to spend your life with."

"Me too, Mom." They were informed the dress would arrive by December, and she figured she was so far ahead of the game that she could take the next six months off. All they had to do was pick a date and a band. Couldn't get easier than that.

"Let's go have lunch and celebrate," Carol announced.

She linked arms with her soon-to-be mother-in-law and laughed. "One store, first dress. This has got to be some kind of record."

"You have always been decisive, and I can say it's one of the things I most appreciate about you," Joy said as she held the door.

"Thanks, Mom." Flicking her remote, the locks on the car opened. "I guess agreeing to marry a man that I've known for less than a month is a pretty good sign that once I find something I like, I grab it."

"Mark is the same way, so you two were made for each other."

"In a hundred ways," Birdie replied as she climbed into the car.

They were enjoying a lovely lunch on the patio of the Hotel Del when Birdie watched Carol pull out her buzzing phone. When her face fell, she knew something was wrong—terribly wrong. "How bad is it?"

Carol ended the call and looked up with tears in her eyes. "Bad."

Leaning forward, she took a deep breath. "Where is he?"

"He's on a carrier and currently stable. They're going to fly him out as soon as possible and assess whether he can wait for surgery or decide if they need to do it on the ship. He's going to be flown to the Naval Medical Center in Virginia."

Birdie pulled out her iPad. "I'll get us on the next flight. Do you mind driving to LAX if it's faster?"

"Whatever it takes," Carol responded as she started making calls.

Joy took her daughter's hand. "I'll take care of everything here."

Birdie nodded and then glanced up from her iPad. "Carol, I can get you out tonight on a flight through Chicago. It has only one stop. I'll take a flight through Dallas. It has more stops, so you should be there before me."

Carol squeezed her. "He's going to be all right. Let's just keep our prayers up."

They called for the check and, by the time they were squared away, Birdie had the flights booked. "He's going to be okay. I'm not giving him a choice because he didn't give me one when I was in a car accident. We're going to have a long happy life together, and he's not getting out of it.

Standing, she moved toward the exit and knew she wouldn't let him get away with less.

No way.

***

NMC
Virginia

Birdie stood against the wall and checked her watch. It was almost one in the morning, and she had been informed that Mark would be arriving any time.

She thought about the little tif they had gotten into a week ago when he insisted they start filling out paperwork for her to be notified if anything happened to him. He had told her it was non-negotiable, and she thought he was being stubborn.

Which he was, thank God. If he hadn't started the ball rolling, she wouldn't have been allowed to receive any updates, and she couldn't imagine how crazy she would've been had that happened.

The fact that she had arrived before Carol only made it all the more important because she had his medical power of attorney, and if something needed to be decided quickly, then she could do it.

Not that it was going to be necessary.

A nurse strode up and tapped her arm. "He's on his way in. The ambulance should be here any minute. He had emergency surgery on the ship, but he'll need additional procedures once we get him stabilized."

"Thank you," Birdie replied as the emergency doors flew open. Seeing Mark on the gurney made her heart flip over. She moved to his side and took his hand as they moved down the hall. He was almost unrecognizable; his face was swollen with gashes all over his cheeks, and both eyes were black and blue. "Mark Frazier, I love you, and you said you would come back to me, so you better keep your word."

The doctor strode up and lifted the chart that was resting on his legs. "Who are you?"

"I'm Birdie James, Mark's fiancée." The doctor nodded and studied the chart and started speaking to the nurses. She listened carefully as they discussed the initial tests. Apparently, he had extensive damage to a lung along with needing reconstructive surgery on his knee.

"Let's get him stabilized, and then we'll do the surgery," the doctor barked as they rolled him into a room. "We're going to do everything we can to put him back together."

Staring down at the man she loved, she knew he wouldn't leave her. She leaned down to kiss his bruised and bloodied cheek and felt a strong urge to kill the sons of bitches who'd done this to him. Realizing he'd expressed a similar sentiment when she'd been hit, she almost laughed. Peace-loving Birdie was gone and had been replaced by someone who would be very willing to exact revenge. Deciding violent thoughts were not going to do any good, she quietly stepped back and stood in the corner as the nurses got him hooked up to an IV and monitors.

"We're going to try and get his temperature down before we take him," One of the nurses said as she checked the monitors.

"Okay, thank you for letting me know." She looked at her beautiful, lethal warrior lying motionless and murmured, "I love you, Mark, and I'm going to be right here."

Knowing it was a waiting game, she took a deep breath and sank into a chair, and started asking God for any blessings he could spare.

Mark had been in surgery for over six hours, and she'd received only one update and hoped it was a good sign. Looking up, she spotted Carol walking in. "You made it." She led her over to the chairs and handed her a bottle of water. "I'm so sorry that you got stuck in Chicago for so long. I should've thought about the weather before I booked your flight."

"Nothing to be done about Mother Nature. All that matters is I made it, and Mark is going to survive."

"I've only gotten one update, and I believe they're still trying to repair the damage to his lung."

"That's what the nurse told me before I came in."

Hearing her name, she looked up and saw a doctor in scrubs walk toward them. She held out her hand for Carol and helped her up. "I hope you have good news."

"The lieutenant is out of surgery, and we're cautiously optimistic. We were able to repair the damage, and now we have to let his body take over and start healing. We almost lost him on the table, but he's got a strong heart and fought back. We see that a lot when we have a SEAL on the operating table. Seems that whatever makes them capable of joining the Teams also makes them great patients."

Her body suffused with heat and her legs collapsed. All she could hear was a loud buzzing sound in her head. After the doctor said, "We almost lost him," her brain blanked out.

Carol sat and took her hand. "Bend over and put your head between your legs."

"He's a fighter, so I think he has a hell of a chance," the doctor stated quietly.

Nodding, the buzzing sound receded, and she took deep breaths. When she felt like the panic had subsided, she sat up. "When can we see him?"

"Soon, they're getting him cleaned up, and it shouldn't be too long," the doctor responded before moving toward the door. "The nurses will keep you updated."

"Thank you." She gulped water and then let out a breath. Turning to Carol, she took her hand. "How have you done this for eleven years?"

"I didn't have a choice. Mark decided this is what he wanted to do, and there wasn't a thing I could do to change his mind. He's not been seriously injured in about eight years. Most of the time, I don't hear about it until months later, when he gets home." She drank some water. "This is only the second time that I've received a call. The Navy only informs you when they think the injuries might be fatal."

"I didn't realize that."

A nurse came out and looked around. "Mark Frazier's family."

Birdie lifted her hand.

"He can be seen, but only one at a time."

Carol stood and squeezed Birdie's hand before following the nurse. She watched her walk down the long corridor and then closed her eyes, thanking God for helping Mark survive.

When it was her turn, she prepared herself before walking into the room. Opening the door slowly, she walked up to his bed as her heart fell through her stomach. She took his hand, leaned down, and kissed his cheek. "I love you, Mark Frazier. Thanks for pulling through surgery."

Holding his hand tightly, she drank in his handsome face. "You rest and take all the time you need." She leaned her head against his gently and promised him silently she would be the best partner he could ever imagine; all had to do was live.

The nurse poked her head in. "Time's up."

"Okay." She gave him one more kiss, then returned to the waiting room and sat next to Carol. They took one another's hands, and Birdie knew how lucky they were that Mark had survived.

CHAPTER TWENTY-NINE

Two days later, Birdie walked into Mark's room, took his hand, and kissed him. "Hi, handsome, you look good today. I love you, and can't wait to see those pretty eyes of yours."

Smoothing out his blanket, she moved his hair from his face and kissed his cheek. "I had a shower and some breakfast, so I'm ready for our day together."

When she saw no movement on his face, she decided it wasn't a bad sign. He was, after all, seriously injured and if he needed several days before he was ready to become conscious, then so be it.

Moving to the chair, she got comfortable and dug her iPad out. She had downloaded a couple of books at the hotel and figured she'd start one now. She took Mark's hand and settled in for their day together.

By the time she was halfway through the book, the doctor walked in and went over Mark's chart. "He's progressing well. All his vitals are strong and, if it continues, then we should see some sign of consciousness in the next twenty-four hours."

"That's great news. I'll let his mom know when she gets here later."

Nodding, he wrote some notes and then left. Sighing, Birdie stood and looked at Mark. "Whenever you're ready." Tilting her head, she decided he needed some moisturizer and lip balm. Lifting her bag, she pulled out her baby wipes, lotion, and Chapstick. "Got to keep your good looks up, Mark. Just because you've been almost blown to pieces is no reason to let things go."

Smoothing the baby wipe over his face gently and slowly, she took in his handsome, strong features and wondered why in the world he had fallen for her.

She wasn't anything spectacular, and he could easily have his pick of any woman in the world. Deciding she might never get an answer, she opened her moisturizer and smoothed some over his face and neck, and then slicked his lips with Chapstick. "There you go; better than ever."

Hearing the door, she looked up and saw Carol walk in. "The doctor was just here and said he's doing well."

"Wouldn't expect anything less," she replied as she took a chair. Holding up a bag, she smiled. "I brought us a snack from the hotel."

"Thank you, that will be a nice change from the cafeteria."

They kept each other company for the rest of the afternoon and Carol decided to return to the hotel around four. "I'll call you if anything changes."

"Are you sure you want to spend another night in the hospital?"

"Of course. I wouldn't get any sleep at the hotel anyway, and I feel better if I can hold his hand."

"All right, I'll see you in the morning."

"We'll be here." Settling into the chair again, she took Mark's hand and went back to her book. "Love you, just let me know if you need anything."

The nurses came in the middle of the night for their scheduled check, and Birdie woke when she heard them enter. Once they were done, she fixed his gown and blankets and then stretched. "Do I try and go back to sleep or just read?"

Cupping his face, she waited. "You're right; I should try and get a little more sleep." She bent over and kissed his cheek and took his hand. Glancing down, she swore she felt movement. "Mark, are you ready to wake up?"

Nothing.

"Okay, when you're ready." She kissed his cheek. "Love you." Feeling movement, she lifted her head. "Okay, twice is not wishful thinking on my part."

She held her breath, and his eyes fluttered open. Pushing the nurses' button, she felt tears slide down her cheeks. "I love you so much."

The door flew open, and two nurses came striding in, and she moved to the side. "I think he's coming back."

"Let's see if he's ready," one of them commented as they called for the doctor and started charting his vitals.

Thirty minutes later, the doctor walked in, and Birdie stood in the corner while they evaluated him. After much discussion, the doctor finally spoke. "Let's decrease his medication and see if the lieutenant commander is ready to join us."

"Thank God!" Birdie exclaimed.

"He's a hell of a fighter," the doctor said as he wrote instructions. "It's a waiting game now."

Birdie nodded and then texted Carol with the information and told her to take her time because the doctor didn't think they were going to see any significant changes until the morning.

After everyone had left, she took his hand and smiled. "I love you."

CHAPTER THIRTY

The morning light slanted across her face, and she woke up with a start; looking around, she tried to get her bearings. Standing, she bent over and touched her toes and cringed at all the tweaks she felt.

"I'm going to freshen up, honey, and then get a cup of tea." She grabbed her bag and headed out.

Once she returned to the room, she straightened his blankets and settled back into her chair. She pulled out her iPad and decided to start working on a song list for their wedding and hoped to have something ready by the time he woke up. Plugging her earphones in, she began choosing songs.

Singing along, she chose several and then felt Mark squeeze her hand. She yanked out the earbuds and looked over. Seeing his mouth move, she moved closer. "Mark?'

"I would know that awful voice anywhere, and I sure missed it."

Standing, she took his face in her hands and kissed him again and again as she cried. "People have always told me how bad my singing is, and I sort of believed them, but I had no idea it was bad enough to wake someone up from a heavily medicated sleep."

"Whatever it takes," he whispered.

Pushing the nurse's button, she smiled. "I won't torture you again until you're fully recovered."

"God damn, I love you Birdie."

"Love you more, Mark. Thank you for coming back to me."

He squeezed her hand. "I told you I always would."

"That you did." Resting her head against his, she felt her heart explode with love and appreciation. They were going to have a fantastic happy ever after, that was for darn sure.

***

Mark looked at his mom while the nurses took his vitals. "Thanks for coming, Mom."

"I will always come."

Mark nodded and then waited for the nurse to finish. When she left, he hitched his shoulder. "What do you think of Birdie?"

"I don't think there is a better woman out there. She invited me to spend the weekend, and we had just finished dress shopping when the call came in informing me that you were injured. She went right into action and had a plan within five minutes. You're going to be in good hands because she never faltered for one second. She arrived before me since I was stuck in Chicago. There was weather that delayed me, and it took forever."

"I knew she was special before any of this happened. I'm damn lucky to have survived this one because we had a lot of QRF that wanted to see us dead." He tried to sit up and then remembered how badly he'd gotten banged up. "We got the job done, though and in the end, that's all that matters. I need to talk to Frisco and get a copy of the after-action report, so I can confirm everything was handled."

"You have more courage than anyone I know, and often wonder where it came from."

"Just doing what's right, Mom. It's not that big of a deal."

"It is, and you know it." She squeezed his hand. "Do you remember anything from the op?"

"We got what we went in for and were doing okay until the rebels woke up and gave us a run for our money. Some asshole got lucky with a hand-held rocket as we were extracting. I remember hearing the explosion, and then the world went black." He moved his hand over the blanket and then cleared his throat. "Travis and I were the only ones injured and the nurse told me he's doing okay. Banged up like hell, but alive."

A nurse came in and disconnected some of the equipment that he was plugged into and changed some of the meds in his IV line. "We're going to try and get you in a wheelchair later on and let you get out of the room for a little while."

"I can try walking, with some help."

She shook her head. "Not with your knee so torn up. They're going to reconstruct it here."

He looked down and recognized the feeling of pain in his knee, and knew it was unlikely he'd return to active duty. All the king's horses and all the king's men were probably not going to be able to put him back together again. He'd already had it reconstructed twice before, and a new bionic knee was going to be nice, but probably not enough to get him back on the Teams.

Taking a deep breath, he nodded. There was a lot to be grateful for, but he wasn't ready to leave active duty.

"We knew it wasn't going to last forever, but it's always a shock when it happens sooner than we think," Carol said firmly.

He looked at his mom. "I always thought that I'd last a couple more years."

"The fact that you've survived this long is a miracle. I know it doesn't feel like that right now, but sometimes the second act is better."

"I guess that I'm going to find out one way or another. At least I have a hell of a woman and a new life to keep me busy." Looking out the hospital window, he felt a wide range of emotions and knew it was going to take some time before he sorted them out. Scraping his hand down his face, he felt a small smile form and realized he had someone to do it with."

***

Birdie walked into the room and went up to his bed, took his hand, and planted a big kiss on him. "Hi, handsome. How's it going?"

He leaned his head against hers and whispered in her ear, "Did you miss me?"

"I sure did."

"Come here and give me a good kiss and show me." She leaned in and pressed her mouth to his, and he answered by sealing his lips over hers and kissing her for all he was worth. Breathing her in, he didn't think he'd ever get enough. He'd come damn close to checking out, and it gave him a whole new appreciation of what he had.

Birdie being at the top of the list.

He slid his fingers through her hair and slicked his tongue past her parted lips and heard her moan. Despite his lousy physical condition, he reacted like he always did and felt himself harden.

Didn't matter where they were or how many injuries he had, she would always have the same effect. Tugging her hand, he laid it over his crotch and grinned against her mouth. "See what you do to me."

"Is that allowed? I don't think that's allowed."

He pulled her against him and laid his mouth on hers. "Baby, it's the best medicine in the world. You wouldn't deny me a little physical pleasure." Pressing their mouths together again, he decided to work on some physical therapy of his own.

They got so caught up in kissing that he didn't hear the nurse come in until laughter filled the room. "Busted."

The nurse looked at them both. "I guess what they say about SEALs is true. I always thought it was a myth."

Birdie sat up, pulled her shirt down, and whispered in his ear. "Don't say anything."

"Wasn't going to."

"I'll give you two some time and be back in a little bit," the nurse said before she walked out, laughing.

"I heard you found a wedding dress, so it sounds like we could get married next month."

"I did find a dress, but we're not getting married next month." Running her hand over his face, she smiled. "Long engagement, remember?"

"How about a winter wedding, maybe December? We could have it the first weekend of

December. I almost died, and the only way to celebrate is to grab hold of life and not hold back."

"I see that you're going to use this 'I almost died' business for everything you can."

"You wouldn't expect less from me."

"True."

"December."

"I'm not competing with Christmas. We can get married in February, maybe the last weekend of the month?"

"How about the first weekend in January? New Year's Eve would be perfect."

"Maybe. I'll make some calls when we get home. Let's get you out of here first and then work on a wedding." Kissing him gently, she rested her hand on his cheek. "I'm sure glad to see your handsome face."

He leaned forward and gently placed his lips against hers, and it felt like the first time he kissed her at the wedding. He had a pit in his stomach, his heart raced, and there was a huge bubble of happiness that wanted to burst out of his chest. Placing his hand on the back of her head, he deepened the kiss and knew Birdie James was a good woman to come home to and was damn glad he'd found her.

Birdie pulled back and laughed. "Let's not tell people how my horrible singing woke you up from a drug-induced sleep."

"Sure, baby, whatever you want. I won't tell anyone as long as you agree to get married as soon as we can."

"That sounds like bribery; are you sure that you want to play that card?"

"I'll play whatever card I feel is necessary if it gets you legally bound to me."

"If that's the way you want to play it, fine. I'll marry you sooner as opposed to later. Just be ready, Mark, because once we're bound, we're never coming apart."

"That's the plan, sweetheart. I love you, and always will." Feeling like there wasn't more happiness possible, he knew that Birdie had finally latched on to him.

A blessing he planned on celebrating.

I hope you enjoyed the first story in the
Coronado series.

Xoxo
Lea

LEA
HART

MILITARY ROMANCE
Witty, hot & delicious

Delicious alpha hero? *Check.* A story sweet enough to make you swoon? *Also check!* Smokin' hot love cranked up to a hundred? *Check and check!* *Come see what happens when hella-hot Navy SEALs meet their match.*

CORONADO SERIES
LATCHED
SNATCHED
ATTACHED
CATCH
FATE
BEWITCHED
HITCHED
SWITCHED
TUMULT
INFATUATED
FASCINATED
COMPLICATED (2022)

ROMANTIC ADVENTURE
Narrow escapes and naughty shenanigans

Romantic Adventure at its sexy best.
Come see what happens when bullets fly along with a few inhibitions.

SAI SERIES
VORTEX
WHIRLWIND
TEMPEST
BESIEGE
BARRAGE

STANDALONE NOVELS

A WHOLE LOTTA TROUBLE
SMITTEN

SWEET & STEAMY
Snickers & surprises

These romances are sweet and steamy enough to
satisfy any craving!
*If you're ready for a tale with a ton of heat dive into these
books and enjoy a witty, delicious ride.*

SPORTS CENTER
SHAKEDOWN
SHOWDOWN
TAKEDOWN

UNMATCHED

HELLA-HOT VEGAS
Heartfelt moments of grace
Deliciously naughty banter that will make you one
more page yourself into the wee hours.
*Come see what happens when these anti-heroes discover
just how deeply they can love. It's a happy ever after that you
won't want to miss.*

TROUBLE SERIES
ROGUE
CHAOS
RASCAL
SCOUNDREL
PATRIOT

SMALL TOWN ROMANCE
It's a lot hotter than you think

If you love heroes who will stop at nothing to win their woman's heart, you're going to love these stories!

Are you ready for a book filled with slow-burning romantic escapades, hilarious moments, and a couple of one-two punch to the feels thrown in for good measure?

HAVEN SERIES
TRUST
TEMPTED

LANDRY BROTHERS
IRRESISTIBLE
INEVITABLE

Lea Hart is a bestselling author of military romance and romantic comedy. She is well known for her steamy sweet, witty novels. She lives in Southern California and manages to keep a firm grasp on her sanity despite the efforts of her teenager. A big glass of wine, the right pair of shoes, and an extra helping of audacity ensure that the daily juggling act is somewhat successful.

Printed in Great Britain
by Amazon

10381201R00165